About the Author

Rufaro Faith Mazarura is a British Zimbabwean writer who grew up in Birmingham and studied English and Creative Writing at the University of Surrey. She works as a podcast producer, bringing stories to life through audio, and has written and produced podcasts for the BBC, iHeartRadio and Seven Stories, The National Centre for Children's Books. *Let The Games Begin* is her debut novel.

Let the Games Begin

RUFARO FAITH MAZARURA

PENGUIN BOOKS

PENGUIN BOOKS

UK | USA | Canada | Ireland | Australia
India | New Zealand | South Africa

Penguin Books is part of the Penguin Random House group of companies
whose addresses can be found at global.penguinrandomhouse.com.

First published 2024

003

Set in 12.5/14.75pt Garamond MT
Typeset by Falcon Oast Graphic Art Ltd
Printed and bound in Great Britain by Clays Ltd, Elcograf S.p.A.

The authorized representative in the EEA is Penguin Random House Ireland,
Morrison Chambers, 32 Nassau Street, Dublin DO2 YH68

A CIP catalogue record for this book is available from the British Library

ISBN: 978-1-405-96541-5

www.greenpenguin.co.uk

Mom & Dad, thank you for everything.
The Other Two, it's canape season.

London, UK
Summer 2024

I

Zeke

Four days before the opening ceremony

Ezekiel Moyo had never looked more handsome than on the front cover of the August edition of *GQ*. It was their annual sports issue and since Ezekiel (or Zeke as everyone called him) was the country's surest hope for a gold medal at this summer's Olympics, it was only right for him to be the face of the magazine.

Zeke had spent the whole photo shoot charming everyone on set. He'd chatted to the hair stylist about his Saturday job at a salon and complimented the caterer on how good the food she'd cooked was. 'Auntie,' he'd begun – because he'd been raised to call every older Black woman Auntie – 'this is the best oxtail stew I've ever had, and my mum makes an incredible oxtail stew.' She'd chuckled and given him another portion. Zeke's pre-competition diet hadn't allowed him to eat it, but if there was one thing he'd been taught growing up it was that if an Auntie gave him a lunch box, he had to take it home.

Zeke had gone back and forth with the security guards about that weekend's football match before spotting a group of assistants shyly trying to catch glimpses of him from the other side of the room. He'd known they were too professional to ask for a photo, even though they'd so clearly wanted to. So, at the end of the shoot, he'd walked over to them with his outrageously charming smile and said, 'This is my first big photo shoot and I'm trying to find a way to remember it all – can I get a picture with you guys?' Their faces had lit up in delight.

The security guards went on to tell everyone they met that he was 'the most down-to-earth lad that had ever walked on to the set of a *GQ* photo shoot'. And one of the production assistants posted the photos they'd taken with the caption: 'This is now an Ezekiel Moyo stan account.'

'And are you looking forward to seeing anyone in particular at this year's Games?' the journalist conducting the cover shoot interview had asked him with a slightly raised eyebrow. Zeke had smiled; he'd known exactly where the journalist was trying to go. But he'd had no intention of following.

'I think I'm just really excited to cheer on all my friends in Team GB,' he'd said.

'And outside of Team GB, is there anyone else you're looking forward to seeing?' the journalist had said, leaning forward, as if getting closer to Zeke would make him more likely to open up. If anything, it had made him more determined to stay closed off. 'Someone from . . . the other side of the pond perhaps?' he'd added. Zeke had tilted his head to the side as if he had no idea what the journalist was alluding to.

He'd been trying to ask Zeke the same question in different ways all day. But Zeke could spot a trap from a mile away.

'I have no idea what you're talking about. Shall we move

on?' he'd said with polite but firm finality. Zeke had started running for Team GB when he was fourteen, done his first big press interview when he was sixteen, and had his first relationship that garnered public attention when he was twenty-one. So he'd spent years practising how to share enough to make for a good story while deflecting enough to avoid conversations he didn't want to have. He'd peppered his answers with funny anecdotes and used his charm to disguise the fact that he approached interviews with the tact of a veteran politician.

And it had worked.

GQ Summer 2024
Meet Zeke Moyo: Team GB's (almost) Golden Boy

Zeke winced a little at the title. The last thing he needed was another headline reminding him how close he was to winning Gold this summer. He was already under enough pressure. But he continued reading anyway.

> The thing is, Ezekiel 'Zeke' Moyo was always going to become a star. He was born for it. He chose sprinting and has the silver Olympic medal to prove it. But with his natural charisma, easy smile and effortless, disarming charm, he could have become anything he wanted to.
>
> Zeke could have played the leading man in a Hollywood film and packed out the cinemas or modelled for a designer fashion label and had the whole collection sell out overnight. Because Zeke has that rare combination of star power and humanity. He's the boy you had a crush on at school, the breathtaking stranger you fell for at a party. We overuse the terms 'It Girl' and 'It Boy',

but as soon as I met Moyo, I knew he had that elusive 'It' so many aspiring stars spend years trying to acquire.

The front cover of *GQ* showed exactly what the journalist was talking about.

They'd taken the photos for the cover at the West London athletics track where Zeke had grown up training. Instead of his Team GB uniform, he was wearing a sleek blue athleisure set custom-designed by Zeus Athletics, his biggest sponsor. He was standing on the running track he'd been practising at since he was eleven and holding his very first pair of running shoes. But nobody who picked up the magazine was looking at the running shoes or thinking about his success story. They were all transfixed by Zeke, who was giving the camera, or the photographer, or anyone who picked up the magazine, the kind of effortlessly charming eye contact, smile and subtle lip bite that made them feel like they were the only person in the world. Whatever 'It' was, Zeke had it.

'It' opened doors – and eight-figure sponsorship deals – but the people he loved didn't care about photo shoots, accolades or the fact that this could be the summer he won his first Olympic gold medal. In fact, it was his family who teased him the most relentlessly.

'Not the pout!' said Zeke's oldest brother, Takunda, before passing the magazine over to his other older brother, Masimba, who took one look at the magazine cover and began to chuckle.

'He's giving fashion . . . couture . . . male model,' said Masimba, laughing.

'Are you seeing these poses?' Takunda said as he imitated

Zeke. Masimba joined in and the two of them began a photo shoot in the canned-food aisle. They loved embarrassing him.

'We're just trying to be like you, Little Z,' said Masimba as he leaned against the tinned veg shelf. He was thirty but reverted to age thirteen as Takunda took photos of him and shouted out exaggerated comments to hype him up.

The rest of the world saw Zeke as an Olympic medallist and heart-throb. But they just saw him as their younger brother.

'Mum is going to cry when she sees this,' Masimba said as they got into Zeke's black Ferrari and drove down the road that would lead them home. Zeke smiled and nodded because he knew his mum *would* cry when she saw the magazine cover. They were a tight-knit family and Mai Moyo, the matriarch of the Moyo family, cried at almost everything her sons did. The magazine cover, which symbolized her youngest son going off to his third Olympics, was sure to make her weep.

Zeke had tried to convince his mum to let him buy her a new house when he'd signed his first seven-figure deal, but she'd refused, saying she wanted to live in the house she'd raised her family in. But he knew the real reason was that the house, with its framed photos and peeling paint, held all of her favourite memories of her husband, Zeke's dad, who'd passed away ten years ago when Zeke was only fourteen. All of his favourite memories of his dad had been made in that house too, so instead of buying her a new house in a shinier part of the city, Zeke and his brothers went home for dinner every Sunday night.

But this Sunday, he knew something was off as soon

as he opened the front door. His mum usually blasted old Zimbabwean gospel music as she cooked something delicious, and definitely not Team GB dietitian-approved, for dinner. But as he walked in and called out a hello, the house was silent. Something wasn't right. He took another step inside and then, all of a sudden, the room burst with sound, colours and people shouting, 'Surprise!'

The crowd of family members who'd been hiding in the corridor and spilling out into the garden threw blue, white and red balloons at him and shouted in excitement. All of Zeke's family and friends were congregated in his mum's living room to celebrate him before he flew out to Athens for the 2024 Olympics. He felt a wash of joy come over him; everyone he loved was right there. Well, everyone except his dad.

He reminded himself to smile as music poured through the speakers and his mum ran over to embrace him.

'Ezekiel!' she called out as she squeezed him. Mai Moyo was double his age and practically half his height, but still tried to pick him up whenever he came home. She hugged him and then looked up with pride before standing back to show off the new shirt she'd had printed out with a baby picture of him on the front and TEAM MOYO 2024 on the back. She had at least twenty shirts with his face printed on.

'This is your best one yet,' Takunda said with a laugh at the photo of Zeke wearing a pair of running shoes ten times bigger than his thirteen-month-old feet.

'Mama, I thought we were just having dinner,' Zeke said, amused, as he looked around at the packed room.

'I only invited a few people, family and friends, *chete*

chete,' she said mischievously as she gestured to a crowd of at least fifty people.

Zeke greeted all of his aunts and uncles, then took photos with his cousins knowing they'd immediately post them online to remind their friends that they were related to someone famous.

But he didn't get the same reception from everyone. As he walked out into the garden, a girl with bright-blue braids and a denim jacket covered in leftist, feminist, anti-establishment pins walked towards him. As she came closer, Zeke noticed that she'd sewn a bright new patch on to her jacket with the Audre Lorde quote: 'The master's tools will never dismantle the master's house'. Zeke sighed; he already knew where the conversation was going to go.

'How does it feel to be representing the colonial institution that is Great Britain at the Olympic Games of the corrupt Olympic Organizing Commission?' asked Rumbi, his seventeen-year-old, non-biological cousin, who'd studied the British Empire for one term's worth of A-level history and never looked back.

'It doesn't feel as bad as you think it is, Rumbi,' said Zeke. Rumbi was the daughter of one of his mum's best friends. He'd known her from the day she'd been born and, while they weren't technically related, or the same age, she hounded him about his political affiliations, or lack thereof, with the intensity of a little sister who'd made it her personal responsibility to keep him down to earth. Lately, she'd been sending him weekly articles detailing everything problematic about each of his sponsors, with messages like 'this felt important to share'. But he handled

Rumbi's comments about 'neo-colonialism and the hostile environment you've chosen to align yourself with' the same way that he handled the firestorms that erupted in his social media mentions whenever he dared to have an opinion on anything other than sports. He pushed down the anxiety, tried not to let it affect the way he saw himself and just focused on his next run.

When Zeke first started receiving interest from big-name athletics coaches as a teenager, he'd genuinely considered competing for Team Zimbabwe instead of Team GB. But Team GB had some of the best coaches and training facilities in the world and . . . well, a lot of money. So, his choice was made – he knew he wouldn't have to worry about sponsorships or the cost of travelling to competitions ever again.

The divisive politics and anti-immigrant rhetoric that he'd lived through for most of his life had stopped Zeke from actually feeling patriotic about being British beyond football games and his friends who worked in the NHS. But while his family was from Zimbabwe, the UK was the only country he'd ever lived in. So, he chose to represent the people and elements of the country who made him feel at home. He knew that if he tried to explain himself to Rumbi she'd probably lecture him about how British wealth was steeped in colonialism, ask if fancy running shoes were enough to compromise his integrity and then pack an Afua Hirsch book into his suitcase for 'light reading'. But he'd made his decision, and it was too late to change his mind.

She shrugged. 'As long as you can live with yourself, and the knowledge that this country only loves people like us as long as we play the role of the good immigrant,' she said with the unshakeably clear-cut sense of right and wrong you could only have at seventeen.

'I can, thank you for checking in.' He put a hand over his heart.

'Weakest link,' Rumbi muttered under her breath.

'Oh, and did the reference I wrote you for that Oxbridge summer school help?' he asked, raising an eyebrow.

'Yeah . . . I got in,' said Rumbi, looking a little bit embarrassed. Rumbi never missed an opportunity to call him out, but she also wasn't too proud to ask him to write her glowing references for internships and pre-university courses. She mumbled a thank you, and then the rest of his cousins, both biological and communal, ushered him into the living room. His aunties sang old Zimbabwean hymns, his uncles gave long speeches, then his mother went into a fifteen-minute-long prayer.

'Jesus Lord! May Ezekiel make good decisions,' she prayed, and a symphony of aunts and uncles chorused 'Amen'.

'May he have journey mercies as he travels to Athens,' she prayed, to snaps and claps from around the room. Zeke didn't really believe in God, but his mother was close personal friends with Jesus. So, he'd long accepted that every birthday dinner, family get-together and competition send-off for the rest of his life would end just like this. With a drawn-out, not-so-subtle prayer that usually aired out somebody's dirty laundry.

'May he be the head and not the tails,' she prayed, to an echo of agreement from all the adults in the room. One uncle, who everyone knew had a gambling problem and typically bet a few hundred pounds on Zeke winning a medal, said 'Amen' extra loudly.

'May he bring honour to Team GB! To Zimbabwe! And to the Moyo name!' An auntie who never left the house without a tambourine shook it in agreement. Zeke was grateful his mum hadn't declared that he was going to bring home a gold medal. But he could still feel the pressure to win building up in his chest.

'And may he not be led astray,' she prayed, in the solemn tone his mother reserved for the final act of her prayers. She left a dramatic pause and then she started to cry. Zeke tried not to roll his eyes; he knew his mum well enough to know exactly where she was going with this.

'Almighty Father, keep Ezekiel away from sin!' she shouted, and the uncles began to clap. 'Keep him *away* from the spirit of wrongdoing!' An auntie whose son was a thirteen-year-old walking headache nodded in agreement and whispered an exhausted 'Yes, Lord'. Zeke bit his tongue.

'From pride! From . . . *drunkenness* . . .' she continued. Technically, his mum was praying for Zeke, but the whole room unintentionally moved their heads in the direction of Uncle Isaiah, who was notorious for getting blackout drunk at every family function and was already on his sixth can of the night.

'Lord God, Heavenly Father . . . keep Zeke's heart *away* from promiscuity,' his mother yelled, prompting his aunts to 'Yes, Lord!' and 'Amen' in agreement. Zeke looked at his brothers, who were trying not to laugh. It was just another regular Moyo family get-together.

Eventually the prayer ended, and he stood in the centre

of the room as each of his aunties and uncles came over to hug him, give him advice and leave with at least three lunch boxes of leftovers each. The house emptied until it was just him, his mum and his brothers.

'Good luck, Little Z,' said Takunda as he picked up his car keys. 'You'll make us proud.'

Zeke didn't really confide his worries to anyone, not even his brothers. But they knew him better than anyone. He could tell they sensed the way the pressure to win was starting to affect him, because they'd spent the last few weeks reminding him that while they wanted him to win his first Olympic gold medal just as much as the rest of the country, they'd be proud of him no matter what.

'Make sure to have fun with it, all right?' said Masimba. Zeke nodded.

'I mean it,' said Masimba, looking him in the eye.

'Just one foot in front of the other,' said Zeke.

'But faster than you ever have before,' his brothers said, echoing the words their dad had always said to them when they were growing up. Zeke could feel a rare sting in his eyes, but he blinked back the tears before they could fall. Takunda glanced over at him with the same concerned look he'd been giving Zeke since he was fourteen. But it had been almost ten years and Zeke still wasn't ready to really talk about his dad. Thankfully, Masimba was good at changing the conversation.

'Also, I should probably tell you to be responsible and that, but . . .' Masimba said with a knowing smile.

'What happens in the Village . . . stays in the Village,' Zeke said.

'Stop corrupting my sweet son!' said their mum as she

walked across the living room to scold them. She had a handy way of forgetting that Zeke was always the one egging his siblings on.

'If only your father could see you now,' Mai Moyo said with tears in her eyes.

Zeke was a solid foot and a half taller than her, but next to his mum he felt small again. Like he was still the fourteen-year-old boy he'd been when his father died, completely helpless in the face of grief. So, he did the only thing he knew how to do, the only thing she ever expected him to do. He put his arm around her shoulder and gave her a hug. For her, that had always been more than enough.

'He would have been so proud of you,' she said quietly.

Zeke nodded, but he could feel the familiar sense of guilt that came back to him now and again. Yes, his father would be proud. But it would be a complicated kind of pride. His father would cheer and celebrate, but there would be a flicker of imperfectly concealed disappointment in his eyes too. Because Zeke had made so many compromises. He was keenly aware of the small choices that had compromised his integrity and all the ways he'd fallen short of becoming the kind of man his dad would be proud of. But he also knew that a life lived on his own terms would never quite fully line up. So, the one promise he lived by was to always cross the finish line knowing he'd done the very best he could.

As Zeke left the house he'd grown up in and drove back to his apartment, he watched the sunset and began to let himself imagine what the next three weeks of his life would be like. The races he would run, the old friends he would see and all the memories he knew he was about to make. Getting to compete in the Olympics for the third time was his greatest achievement. He'd spent his childhood dreaming about it and most of his life training for it. He was the bookies' favourite to come first in the 100-metre final and everywhere he went people told him they knew he could bring home that gold medal. And Zeke wanted to bring home that gold medal. To hear the crowd erupt into applause as he crossed the finish line and to know that he'd finally reached the pinnacle.

But as he stood in front of his suitcase checking he had everything he needed, he could no longer deny the sense of dread slowly building up in the centre of his chest. Now that he was alone in his room, where there was no one to impress, he could feel his doubts rising to the surface.

There was so much riding on these Games. A gold medal to win, a personal record to break and a country to make proud. He knew that he could run the race, but he was terrified of what came after he crossed the finish line. When he'd won the medal that hung above his mother's mantelpiece – a stunning silver reminder of his last Olympic Games – he'd felt more joy than he'd ever experienced before. But once he'd left the stadium, the crowd and the applause, that joy had quickly faded into something darker, something more difficult to explain. A wave of emotions that had brought him to his knees. For the first time in his life, he'd truly fallen apart.

And Zeke couldn't fall apart again.

2
Olivia

Four days before the opening ceremony

'Can you tell me about a challenge you've experienced and how you overcame it?' asked the man on the other side of the video interview.

Olivia Nkomo was perfectly composed as she maintained eye contact through the screen. She looked up for a second as if she was deep in thought. But the reality was that she'd rehearsed her answer to this question a hundred times before. She had a more successful interview-to-coveted-internship record than anybody she knew. So, she was an expert at delivering exactly what the person on the other side of the table wanted to hear. And if she was honest, the question was easy to answer, because Olivia Nkomo had experienced more than her fair share of challenging moments at work.

She'd spent her time at university trying to add as many things to her CV as she possibly could. Even if it was uncomfortable sometimes . . . Like when she'd found her investment banking supervisor sniffing a line on the sink of the ladies' bathroom less than ten minutes into the company-sponsored welcome drinks. Or the strange summer she'd spent working at a crisis PR agency for musicians whose problems ranged from leaked private photos to criminal court cases. On the second week, she'd been asked to drive her manager's *incredibly* expensive Mercedes across London to hand deliver a parcel to the home of a celebrity who'd *just* narrowly avoided a prison sentence for third-degree murder.

'Innocent until proven guilty,' her manager reminded her.

'But the only reason the evidence got dismissed was because—' Olivia started.

'Innocent. Until. Proven. Guilty,' her manager said.

Olivia tried not to think about which cover-up had paid for their Michelin-starred £200-per-person team dinners. She'd quietly sent in her resignation and donated a small chunk of her savings to charity. But all the donations and long hot showers in the world couldn't cleanse her from the dark whispers she'd heard while waiting for the office kettle to boil.

Then, in the summer of her second year of university, Olivia interned at a major tech company. Yes, *that* tech company. They'd given the interns free catered breakfasts to distract them from the fact that it was four weeks of unpaid work. And reminded them that the prestige the month would add to their CVs far outweighed the toxic culture they'd have to experience while they were there. When the date of their 'not mandatory' but definitely mandatory office summer party came around, Olivia found an excuse to leave her team so she could go and play snooker with the other interns. She'd admitted that she didn't know the rules of the game, but instead of one of the other interns giving her tips, she'd felt the presence of a man who worked in accounts hovering over her. He was taller than her, older too. Maybe in his forties. He'd slowly put his hand on her shoulder and muttered that he would 'teach her how to play'.

Before she could politely say no, he'd placed the snooker stick between her finger and thumb. Her whole body had frozen as he'd covered her fingers with his sweaty hands. She'd glanced around the room for an escape route, for an excuse to leave. But instead found reasons to maintain her composure. There were way too many important people in the room to risk drawing attention to herself. The head of her department was a couple of steps away talking to the company's bigwigs. The other interns just watched, taking in her discomfort and standing in it like it was their own. The man from accounts pressed his whole body up against hers, squeezed her fingers with his clammy hands and leaned closer. His vodka-and-lime-scented breath condensing on her shoulder.

But Olivia couldn't make a scene.

So, she'd just stiffened up, counted to ten and then said that she needed to go to the bathroom. At which point he'd finally let her go.

As she stood in the toilet cubicle, she told herself that if she'd been out in the real world, she would have said something. She would have done something. If a creepy older man had pressed his body against hers at a bar, she would have shaken him off, shouted at him and left. But in a room full of people who could give her a glowing recommendation or a prestigious job after she graduated, she knew she would gain nothing from causing a scene. Instead, she'd splashed some water on her face, pretended it had never happened and moved on.

Because unusual, expensive and sometimes uncomfortable experiences were just the price you paid to work at prestigious companies when you were a couple of months away from graduating into a recession. So, when the interviewer asked her, 'Can you tell me about a challenge you've experienced and how you overcame it?' she gave her most polished answer, talked up an internship she'd done last summer at an NGO and dropped an obscure sports reference that made him sit up and smile. Olivia left the call knowing she'd done pretty well, but even she was surprised when she saw an email with the subject line 'Congratulations!' in her in-box. She'd spent hours in the library, interned during every university break and meticulously plotted out her career in the hopes that it would lead to what she'd been dreaming of her whole life. And now she'd finally done it: Olivia had landed her dream job at the Olympics. A dream she'd been working towards since she was eight years old.

It had all begun during the summer of the 2008 Beijing Olympic Games. Her parents had made three big bowls of popcorn, turned the television on and joined millions of people around the world to watch the opening ceremony. Olivia had a vague memory of a teacher telling her class about the Olympics, but it wasn't until her eight-year-old self sat on the sofa in front of the TV and watched it for the first time that she began to understand why her parents were so excited for it. She'd watched the opening ceremony performers fill the stage and tell a story through song and dance, completely mesmerized by what was unfolding before her eyes. She'd tuned in the next day to watch the synchronized swimmers and stared at the TV in awe as she realized how much discipline and practice it had taken them to get there. She'd watched a documentary about one of the cyclists who'd gone from growing up in a slum to winning gold, and marvelled at how sports could change somebody's life. That summer, Olivia spent hours in front of the TV watching different competitions every day, going to the library to read up on the sports and then trawling the TV guide to find documentaries and films about the most legendary athletes. By the time she and her parents gathered back around the TV to watch the closing ceremony fireworks, Olivia had become so swept up by the magnitude of it all that her vision for what she wanted to do – or more specifically, where she wanted to work – had become crystal clear.

She couldn't help but be pulled in by the magic of it all and covered her walls with posters displaying the official artwork for every Summer Games in the last fifty years. Her parents trawled vintage shops and online auctions to buy her Olympic memorabilia for her birthday. And ever since that first Olympic opening ceremony, she had dreamed of a life spent travelling around the world to follow those five intersecting rings. She wasn't an idealist in her normal life, but something about the way the Games crossed borders, languages and political lines gave her something to believe in. A belief strong enough to plan her life around. And now, she was finally about to see it come true. Because she'd landed an internship at the Games and in just a couple of days she'd be heading off to Athens to watch her dream come to life. She just needed the perfect outfit for it.

*

'Olivia, baby girl, you look incredible,' her mum, Mai Nkomo, said, gently wiping her eyes with a tissue, from her seat outside the changing rooms. Olivia could've come out wearing a dress made of rags and her parents would still have said she looked like a supermodel.

But as she looked at herself in the mirror, she realized that she did look really good. She was wearing a majestic emerald-green suit, tailored to perfection. She'd seen the price tag while she was getting dressed and had grimaced at the total. She knew her parents couldn't afford it. She'd planned to take it off and lie to them, saying that it didn't fit right to give her a chance to grab something cheaper, but they'd called her out before she could come up with a reasonable excuse.

'My beautiful, intelligent, successful girl. Give us a twirl!' her dad, Baba Nkomo, said.

Olivia did a little twirl and tried not to feel too embarrassed as she watched the shop assistants on the other side of the changing rooms smile. She was twenty-three years old.

'I can already see it,' her mum said, standing up in excitement. 'You walking into those offices, looking like a smart, sophisticated professional and wowing them all.'

'Shaking hands with high-flyers, impressing them with your brilliance . . . my daughter the Olympic lawyer.'

'Dad, I'm not a lawyer yet.' Olivia had done a three-year law degree and a master's, but she hadn't started her legal practice course yet. 'And it's not a job, it's just an internship,' she said, trying to manage the narrative before she became the number-one topic of the WhatsApp groups her parents and their friends filled with messages about how well their kids were doing.

'But I can already see the finish line,' her mum said, walking over to hug her as they looked in the mirror together. Olivia hugged her back, smiling at their reflection.

She tried to talk her parents out of buying the suit; said that she already had the perfect outfit at home. But they were stubborn. She knew they were too proud to admit they couldn't afford it and would be deeply offended if she offered to pay for it. So, she hugged her mum again and resolved to pay them back by buying their groceries for the month. They would never accept money from her, but they wouldn't say no to a kitchen full of food.

Olivia's parents had taken her to buy a new school uniform for the first day of school every single year since she was four years old. Even when money was tight and they would have been better off buying something second-hand. When she'd started getting internships and new jobs, they'd continued the tradition, taking her to department store clearance racks and high street sale days instead of school-mandated uniform shops. Her dad always reminded her to dress the part, and her mum told her that the right outfit was the key to walking into any room feeling like she belonged there. So, when she'd seen the gorgeous emerald-green suit displayed in the shop window, she'd immediately known that she'd found the perfect outfit to kickstart the most important job of her life. And to achieve the goals her parents had been working towards for most of *their* lives too.

When Olivia's parents had left Zimbabwe for the UK in the '90s, they'd been young, hopeful twenty-somethings. Following the dream that so many before and after them had spent their lives chasing: a better life in the UK. They'd met at law school in Harare, got married less than a year later and arrived in England fresh-faced and ready to make a life for themselves.

But they'd quickly become disillusioned. First-class degrees from third-world countries didn't mean anything in their cold, grey new home. The years they'd spent studying had come to nothing. Fancy law firms didn't want to hire an immigrant with a thick accent from a country they only knew about in terms of dictators and poverty. So, they'd both retrained, promising themselves they'd find their way back to becoming lawyers one day. But that day had never come. Her mum had become a law teacher. The secondary school students she taught made fun of her accent and pretended not to understand what she was saying. But she stayed up late to make safeguarding calls and ran a summer lunch club for kids who likely wouldn't get a good hot meal if they weren't at school. And her dad had got a job as a social worker – he spent his days and nights trying to help vulnerable adults in the face of a council whose budget shrank every week.

The better life they'd dreamed of amounted to working long hours to barely make ends meet, and living on the other side of the world in a city that would never feel like home. But then they looked at her and Olivia *knew* that, in their eyes, all their hard work had been worth it. She would be the one to achieve everything they hadn't been able to. Their daughter, their only child, was a product of their wildest dreams.

3
Olivia

Three days before the opening ceremony

'Are you ready to fall in love with a hot Greek boy, become a sun-kissed goddess and have the best summer of your life?' said a familiar voice. A moment later, Olivia was pulled into an espresso-scented hug by her favourite person in the world: Aditi Sharma.

'Uh, I'm ready to ace this internship, be offered a full-time job at the OOT *and* have the best summer of our lives,' Olivia said as Aditi hugged her even tighter.

Aditi Sharma was the type of girl you could tell all your secrets to without suspecting for a moment that they would leave the room. Her long wavy black hair, golden-brown skin and curves looked good in everything. They'd met on the playground at the age of five and had been inseparable ever since. She was the human personification of sunshine.

'I'm so proud of you, Liv!' Aditi said, putting her hands on either side of Olivia's face. They'd been talking about her Olympic dream for years. As soon as Olivia had secured the internship, her best friend had begged to come along for the ride. Aditi was a full-time iced coffee influencer with a side gig doing graphic design for a tech company. She could basically work anywhere, so they'd found an apartment in Athens for the summer. To nobody's surprise, Olivia's internship was unpaid, so she used a chunk of her overdraft to pay for the flight, an even bigger chunk of her credit card to pay for the Airbnb, and ignored the financial hell she could feel herself falling into. Because it was the Olympics! She'd deal with all of that once she secured her graduate job.

They walked through the airport together, passed security and browsed the bookshop as they waited for their gate to be announced. They tried on fancy perfumes in the duty-free section and imagined what the weeks that lay ahead of them would be like once they landed in Greece.

'So, will *Summer Olivia* be joining us this year?'

Olivia paused what she was doing and turned to face Aditi.

She and Aditi had spent years saving for the summer after their nineteenth birthdays. Neither of them had ever been on a holiday abroad so they'd planned and plotted a girls' trip straight out of their dreams. They read travel blogs, watched holiday vlogs and searched 'safe, non-racist cities for young women' before settling on Portugal. At first they'd been having a great time. But then, on their fourth day of exploring Lisbon, Olivia met Tiago: a tall, devastatingly handsome Portuguese boy who worked at the hostel where they were staying. He took them to his favourite bakery to try delicious pastéis de nata, showed them gorgeous views of the skyline from all around the city, and then kissed Olivia while they walked on the beach at sunset. Olivia fell for him – fast. At one point she'd turned to Aditi and said, 'I think the sun is going to my head; summer makes me reckless,' and thus the nickname was born. But this year she was determined to keep her head on straight.

'Summer Olivia is permanently retired,' said Olivia adamantly.

'But she's so much fun,' Aditi said with a mischievous smile.

'She's fun until she gets distracted and starts making bad decisions and lets the sun get to her head and almost turns my life upside down,' Olivia said, recalling the last time her summer self had taken the reins. She'd wound up using her credit card to book a last-minute flight and had cried on the plane for her whole journey home.

'But remember how much fun we had?'

'And remember how I almost didn't come home?'

'Would that have been so bad?' Aditi smiled.

'You only say that because if I'd uprooted my life for *that boy*, visiting me would have given you a reason to spend every August on a Portuguese beach,' Olivia said, raising her eyebrow. She laughed as the expression on Aditi's face changed. 'This time, *the plan* comes first,' she said, tapping the top of her suitcase to emphasize each word.

After the impulsive, almost disastrous summer of 2019, Olivia had gone home and meticulously mapped out how she was going to live out the next few years of her life. She'd made a five-year plan, stuck it above her desk and promised herself that she would do everything she could to achieve every goal on her list.

'And what's the plan again?' Aditi knew every step of *the plan*, but she also knew just how much Olivia liked talking about it.

'Years one to three, get a first-class honours law degree at UCL and intern at each of the big four,' said Olivia.

'Tick,' said Aditi with a grin.

'Year three, spend the summer interning at an Olympic-adjacent company in New York and get into LSE for my master's.'

'Tick,' said Aditi drawing a tick in the air.

'Year four, KILL my master's programme, win an academic award and intern at a bunch of tech start-ups and NGOs.'

'Tick!' shouted Aditi, squeezing Olivia's arm.

'Then start year five by interning at the Olympics and end it having secured my dream job at the Olympic Organizing Commission or the UN,' said Olivia as they headed over to their gate. 'Then the rest of my twenties? Total world domination. By twenty-nine I'm either on the *Forbes* Thirty Under Thirty list or a Nobel Prize nominee, you know?' She laughed but they both knew she wasn't joking; she ran on pure unfiltered ambition.

'Or both!' said Aditi. Olivia could always count on her best friend to be her number-one hype woman. On the plane, they synced up their screens to watch the same movie together during their flight. When they were above the Austrian mountains at the halfway point between England and Greece, Aditi took out her toiletry bag and – to the complete bewilderment of the middle-aged man sitting beside them – began her six-step skincare routine. Olivia accepted a face mask, closed her eyes and smiled.

This summer was her chance to take a huge step towards achieving the dreams she'd spent her whole life thinking about. And to make it in ways her parents had long ago stopped believing they could. She just couldn't afford to veer away from the carefully crafted plan she'd made for herself.

'Ladies and gentlemen, this is your pilot speaking,' came the voice from the speakers above. 'We're about to land in Athens where the temperature is thirty-four degrees centigrade. If you look to the left, you'll see the majestic hills and the Acropolis.' Olivia glanced over to the left and caught a glimpse of the city from the windows on the opposite side of the plane.

'And if you look to the right, you'll see what I know so many of you have come to Athens for this summer,' he said. Olivia looked out of her window as the plane began its descent. She could see the city sprawling out across the horizon. And then she looked closer. There it was, standing apart from everything else in the city: the Olympic Stadium. She had spent years planning for this, months preparing for it and her whole life dreaming about it. Now, it was finally within reach.

4
Zeke

One day before the opening ceremony

The Team GB uniforms had arrived at Zeke's apartment three weeks ago in hand-delivered boxes tied with blue ribbon. He was lifting weights while watching and analysing one of his old races. But as soon as the courier handed over the boxes, he'd stopped everything. He'd placed the first box on his coffee table, gently unfolded the ribbon and slowly lifted the lid. Inside was a fresh white jacket. It had a British flag on the left, 'Team GB' on the right, and his full name on the back. As he'd looked at his reflection in the mirror, the reality sank in: he was really going to Athens for his third Olympic Games.

When Zeke arrived at the airport terminal on the day the team was scheduled to fly to Greece, he was surrounded by an excited crowd waving red-white-and-blue flags as they cheered for each athlete that walked past. There were news reporters and TV cameras lined up on either side of the entrance. A group of schoolkids held flowers and 'good luck' signs. One girl spotted him and nudged her friend, sending a ripple through the sea of supporters until they were all shouting his name.

'Zeke!' called a voice that he instantly recognized. He

turned around to see one of his friends, Anwar, a Team GB javelin thrower. The whole team was inside the airport terminal. They played different sports and only got to see each other a few times a year, so each team trip felt like a full-blown reunion.

'I see you ordered a shirt two sizes too small again?' said Camille, one of the high jumpers.

'Especially for you, Camille,' Zeke said, flashing her a smile. He turned back to greet another friend. 'What are you listening to, Frankie?' he asked. Frankie was a long-distance runner who always listened to audiobooks during his marathon training sessions.

'*A Little Life*,' said Frankie.

'Whoa, are you okay?' asked Zeke, surprised. He'd read the book last summer and, like everyone else, he'd finished it feeling a little bit broken.

'It's not exactly light-hearted, is it?' said Frankie. 'But it's thirty-two hours long, so perfect for training.'

The team checked their tickets to see who was sitting next to whom on the plane. There were over four hundred athletes at the airport. Fencers, cyclists, rowers, gymnasts, boxers and athletes who competed in events that the average person would never even have heard of. It was the best thing about the Games: feeling part of something way bigger than yourself. Being in a team with athletes who'd grown up across every corner of the country and made a home for themselves in sports centres, fields and waters. They'd spent their whole lives training for this moment. So laser-focused on their goals that they'd missed out on birthday parties, holidays and carefree weekends with their friends to dedicate every single day to mastering their sport.

And the time spent was more than worth it, because now they were about to compete with some of the best athletes in history.

Zeke remembered the day he first got the call. He'd competed in local and regional running competitions throughout his childhood and he and his dad had met with plenty of coaches over the years. They'd spent car journeys strategizing his career and evenings researching runners like Linford Christie, Usain Bolt and Tyson Gay to learn from their technique. But Zeke got the call from Coach Adam, inviting him to join Team GB, less than a month after his dad's funeral.

He'd gratefully accepted the offer to join the team, but he'd felt a deep wave of sadness, knowing that his dad wasn't around to give him advice any more. His dad's death had been sudden, a heart attack nobody saw coming. And Zeke had been too young to realize how many questions he'd one day wish he could've asked. If he'd had an inkling that his dad wouldn't be around by the time he became an adult, Zeke would have paid so much more attention. He would have sat in the car and listened to every lecture and unsolicited piece of advice. Taken his headphones off and asked to hear all of his dad's favourite stories. Asked him how to live, how to be a good man and how to know if he was doing things right. Because despite his mother and brothers' reassurance, he was never quite sure that he was doing anything right.

Zeke and the hundreds of other Team GB athletes made their way on to the airport concourse and got into formation. They adjusted their matching kits as photographers aimed their cameras towards the plane that was about to fly them to Athens.

'When was the last time you saw *Miss USA*?' said Anwar, elbowing Zeke as a magazine fell out of Camille's bag.

'I have no idea what you're talking about,' Zeke lied. His friends looked over at him with amused, questioning eyes.

'Oh, so you're not familiar with . . . *her*?' said Camille as she picked up the magazine and handed it over to him.

The July cover of *American Vogue* was a group photo of the stars of Team USA's gymnastics team. There was Sade Ambrose, a nineteen-year-old from Michigan who'd nailed a flip that only two other gymnasts had ever been brave enough to do before; Ming Zhang, a twenty-year-old from Maine whose vault routine was unparalleled; Kristen Lewis, a twenty-three-year-old from Arizona who was a marvel on the beam; and Ava Johnson, an eighteen-year-old New Yorker whose floor routines went viral.

The headline on the front cover was THE FEARLESS FIVE and Ava, Ming, Kristen and Sade were all standing in the middle of an orchard wearing beautifully ornate gold-leaf crowns. But at the centre of the photo, staring directly into the camera with piercing dark-green eyes, her long brown hair curling over her shoulders, was the girl that everyone wanted to know more about: Valentina Ross-Rodriguez. She was the five-time medal-winning star captain of Team USA's women's gymnastics team. At twenty-four, she was already acknowledged as one of the greatest athletes of their generation.

And she was Zeke's ex-girlfriend.

The captain of Team GB walked to the front of the line, faced the athletes and said, 'Okay, everyone smile and say "team" in three . . . two . . . one!'

Zeke, ignoring his teammates' questions, looked directly into the camera and smiled. It was going to be a very interesting summer.

Athens, Greece
Summer 2024

5
Olivia

'Olivia, you need to read *Directing the Montage of Your Life*!' Aditi insisted.

'Aditi, I love you. But I'm not reading something called *Directing the Montage of Your Life*.' Olivia was deeply sceptical of her best friend's 'life-changing' self-help books. Mostly because they had corny titles like *The World's Your Oyster (Bar)* and . . . *Directing the Montage of Your Life*.

'Right, so since you never take any of my *very good* recommendations, the idea is that everything's exciting if you look at it that way.'

'How do I romanticize this?' Olivia positioned her phone camera towards the vending machine next to the bus stop where she was about to catch a bus to the Village.

'It's a Greek vending machine! Have you ever seen that brand of chocolate before?'

'No. I'll take a photo for my scrapbook,' she said drily. 'Okay, how about this phone box?'

'It's an ancient artefact of a time before the Uber app.'

'You're ridiculous,' Olivia said, amused by her best friend's unflinching commitment to magical thinking.

'I'm a storyteller.' Aditi grinned from Olivia's phone

screen. She moved through life with a sense of ease and wide-eyed wonder. She saw magic in everything, and while Olivia didn't, her best friend never stopped making her want to. That's probably why they'd stayed friends for so long. They were similar in all the ways that mattered but different in all the ways that made life fun. And Aditi was always trying to get Olivia to have more fun.

'I've been thinking about Summer Olivia,' she began.

'Not this again.' Olivia shook her head as she took a swig from her water bottle. The Athens heat was starting to get to her.

'Hear me out. What if that summer wasn't a fluke?'

'It wasn't a fluke, it was a mistake,' Olivia insisted, remembering how she'd allowed herself to fall so in love with Tiago that she'd considered deferring her studies to go travelling with him. But then she'd gone to his apartment one night to surprise him. There, she'd been greeted at the door by his gorgeous, incredibly angry, *long-term* girlfriend. Tiago had been hiding them from each other all summer, and Olivia had been too caught up in her feelings to see the signs.

So, impulsive, carefree Summer Olivia wasn't going to be making an appearance in Athens. But before she got off the phone with Aditi as she arrived at the Village, she did promise to immortalize that morning with a first-day photograph.

She walked over to a statue of the five Olympic rings and popped her phone on a fence to try to take a photo. After her third attempt, a guy came over to help her.

Olivia's eyes widened. She'd known that she'd eventually see an athlete in real life; it was the Olympic Village after all. But she hadn't expected to meet one so soon after arriving. He was wearing a white-and-red tracksuit and had the kind of tall, strong build that made it obvious he was there to compete. But Olivia would have recognized him in the middle of a crowded supermarket. Because he wasn't just any athlete, he was Haruki Endō, the star of the Japanese swimming team. He'd won a gold medal at the last Olympic Games, just done a big fashion campaign with Louis Vuitton, and was on track to win even more medals that summer. Olivia was completely starstruck.

'I can take a photo for you if you want,' he said, walking over to her with a smile.

'Thank you. My best friend would kill me if I didn't take a good picture,' said Olivia.

'You've got to get the first-day photo. You never know what it'll mean to you in five years,' he said.

Olivia smiled at the camera and tried not to think about the fact that she was speaking to a multi-medal-winning Olympian.

'Is this all right?' he asked, coming closer so she could see the photo. Her braids were in a ponytail with two perfectly curled sections gently framing her face. She was wearing brand-new heels and the sleek green suit her parents had bought her especially for today. Olivia was glowing.

'It's perfect, thank you,' she said, nodding like a bobble-head. She was doing such a bad job of playing it cool that as she reached out to shake his hand the iridescent note-book that was hanging precariously out of her bag fell out. Haruki bent down to pick it up.

'You're welcome,' he said, putting his hand out to shake hers. 'I'm Haruki.'

'I'm Olivia,' she said,

'*I am feeling very Olympic today*?' he said, reading the words inscribed on the notebook. Olivia felt a tinge of embarrassment; it seemed corny out of context.

'It's a quote from—'

'*Cool Runnings*?' said Haruki in recognition.

'Yeah,' Olivia said, pleasantly surprised. 'It's my favourite movie,' she admitted.

'You've got to love an underdog story,' said Haruki, giving her the kind of smile that had created a fervent fandom of teenage girls.

Olivia knew that Haruki hadn't been born into wealth; he'd become an Olympic swimmer by training at a local swimming club while his mum went to work at the weekends. She felt a sense of understanding pass between them.

'Well, I've got to go to training now . . . but I'll see you around!' He walked away with a nod and one final smile.

Maybe she *would* see him around? The summer that lay ahead of her seemed so rich with potential that it almost felt too good to be true. The sun was shining and the Village was more stunning than she'd imagined it would be. Everywhere she looked there were busy officials with security lanyards and headpieces walking across the park with purpose, and energetic volunteers giving directions while holding up brightly coloured signs. The energy was like the first morning of a festival and, for the first time in a long time, Olivia felt like she was exactly where she was supposed to be.

6

Olivia

One day before the opening ceremony

She looked good, she felt good, and for the next two weeks, Olivia would be joining the Olympic International Relations and Diplomacy team as their summer intern. She looked down at her phone to check the time. She was an hour early; everything was going according to plan.

When she got to the first security checkpoint, she showed the guard her email confirmation. He checked her passport and then pointed her in the direction of the long line for the next security checkpoint. Her feet began to ache after minute five, she regretted wearing heels after minute ten and debated going barefoot after minute eighteen. But it was her first day, and she had to make a good impression. She wasn't going to be the girl who took her heels off in the middle of the Olympic Village. She just needed something to distract her from the pain. So, she opened LinkedIn and began to type.

> @OliviaDNkomo: I'm so excited to share that I have the honour of spending the summer working with the OOT as their summer International Relations and Diplomacy intern.

She attached the photo of her standing next to the Olympic

rings, then posted it, feeling a spring in her step as she walked to the final security checkpoint. By the time she got to the front of the queue, her mum, who had push notifications for her, had commented 'From Harare to Athens! Incredible! Sharing this with my students!' Olivia shook her head and laughed, knowing that a screenshot was probably already making its way through one of the many Zimbabwean auntie WhatsApp groups her mum was a part of. But, for once, she didn't mind. Wasn't every daughter of immigrants' tale an underdog story?

'Welcome to the Olympic Village, please scan your QR code ID,' said the bored security guard from inside a glass booth. But Olivia didn't have a QR code ID. She scrolled through her emails and searched through her spam, but there was nothing.

'What department did you say you were in again?' the security guard asked.

'International Relations and Diplomacy,' she said.

'Hmm, you're not on that list. Are you sure you have the right department?'

Olivia reached into her bag to pull out her confirmation letter, but as she did so, something shifted. The security guard gave her a strange look, picked up his walkie-talkie and muttered some incomprehensible words into it. Instantly, Olivia was surrounded by a group of very serious-looking men who began to lead her away from the gate, creasing her perfectly steamed suit in the process.

'Hey! What are you doing? Where are you taking me?' she said as they rushed her along. Her heels were already aching, but being marched along the cobbled pavement was making them even worse.

'You have not been cleared by security to be in the Village,' one of the guards said sternly. 'And from the looks of it, this is a fraudulent confirmation letter,' he added, looking at her suspiciously.

'Fraudulent . . . what are you talking about?' she asked. Olivia had no idea what they meant. But she'd studied foreign imprisonment for exactly two weeks in her second year of university and decided that now was the time to advocate for herself.

'You can't detain me without cause! You've got to read me my rights!' she said, unsure whether any of the things she was saying applied to security guards. 'You don't even have police badges.' But they continued to escort her in the direction of a discreet building just outside of the Village. As she protested, she noticed a group of volunteers glancing over at her and then looking away. As if making eye contact with her would incriminate them too. She was mortified.

The guards passed her over to a female guard who made her take off her shoes, hand over her belongings and walk through yet another metal detector. She was relieved to be able to get rid of the heels for a moment, but was annoyed that they'd made her part ways with her phone before she could google what she was supposed to do in a moment like this.

They put her into an all-white windowless room and seated her in a chair nailed to the ground. *Was this Olympic jail?* she wondered. *Did she need a lawyer? Was she about to be interrogated?* She was mentally mapping out scenarios and trying to remember what she'd learned about foreign imprisonment when the door opened and a tall, gangly man with a worried look on his face walked in.

'First of all, I'm really sorry that they detained you like that,' he said, sounding panicked. 'I am an ally of the Black Lives Matter movement and . . .' Olivia did her very best not to roll her eyes; of course this conversation was going to start with a disclaimer. She wanted to tell him to calm down and cut to the chase. But the man was on a roll.

'It's never acceptable to detain a person of colour without cause and those guards do not represent the values of diversity and inclusivity at the heart of the Olympic Games and OOT and—' Olivia could already tell that he'd played out the PR disaster he would have to deal with if anything bad happened to her. But she really didn't have the energy to comfort a white person who was so clearly looking for reassurance that she didn't think he was racist.

'Could you just tell me what's going on?' she said with a sigh.

He looked nervous. 'I'm Noah, head of recruitment here at the Athens Olympics, and there's been a bit of a mix-up with your role this year.'

Olivia's heart began to sink, the way it always did when she could sense bad news on the horizon.

'There were originally going to be two International Relations and Diplomacy interns. We sifted through hundreds of applications and went through a rigorous interviewing process,' he said.

Olivia nodded.

'However, we made a . . . clerical error.'

Olivia sat up straighter in the chair and frowned. Noah looked everywhere but at her.

'During the recruitment process, the team decided to make it a paid internship but the department didn't have the budget to fund two paid internships and so we had to cut it down to just one intern. And, unfortunately, the team decided to go with the other applicant. Though I take full responsibility for this mistake, somebody was supposed to get in contact with you and take you off the new recruit mailing list, but unfortunately . . .'

Noah was still speaking, but Olivia didn't need to hear any more. She'd spent years planning her path to the Olympics and made pretty much everything in her life secondary to achieving her greatest dream. She'd cut into her overdraft, dipped too deep into her credit card and pinned her hopes on this one perfect summer. But her vision was dissolving. She was already well acquainted with disappointment, but this one really stung.

'So, if I'm understanding you correctly . . . I flew to Athens for an internship that's not going to happen?' Olivia asked calmly.

Noah winced. 'I'm sorry, but yes, that is the case,' he said, looking up at the ceiling, down at the floor and then over at the door to avoid making eye contact with her.

Olivia wanted to protest. To insist they'd got it all wrong and to fight for the place she knew she deserved. She'd already made a mental list of questions that would pick Noah's story apart. But as she looked around, she sighed. Just like when she'd driven the Mercedes to the house of the probable murderer, and when she'd said nothing to the creepy snooker table man who'd made her hate the smell and taste of limes, sometimes it was easier to detach and move on than fight. There was nothing to be gained from speaking her mind in a place like this. The 'angry Black girl' label was the kiss of death and she still wanted to get

45

a job here one day. So, instead of fighting it, she decided to find a way around it. Her best option, she reasoned, was to convince them to give her something, anything. And then work her way up to the top.

'Well, Noah, I came all the way to Athens.' She did her best to maintain her composure. 'There's got to be something I can do for the rest of the summer, right?' She wanted to seem determined, not pushy.

God, all she ever did was try to seem determined but not pushy.

Noah fidgeted and looked around as if trying to find a solution in the walls. Then his face lit up.

'Yes, there is. We have one last space in another department that you can join.'

Olivia gritted her teeth and listened to what he had to say.

7
Zeke

One day before the opening ceremony

'Zeke, wake up! Look!' said Anwar.

Zeke had fallen asleep almost immediately after getting into the Team GB shuttle bus from Athens International Airport. But at the sound of Anwar's voice, he woke up and looked out of the window. His eyes widened as he realized what he was seeing. The gates, the signs, the red, blue, green, yellow and black rings.

'The Village . . .' said Frankie. Suddenly everyone on the shuttle bus was looking out of their windows. The road leading up to the gates was lined with a row of sycamore trees that looked magical in the sunlight. The newly built training facilities, accommodation blocks and competition venues were dazzlingly high tech. And there were athletes from all around the world in colourful team uniforms piling out of shuttle buses. Zeke had been to Rio and Tokyo, but the first moment on Village grounds never failed to take his breath away. The gravity of it all was overwhelming. It was a strange mixture of grief and joy.

The Olympics had been his *and* his dad's dream, yet only one of them would ever step into the Village. Zeke tried to shake off the complicated feelings. He'd spent his whole life making sacrifices for this.

But there was more to the Olympics than competing. When the *GQ* writer who'd interviewed Zeke had asked him what his favourite part of the Games was, Zeke had answered immediately – the Village.

Because the Olympics threw together hundreds of young, hot, athletic twenty-somethings from around the world and let them play sports and party for two weeks. Well, party within reason.

'What happens in the Village, stays in the Village . . .' said Zeke and the whole bus began to groan. It was Zeke's favourite game. 'What happens in the Village, stays in the Village, but do you remember the time *somebody* got black-out drunk and security found them running around the stadium at three a.m. wearing Team GB Speedos . . . and nothing else?'

Harry, the shot putter who had done exactly that, laughed from the front of the shuttle bus. 'Okay, what happens in the Village, stays in the Village, but do you remember the morning when we saw two members of the Croatian rowing team leaving Frankie's room . . .'

Frankie shouted in protest, 'What happens in the Village, STAYS in the Village!' Frankie wasn't as innocent as he looked. 'I mean it,' he said, blushing. 'Okay, what happens in the Village, stays in the Village, but do you remember the time *someone* set up fireworks to ask someone to go on a date and then got interrogated by the actual Japanese FBI?'

'They were just really active sparklers!' protested Zeke, 'and anyway, they weren't mad at me, they just couldn't understand how I'd got them into the Village.' He shrugged.

'Now that I'm thinking about it, how *did* you get fire-works into the Village?' asked Anwar.

'Even more surprisingly, how did you get Valentina Ross-Rodriguez to be your girlfriend?' said Camille with a smirk as the whole bus laughed.

'And how did you fumble the bag *so* badly?' said Frankie. They were always teasing him about Valentina.

Valentina Ross-Rodriguez was Zeke's first love. And when he'd fallen, he'd fallen hard. Zeke and Valentina had met at the Tokyo Olympics when they were twenty-one. They'd locked eyes during the opening ceremony, become inseparable for the rest of the month after the Games, which they'd spent exploring Japan, and by the end of the summer they'd started what would become a two-year long-distance relationship. Zeke had been completely infatuated with her, convinced himself that they were soul-mates. If she hadn't broken things off, he probably would have asked her to marry him. But that was in the past now.

'All right, all right. My fault for starting the game,' said Zeke. 'But remember the time somebody threw an open-invite hall party that got so wild we all ended up in disciplinary?' The whole team cheered as they remembered the epic party they'd enjoyed in Tokyo after Camille had won her first Olympic medal.

'But it was worth it, right?' said Camille, and everyone shouted in agreement. The athletics team had been given a seven p.m. curfew for the rest of the Games for causing a 'serious disturbance', but it was still one of the best parties Zeke had ever been to.

'I've had three years to practise, so this summer's hall parties are going to be legendary,' Camille said. Camille's

parties *were* pretty legendary. The halls of the athletes'
apartments had the same energy as the halls of a student
accommodation block the night after exam week ended.
But before anyone could ask her what she was planning
for this year, one of the GB officials at the front of the
shuttle bus stood up.

'Guys, I already have to babysit the rugby team since
they make a mess everywhere they go,' he said, shaking
his head with the weariness of a man who'd sat in one too
many party-related disciplinary committee meetings.

Camille turned around to whisper to Zeke and Anwar
through the gap between her seats. 'I brought a whole bag
of party decorations.'

They got out of the bus, collected their suitcases and
walked to the athletes' section of the Village in a crowd
of Team GB branded uniforms. Volunteers looked over
and pointed at them and Olympic staff glanced over in
excitement. When they reached the athletes' plaza, Zeke
looked up and spotted the international flags hanging from
the apartment blocks all the athletes were staying in. This
year, they were tall, bright, modern buildings surrounded
by newly planted trees and perfectly landscaped gardens.

'Excuse me, are you Ezekiel Moyo?' said a quiet voice,
squeaking a bit at the end. He looked down and smiled at
the two girls wearing the uniform of the Italian team.

'Can we get a photo with you?' the girl on the right
asked.

'Of course,' said Zeke warmly as Anwar took one of
their phones to take the photo. The girls squealed their
thanks and then ran back to their team.

'My bet is gymnastics. They look about twelve,' said

Frankie; they always made a game of guessing what sport someone played based on their first impressions.

'I feel like synchronized swimming,' said Camille. 'They're tiny and look exactly the same. It would be a waste not to use it to their advantage.'

'The Caruso twins?' said Coach Adam, the head coach of the athletics team. 'Four-times gold-winning fencers, they're absolutely lethal when they have their masks on.'

'How do you even know that?' asked Zeke.

'I know everything,' Coach Adam said matter-of-factly. 'The way I know that *somebody* was planning a first-night hall party.'

They all groaned.

'But, Coach, it's essential to team bonding,' said Camille.

'You can bond on the track during practice. Come on, you know better. Subpar athletes party . . .'

'Medallists go to sleep,' they said in unison as they arrived at GB House. They ran up the stairs to go and see their rooms. Zeke's favourite moment after arriving at a competition was always looking out at the view from his temporary bedroom. He pulled back the curtains and stared out at the sea of athletes' apartment blocks. He could see dozens of buildings adorned with flags. Sweden house and the Peruvian block, the Nigerian apartments and Italy's building. He snapped a picture of a set of windows decorated with Zimbabwean flags, sent it to his family then tapped on a new message notification.

Haruki: WE'RE NEIGHBOURS!

Haruki Endō, his best friend, was a swimmer on the Japanese team. And this year Japan House was just a three-minute walk away; a major upgrade from their usual fourteen-hour flight. But before he could reply to Haruki, another message popped up on his screen. Zeke smiled. It was Valentina Ross-Rodriguez. He felt his heart quicken for a second the way it used to whenever he got a text from her. But then it slowed down again. They were just friends now, after all.

Valentina: can't believe you followed me all the way to Greece

Zeke: you broke up with me by text, you left me with no other choice

Valentina: leaving a trail of broken hearts wherever I go isn't easy for me either

Zeke laughed. He could hear the way Valentina would say that.

Zeke: when can I see you?

Valentina: Coach Lydia basically has the team on lockdown until our competition

Zeke: opening ceremony after-party then?

Valentina: if you can find me

8

Olivia

Noah, the HR manager, had told Olivia that they needed an 'all-rounder' volunteer who could jump into different departments whenever they needed help. Her options were either to go back home knowing she'd wasted hundreds of pounds to get to Athens, or to fake gratitude and say yes to yet another summer of fetching coffees, replacing toilet rolls and packing envelopes, without even being able to call it an internship.

What she'd really wanted to do was to tell him that he could take his clearly made-up 'all-rounder' role, stuff it between the shaking lips of his insincere smile and choke on it. But Olivia had spent enough time overhearing conversations in corporate offices to know that everything she said in anger could and would be used against her, especially if her CV were to land back into an Olympic HR in-box for a future job. So, she'd accepted his lacklustre offer, followed him out of Olympic prison and hated herself a little for being so agreeable.

Noah had led her to the other side of the Village and introduced her to one of the volunteer managers, who'd taken her through the most detailed training session of her life. It turned out that the 'all-rounder' volunteer gig wasn't actually a fake role, it was pretty intense. She'd been looped into a training day for new volunteers and in the last five hours she'd been taught how to administer first aid, how to drive a golf buggy and how to successfully escort 2,000 people out of a building in case of a fire. She'd been on an extremely detailed tour of the Village to get familiar with all the different nooks and crannies and then she'd gone to the volunteer centre to be given a bright blue-and-yellow volunteer uniform to wear for the duration of the Games. 'Volunteering at the Olympics' didn't have the same level of prestige as 'working at the Olympic Organizing Commission in the International Relations and Diplomacy team' would have. But, by the end of the day, Olivia had accepted her fate. She sat on a bench in the middle of the Village and gave her feet a moment to recover from the hell she'd put them through.

When she looked at her phone, she was greeted by a sea of messages from old friends, colleagues and distant family members congratulating her on the internship. Her mum's proud-parent screenshot had travelled across group chats at the speed of light. She grimaced at the realization that eventually they'd all find out that things weren't going as smoothly as she'd planned. And that her parents would be sad when they found out the daughter they'd told their friends, students and colleagues about wasn't the bright success story they thought she was.

But Olivia was nothing if not determined; she would find her way to the top before anybody back home found out. And if she hadn't picked up her phone to delete the

LinkedIn post, maybe she could have shrugged it all off and decided that any opportunity was a good opportunity if she made the most of it. But as she scrolled, her eye caught on a photo of a guy around her age posing in a perfectly tailored suit in front of the Olympic rings. As she read, she began to taste something angry and acidic in her mouth.

'Lars. Lindberg,' she whispered as soon as Aditi answered the phone.

'The whispering is a bit ominous – you're freaking me out,' Aditi said.

'Lars *fucking* Lindberg,' she said, her whisper now sounding like a hiss.

'Lars Lindberg as in the guy we went to uni with?'

'Lars Lindberg as in the silver-spoon-fed, winters-in-Aspen, barely-showed-up-to-lectures Lars Lindberg. He stole my job! Well, he was given my job. And if my sources are correct, he's got VIP tickets to the opening ceremony,' Olivia said, thinking about the photo he'd just shared on his Instagram story.

'And are your *sources* . . . Instagram?'

'Maybe,' she said defensively.

Olivia had first encountered Lars Lindberg a couple of weeks into her first term of university. While he'd been on the same law degree as her, she'd almost never seen him at lectures or seminars. But Lars was the biggest name on campus, and the furthest thing away from an underdog. He threw sprawling parties in his family's house in Chelsea, his mother was a major donor with her own plaque outside of the university library, and the family history section of his father's Wikipedia page was filled with blue hyperlinks.

Lars wasn't just well off, he was private-jet, Swiss-private-school, never-lifted-a-finger, crazy, *stupid* rich.

His Instagram was littered with photographs of him talking to world leaders at fancy black-tie galas, jumping into sunset-framed infinity pools and eating five-course meals of teeny-tiny Michelin-starred dishes. Then there were the *I'm socially progressive and care about people and the planet* photos to balance out the *No I won't answer your question about where my family's money came from or why my dad's business manager spends so much time in the Cayman Islands* photos. Lars collecting plastic from the ocean, Lars helping to build a school in Nepal and, of course, Lars posing with a group of Black kids he didn't know outside a village hut in Kenya.

But it wasn't the old money or performative activism – which he only seemed to do when his family's business was in the news for something ethically murky – that bothered her. It was the fact that while Olivia had to plot, strategize and negotiate her way into every room she'd ever stepped into, Lars had breezed through university, getting every internship, award and opportunity she'd wanted with barely any effort. And now here he was with his family-crested ring and floppy posh-boy hair. Making a fun summer anecdote of the job that Olivia had spent years dreaming about. And unlike Olivia, who'd put herself into financial hell for an unpaid internship that wasn't happening any more, Lars was getting paid.

'Olivia? Are you okay?' asked Aditi.

Olivia was sitting on a bench in the middle of the Village breathing heavily and ferociously scrolling through her phone. She definitely wasn't okay. She could only imagine how strange she looked in a sea of smiley, upbeat volunteers.

'I have to go,' Olivia said, standing up.

'Are you sure? We can talk about it.'

Olivia knew Aditi wouldn't judge her, but envy was an ugly emotion; there were just some things she kept to herself.

'Yeah, I'll see you when I get home,' Olivia said, feeling deflated as soon as she ended the call.

At some point in every internship she'd done the HR department had ushered the girls and the Black and Asian interns aside for some sort of panel that almost always revolved around the topic of imposter syndrome. The speaker would talk about how they, as someone under-represented in the industry, had felt like an imposter and questioned if they were really smart, talented or competent enough to be the best at their job. And each time, Olivia had nodded and clapped along because she knew that was what she was supposed to do. But the thing was, Olivia had never felt like an imposter.

In fact, when she'd done her first (unpaid) summer internship at a high-powered law firm, she'd looked around at the room of private school boys and kids of law firm partners and thought: *If anyone's an imposter here, it's them, because at least I know how hard I worked to get here.* She would go into the office an hour earlier than she needed to so she could get ahead. Spent the weekends reading up on legal cases so she could always be overprepared. And had almost maxed out her overdraft by spending the whole summer paying to commute into the city, buying new outfits to fit in and going to every after-work drinks and social activity she could to keep up with her colleagues.

So, when she'd looked around to see people who'd done

a fraction of the work she had done to get there, working half as hard as her, she'd thought *Why would I think I'm the imposter when I'm clearly outpacing all of them?* But it still stung to be reminded that rich boys with well-connected dads would always finish first.

As she watched Lars's Instagram story, Olivia began to feel a familiar sense of disillusionment. It crept into more and more of her life each year. Yes, it was mostly jealousy – and Olivia hated feeling that way. But there was more to it than that. It was a confirmation of what she had long known but foolishly allowed herself to believe she could defy. That she was always going to have to work three times as hard to get half as far. No matter what new hobbies she picked up, books she read and anecdotes she rehearsed, she would never be the first choice in a draw between a girl like her and a guy like Lars. And no matter how much money she spent on fancy clothes, the world she wanted to work in wasn't set up for people like her.

As she walked through the Village, the disappointment she'd felt earlier began to fade away. In its place came a quiet, searing, contained rage. It was the only kind of rage she allowed herself to experience, and it was rising up faster than it ever had before.

She'd spent so much of her life managing her emotions and carefully curating her personality so that nobody could ever throw an 'angry Black girl' label at her. But she was angry. Angry she'd worked so hard only to be denied at the very last second. Angry that she'd spent such a huge chunk of her savings to fund a summer that was dissolving right in front of her. And angry that she was going to have to go back to the drawing board and plot out a new way to get to the other side of her five-year plan. So, on that day in Athens, Olivia allowed herself to walk through the Village with blood in her heels and a scowl on her face.

9
Zeke

One day before the opening ceremony

Zeke and Haruki Endō met for the first time at their first Olympic Games in Rio. They had bonded over the fact that they were both fiercely competitive when it came to their sport yet incredibly easy-going when it came to everything else. Now, at twenty-five, Haruki was six foot seven with broad shoulders. He had the kind of bright, boyish face that won him a fierce fandom – there were thousands of fan accounts dedicated to him and just as many spicy fanfiction stories. Usually, his teenage fanbase wrote him in the role of the intense, brooding athlete that was way too focused on winning gold medals to date. In fiction, Haruki was the introspective type who only had time for casual but incredibly steamy situationships that usually involved late-night swims and rushed moments in changing rooms. But, in reality, Haruki was a hopeless romantic. And when he had a crush, his best friend, Zeke, was the first to know.

'Honestly, I just feel like the love of my life is somewhere in the Village,' said Haruki as the two of them walked across the gym towards the treadmills. They always trained together on their first day in the Village.

'I thought the love of your life was in Tokyo, or Rio, or

London,' said Zeke, teasing him. Haruki had never been in love before, but he'd been saying he was going to fall in love in the Village for as long as they'd known each other.

'No – for real this time. It feels like fate.' They stepped on to their treadmills and started running. Zeke was well-versed in his friend's theories on infatuation and his much slower running pace. And this wasn't the first time Haruki had spoken to a girl for five minutes and started talking about fate. Haruki had two older sisters who'd raised him on a solid diet of romcoms. And his parents had met at a swimming pool on New Year's Day twenty-six years ago. He was born to be a hopeless romantic.

'So, what is it about this time that feels different?'

'The chemistry, Zeke. The chemistry. All I did was take a photo of her by the Olympic rings, but I just felt like we clicked,' he said, smiling into the distance the way he always did after meeting a girl he liked.

'Do you have her number?' asked Zeke.

'Well, no,' said Haruki, who hadn't thought that far in advance about how he was going to reunite with the love of his life. 'You're so obsessed with practical things, Zeke. Love finds a way.'

'And you spoke to her for how long?' asked Zeke.

'Three minutes . . . but we have the same favourite movie! Did I tell you that? She loves *Cool Runnings* too. That's got to be a sign, right?' Haruki said.

Zeke didn't have the heart to tell him that pretty much everyone liked *Cool Runnings*.

'I just feel like I already know her, you know? We only spoke for a short time, but it just felt . . . easy.'

'What's her name?' said Zeke, curious.

'I . . .' began Haruki nervously. Haruki wasn't just a star athlete; he was a celebrity. He met a few dozen of his fans every time he went out and, while he tried to be present in each interaction, he heard so many names that he couldn't hold them all. But he never forgot faces.

'Something with an *a* or a *v* or an *o*?' Haruki said, looking panicked as he realized that thousands of people walked in and out of the Village every day. 'Wait, I'm never going to see her again, am I?' he said, laughing in despair at the reality of the situation.

'You'll find the one, eventually,' said Zeke, teasing him.

'Easy for you to say. You and Valentina met in the Village and look how that turned out,' he said, increasing his speed to catch up with Zeke, who couldn't help but turn every training session into a race. Haruki was stronger than Zeke in almost every way – he was a swimmer, after all. But Zeke was one of the fastest men in the world.

'Valentina and I broke up, remember?' Zeke said, running faster.

'I don't believe that for a second,' Haruki said, matching his pace. Haruki was captain of the ValenZeka fan club, there was no convincing him.

'We did!' said Zeke. He'd spent the past year trying to persuade Haruki that he and Valentina really were *just friends*, who were never getting back together.

'Let me know when you pick out the engagement ring,' Haruki said in a sing-song voice, trying to keep up, although Zeke's Olympic-medal-winning speed left him gasping between words. 'Zeke, you're so competitive it's annoying,' he said, turning the pace up on his treadmill again.

'You only say that because you're losing.' Zeke increased his speed again. Haruki glanced over and did the same thing. Zeke felt sweat dripping down his back and Haruki ran out of breath. The swimmer threw his arms up in defeat and stepped off the treadmill. As he walked over to the water fountain, Zeke followed.

'When else in our lives are we ever surrounded by this many people who are, one, the same age as us, two, as obsessed with sports as us. And three – understand exactly what it's like to have a life like *this*,' Haruki said as he made his way to the window on the opposite side of the room. He gestured outside. 'If there's any place to fall in love, it's the Village.'

Haruki wasn't wrong. There was a certain romance about the Village – even hardened cynics walked on to the grounds and started to believe that anything could happen.

10

Zeke

One day before the opening ceremony

If Zeke had met Olivia when they were twelve, they probably would have become friends. Zeke would have laughed at Olivia's quick, scalding wit and Olivia would have smiled at Zeke's boyish sense of humour. They would have been put next to each other in Year Seven maths because a teacher would have figured out that Olivia's focus would rub off on Zeke and that Zeke's easy-going nature would rub off on Olivia.

If they'd met at seventeen, they would have run for head boy and head girl and spent the year antagonizing each other. Olivia would have rolled her eyes at Zeke's teen-age humour and Zeke would have shaken his head at the fact that Olivia always had to be right. They would have hooked up at the last sixth-form party before results day and it would have been earth-shattering.

If they'd met at university when they were nineteen, they would have become debate club partners. And if they'd met at eighty-six in a care home, they would have become fierce bingo rivals. There were a dozen alternate universes in which Olivia and Zeke could have first met. But on that day in Athens at the end of July, they met when Olivia was

64

falling into a pit and Zeke was slipping into the worst version of himself.

After his morning workout with Haruki, Zeke and his teammates gathered around the track for their first practice. One of their team traditions was to watch each other practise on the first day. Usually, they competed at the same time, so they rarely got to cheer each other on. But on that first day, they all sat around the empty athletics field and watched their teammates do what they did best. They clapped as Sammy Nolan, the triple jumper, skipped three times and landed on the sixteen-metre mark. They cheered as Amina Abbas, the pole vaulter, defied gravity by launching herself over the five-metre bar. And shouted in excitement as Harry Campbell, the shot putter, spun around with the elegance of a dancer then threw the shot with the might of a warrior.

When it was Zeke's turn to practise his 100 metres, he gave it his all. The first-day team training was just a warm-up. But Zeke surprised himself, his teammates and all their coaches by reaching the finish line so quickly that he unintentionally beat his own record. He was high on adrenaline and fulfilled ambition.

As he walked across the Village, an excited group of teenagers wearing the uniform of the Guatemalan team ran towards him. There were thousands of athletes in Athens that summer, but Zeke was an *athlete's* athlete. In the same way that incredibly famous actors fan-girled over Meryl Streep or award-winning musicians got starstruck near Beyoncé, other athletes became awestruck when faced with Zeke Moyo. He was a star, and he didn't hate the attention.

He took a group photo with the Guatemalan teenagers and wished them luck with their diving competition. When he went to get a post-workout smoothie, he noticed how the girl working at the juice bar let her eyes linger on him as he walked in. Then he smiled to himself on the way out as he saw the number she'd scribbled on the back of his cup. Maybe he *would* call her.

After he left the juice bar, he scrolled through his mentions and laughed at the thirst tweets people had attached to the photos he'd taken for his *GQ* cover shoot. Somehow, he'd become the internet's crush of the month. With the sun on his arms and the world at his feet, Zeke began to walk across the Village like it was his own personal kingdom. His mum was always quoting Bible verses about humility and scolding him through pointed prayers like, 'Humble my son, Almighty God! Make him remember that the Olympian is also a boy who must take out the bins at his mother's house.' His brothers teased him down to earth, and his teammates were so talented that he never got complacent. But when Zeke was having a good day, he stepped into the most confident version of himself and became capital 'E' Ezekiel Moyo.

If Zeke hadn't beaten his own record that morning, he wouldn't have put on his noise-cancelling headphones to listen to his favourite playlist. If the Guatemalan teenagers hadn't treated him like a god, then he wouldn't have felt like one that afternoon. If he hadn't been allowing his own hype to get to his head, he would have noticed Olivia walking across the pavilion at 3.28 p.m. on the fourth Thursday of July.

If Olivia's first day had gone according to plan, she

wouldn't have even been walking past the athletes' apartments that day. If she hadn't seen Lars's Instagram page, she wouldn't have been as annoyed as she was that afternoon. If she hadn't been so focused on the photo of Lars with his arm around a tall, silver-medal-winning sprinter, she would have noticed Zeke as he walked across the pavilion at 3.28 p.m. on the fourth Thursday of July.

If Olivia hadn't had such a terrible day and Zeke hadn't had such a brilliant day, they would have never crossed paths. But they did. And before either of them had the chance to look up and realize they weren't the only person walking on the path, they crashed right into each other.

11

Olivia

One day before the opening ceremony

Olivia collided headfirst into a tall, solid wall. The wall fell down and she fell with it. One second she was glaring at her phone screen, and then the next she was descending to the ground and holding on to what was not in fact a wall, but instead a tall, muscular man. It happened so quickly that she couldn't take in the details of the collision. Still, she was pretty sure he'd been the one to cause it. But rather than accidentally knocking her to the ground – which, with his height and weight, should have been the natural gravitational outcome – she'd been the one to fall on to him. He lost his balance, fell backwards and took her down with him.

She looked down and instantly recognized who she'd just fallen on top of. Zeke Moyo. The silver-medal-winning track star of Team GB athletics. She'd watched Zeke win his 100-metre final at the Tokyo Games from her parents' living room and cheered along with the rest of the country as he stepped on to the podium. Everybody back home was a Zeke Moyo fan – he was a national treasure. And as she looked down at him, it became pretty clear why he'd won the status of a heart-throb too. His ridiculously fresh trim, perfectly sculpted face and warm brown eyes were impossible to miss. Objectively, he was a stunningly handsome man. If she'd collided with him that morning outside the Village gates, she would have been knocked off her feet in a *very* different way. But Olivia had met Zeke at the worst possible moment. Only seconds after finding out that Lars Lindberg was friends with Zeke.

Olivia had just seen a photo of Lars sitting on a beautifully set outdoor dining table overlooking a crystal-blue slice of the Amalfi Coast. And Zeke was at the table with him. In fact, Zeke had just signed a multi-million-pound deal with Zeus Athletics. The Lindberg-owned family business was one of the biggest sponsors of this year's Games, which had no doubt been the reason why Lars had got the internship that she'd worked so hard to earn. Well, that's what Olivia assumed.

So, she couldn't help but instantly loathe Zeke.

'At least buy me a drink before you pin me to the ground,' Zeke said, his voice smooth as he looked into her eyes and smiled. It was the kind of smile he knew how to wear well. One that formed slowly, curved to the right and clearly charmed everyone he met. If she hadn't been in such a foul mood, she would have admitted that there were worse places to fall than on to Zeke Moyo's lap. But he'd ruined her suit.

Her parents had forked out way more than they could afford to make her feel like she belonged in a place like this. And now the suit was covered in green juice and smelt like apples and limes. Olivia hated limes.

'Sorry,' she said, passive-aggressively.

'It's all right, it was just an accident. I'm not upset—'

He clearly wasn't hearing her tone right, so she interrupted him.

'No. Sorry is the word *you* should be looking for,' she said plainly. 'You should be saying "I'm sorry for running on a public path, crashing into you and spilling a whole cup of green juice all over your brand-new suit" . . . because that's what you've just done.' The stain was the cherry on top of an already bad day.

'Well, some of the juice fell on me too. And I'm pretty sure I'm the one who was thrown to the ground,' he said casually.

'Are you blaming *me* for this?' she said indignantly.

'Well, you weren't looking where you were going either,' he shrugged.

Olivia couldn't stand the way he was smiling up at her as if he thought she was happy to be in this position. Or the fact that she couldn't break eye contact with him. Or that she couldn't deny how handsome he was up close. So she climbed off him and stood up, immediately regretting the move as she felt the sharp sting of the blisters at the back of her ankles. She tried to distract herself from the pain by reaching into her bag for wet wipes to dab some of the juice off her suit. He stood up too.

'For the record, I wasn't running, I just have long legs, so I move quickly—'

Olivia glared at him. She was usually pretty good at biting her tongue and moving on. But after her day from hell, she couldn't help but say exactly what she was thinking.

'You know that who you are doesn't give you an excuse to do whatever you want, right?' she said. 'That being an athlete or *whatever* doesn't mean that you can just walk around the Village like it's your own personal kingdom?'

'I don't know what your problem is, but I don't think it has anything to do with me,' Zeke said. Then he reached out, put his hand over hers and silently pulled three wet wipes out of her almost-empty packet to wipe the splatters off his shirt. He didn't glance away from her for even a second.

Olivia was appalled to the point of speechlessness. Partly because he was right, but more at the audacity he had to take something that belonged to her without asking. It was the second time that had happened to her in just one day. She knew that if she stayed, she'd definitely say something she would regret. So, she put her bag on her shoulder and turned her incredibly painful ankles to leave. But Zeke was still talking.

'I can pay for your dry-cleaning if you want. My treat,' he said with a bemused smile.

The patronizing way he said 'my treat', and the fact that he still hadn't apologized, infuriated her.

'I can pay for my *own* dry-cleaning.' Her words were venom.

'You should also try being *nicer* to strangers, it will get you *a lot* further,' he said, looking up at her with a raised eyebrow.

Olivia hated the word 'nice'. Being 'nice' only served to make other people comfortable while they chipped away at her. 'Nice' was no longer a priority. And, while it probably wasn't wise to offend an Olympian when her future was already up in the air, for once, she just didn't care.

She took a deep breath, held his gaze and then opened her mouth.

'Okay, I'll be nice. *Politely*, go to hell.' She immediately regretted it, but the words were already out of her mouth. So she winced and walked away.

I 2

Zeke

One day before the opening ceremony

Zeke was standing in the middle of the Village, covered in green juice, reeling from the fact that a girl he'd never met before had told him to go to hell. If he was honest with himself, it probably stung more because he'd spent most of their interaction thinking about how stunningly beautiful she was. Marvelling at how the sun lined her silhouette with gold, transfixed by the way her eyes sparkled as she glared at him and noticing how her soft, full lips were framed with the faint lines of someone who smiled a lot.

But that was beside the point. Because, honestly, he was offended.

She didn't know him, but she'd levelled a whole range of criticisms about his character based on a three-minute interaction. Yes, he probably should've just said sorry because, the truth was, he *hadn't* been looking where he was going. And maybe telling her to be nice and taking a few of her wet wipes without asking hadn't been the best call. But, still, had he really come across badly enough for her to react like that?

He played the conversation back in his head to figure out if he'd said something inexcusable or accidentally hurt her on the way down. But his mind just kept drifting back to *her*. To her long brown braids and the urge he'd felt to brush a few loose curls behind her ears. To the way her skin glistened a little in the sunshine and the brief moment their bodies had been pressed up against each other. She'd smelt like a heady mixture of vanilla and summertime. And she'd sounded so hot as she told him off.

As he wiped some of the juice off his shirt, Zeke noticed an iridescent notebook lying on the floor beside him. It was hardbound and the words I AM FEELING VERY OLYMPIC TODAY were inscribed on the front. On the spine was a name: *Olivia Nkomo*. Her surname was Zimbabwean, just like his. He shook his head. If he ever told his mum that he'd met a Zimbabwean girl within hours of arriving in the Village, he would never hear the end of it.

He opened the notebook. It was empty, except for the first page.

Olivia's Post-Olympic Plan (according to Aditi, your best friend who knows you more than anyone else in the world)

1. *Ace the OOT internship until they beg you to stay for ever (which they obviously will)*
2. *Figure out how to become an ethical billionaire & make the Forbes list*
3. *Achieve (benevolent) WORLD DOMINATION*

PS: HAVE FUN!!!

Aditi xxx

Zeke smiled to himself as he read the last step in the three-point plan. Aditi painted a pretty interesting picture of the girl Zeke had just met. The Olivia he'd encountered was fiery, disproportionately annoyed and maybe a little bit right. But the version of Olivia that Aditi knew seemed determined, strategic and deeply loved by her best friend. If his instincts were correct, she was probably the kind of girl who couldn't live without her notebook. So, Zeke had no choice but to find her and give it back. He just had to figure out where to find Olivia.

13
Zeke

The day of the opening ceremony

The Olympic opening ceremony was always a spectacle, and Athens 2024 was no exception. In fact, because Greece was the birthplace of the Olympics, the Greek committee had stepped up their game more than any other host country before them. The Olympic Stadium had cost just south of a billion pounds to build and when people around the world, across all twenty-four time zones, turned on their TV screens to watch that very first night, they could instantly tell why.

It was eight a.m. in Honolulu and a woman had just come home from her morning swim. She turned her laptop on as she cut up a bowl of fruit and ran to her sofa to hear the first beats of the introduction music start to play.

It had just hit one a.m. in Jakarta and three generations of a family were gathered together in their living room. The youngest son, a five-year-old who'd started learning how to play football just the week before, watched in awe as the first flash of colour appeared on the TV screen.

At nine p.m. in Nairobi, a group of university students gathered around an outdoor screen. At three p.m. in São Paulo, a man who'd once dreamed of becoming a gymnast turned the orientation lock on his phone. And at six p.m. in Reykjavík, two newlyweds looked for the remote to turn on their hotel room TV. They were all there, waiting with bated breath, ready to watch the opening ceremony.

The stadium dissolved into complete darkness and their TV screens went quiet. The commentators stopped speaking and everyone looked up in anticipation. Then it began.

A bright flash of light leaped out on to the stadium as a golden bolt of lightning began to form on the ground, crackling and spreading across the floor until it exploded and filled the stadium with light. The light revealed a gorgeous stage in the shape of a mountain. It was Mount Olympus, the home of the Greek gods. And as music began to fill the stadium, people dressed in white wearing green leaf wreaths began to walk out of hidden doors and make their way on to the stage, forming a crowd of people playing the role of Ancient Athenians.

Zeke Moyo had stayed up late or woken up early to watch every Olympic opening ceremony since he was eight years old. But watching this one, knowing that he'd be inside the stadium by the end of the night, made the whole thing feel even more magical.

Zeke, Team GB and all the other Olympic teams couldn't enter the stadium until it was time for the athletes' parade. So, they were sitting in a field outside the stadium watching it on a set of big screens.

A man dressed as Zeus, the Greek god of sky and thunder, walked out on to the stage version of Mount Olympus that had been created in the middle of the stadium. He had a long white beard and the regal demeanour of a king. What followed was a majestic performance portraying the beginning of the ancient Olympic Games through stories, songs and meticulously choreographed dance.

Zeke kept asking one of the Greek volunteers what it all meant. But he didn't have to understand every detail of the story unfolding before him to be completely mesmerized. It was the most incredible performance he'd ever seen.

People of all ages, races and appearances began to fill the stage as the music grew louder and more ethereal. The audience watched on in wonder as they heard stories about Ancient Greece, learned about the country's history and discovered the city's role in the creation of the ancient Olympics.

Zeke watched gravity-defying stunts, marvelled at all the incredible layers of the set and clapped after each song, dance and performance that made up the first third of the ceremony.

Once the performances were done and the crowd got up to applaud the show they'd just seen, Zeke and the rest of Team GB formed an excited line behind their flag-bearers to join the athletes' parade. As each team walked in, the audience welcomed them with rolls of applause, whether they had over six hundred athletes like Team USA or a small but powerful delegation like the Refugee Olympic Team. When it was time for Team GB to go in, Zeke and his teammates walked out into the stadium to an even louder round of applause than Zeke remembered hearing in Tokyo.

Zeke's eyes widened; he could feel the goosebumps springing up across his skin. The audience was a glittering wave of colourful shirts and beaming smiles. He could see the flags of every country he could possibly imagine hanging down from the rafters. The energy was infectious. As he walked, ran and danced around the perimeter with his teammates and oldest friends, for a few minutes all his worries and questions about what came next melted away. All he could do was hold his friends tight and stare out at the stadium in awe. If this was the pinnacle, it would be more than enough.

Once each country's team had walked in and the athletes were seated around the stage, the stadium dimmed to complete darkness. Classical music filled the air and the screens lit up with a live video of one man running through Athens with a flaming torch in his hand. Then he was surrounded by a sea of excited children, running alongside him with their own makeshift torches. He passed the torch on to an older woman, whose eyes filled with tears as she approached the stadium. The world watched as nervous local heroes, famous athletes and legendary Athenians passed on the torch, until at last they entered the stadium. The final link in the chain walked up on to the stage and lit the fire. The crowd erupted into applause.

The 2024 Athens Olympic Games had officially begun.

14
Olivia

The day of the opening ceremony

Olivia hadn't left the house that morning thinking she would end the night performing a Mariah Carey duet with a Bulgarian weightlifter to a rowdy crowd of Australian water-sports champions. But nothing about the time she'd spent so far in the Olympic Village had gone the way she'd expected it to.

Olivia had decided to make the best of things. Lars Lindberg had her internship now and, as much as she wanted to march back to the HR office and give them a piece of her mind, she knew that at this point it was up to her to find a solution. To take the scraps she'd been given and carefully craft them into something beautiful. So, Olivia was determined to ace her second day.

As an 'all-rounder' volunteer (she was still workshopping how to make it sound more prestigious on her CV), her job was to answer walkie-talkie calls and travel around the Village helping people in different departments who needed a spare pair of hands. Her office for the next two weeks would be the reception desk of the Athletes' Hub. When she arrived, she was greeted by a tall, tanned guy wearing a volunteer uniform. He had curly blond hair and an incredibly friendly Australian accent.

'Olivia? Hey! I'm Arlo, so excited to meet you!' he said as he reached out to shake her hand. He had the energy of a golden retriever.

As he showed her the ropes, Olivia tried to keep the conversation focused on work and how she could become the very best at it. She still had to find a way back to her dream career at the Olympics, after all. But Arlo loved to chat. She found out that he'd been travelling around the world for the past four years: 'It was a gap year that went completely out of control!' That he'd alternated between teaching surfing classes and working at coffee shops. And that he was staying in Athens with his boyfriend's family while he volunteered at the Games. Arlo was in the middle of telling her about the 'absolutely mind-bending' surfing trip he'd taken in Bali when Olivia's walkie-talkie buzzed.

'First walkie-talkie call!' Arlo said enthusiastically. The call was from one of the volunteers working in Canada House, whose athletes had just run out of bathroom towels. So, Arlo and Olivia grabbed their walkie-talkies and made their way to the laundrettes. As they walked around the Village, Olivia quickly realized that Arlo seemed to know everyone. When they got to Canada House, he asked the concierge about her five-year-old daughter. He asked if the cleaner had enjoyed the shawarma at the restaurant Arlo had recommended to him, and whether the security guard had caught up on the latest episode of the Korean crime drama they were both obsessed with. Olivia trailed behind, trying to look friendly as Arlo flitted around like an excited puppy. His unbridled enthusiasm was infectious and as the two of them walked around running errands, she vowed to be a bit more like Arlo. And to say 'yes' to everything that came her way.

When she was asked to handwrite 200 names on to the tickets being sent to national delegates, she said yes. When she got a walkie-talkie call to pick up all the sweaty towels the German rugby team had used after training, she said yes. And when Arlo asked her what her plans were for watching the opening ceremony that night, Olivia said . . .

'Can you stage a walkie-talkie call that gets us into the stadium?'

'No, but I can get you into the second-best watch party in town,' Arlo said.

So, Olivia said yes.

Arlo had arrived in Athens months ago. He'd been volunteering on the preparation side of the Games and had become the self-appointed social secretary of the Village volunteers. So once their shift ended, Olivia and Arlo headed to the other side of the Village and into a bustling sports bar that the volunteers were commandeering as their own. They were surrounded by a crowd of people wearing the same matching blue-and-yellow uniform. Arlo introduced her to more people than she could possibly keep count of. Usually, Olivia dragged Aditi along to every social event she went to, but she was at a food influencer party that night in the centre of Athens. And she didn't have the security credentials to get into the Village, anyway. However, Arlo was the perfect friend-making wingman and soon Olivia felt completely at home with the volunteers.

As she settled into the atmosphere, she began to feel excited about her summer again. According to Instagram,

Lars Lindberg was watching the opening ceremony from a VIP booth in the stadium with all the OOT executives Olivia had worked so hard to research. But she was sitting in a big sprawling viewing party watching it with people who'd spent their whole lives following those five intersecting rings. People who loved the Olympics just as much as her and weren't afraid to show it. She decided that this was just as good.

The volunteers were completely mesmerized by the opening ceremony unfolding just a short walk away from them. When the performers on stage did something spectacular, everybody clapped. When the story being performed got emotional, some people wept. And when it was time to watch the athletes' parade, they cheered for every single country. Olivia took a photo of the ten-person strong Zimbabwean team and sent it to her dad, who texted her back saying 'by the time you run the Olympics, that will be a 100 person team'. Olivia shook her head, realizing that eventually she would have to tell her parents the truth. But before she could dwell on it, she got distracted by the party. The volunteers really were her kind of people. She talked to a Scottish guy volunteering in the accreditation office about how much they'd both loved listening to the London 2012 Olympic soundtrack. She chatted to an Indonesian woman volunteering at the ticket office about how she travelled the world working at events just like this. And she split a big plate of chips and dips with a group of Brazilians volunteering in the transport department as they told her about all of the best places in the Village that weren't on the official map. When the final section of the ceremony began, the crowd came to a hush again as they watched the torch relay in wonderstruck silence. The 2024 Athens Olympic Games had officially begun.

Olivia was ready to leave the Village, head back to the apartment she and Aditi were staying in and call it a night. She had to wake up on time the next morning for her second official full day. And she was planning on applying for new jobs to get her life back on track in time for September. But as she mapped her route back home, Arlo found her and put an end to her plans for an early night.

'Olivia, you are not going home, we have *parties* to go to,' he said with a glimmer in his eyes.

Olivia had heard rumours about the Village after-parties. About the drinking games, wild dares and noisy bedrooms. That in London 2012 a whole team of French volleyball players had ended the night skinny-dipping in the River Lea. And that during Rio 2016, a group of Canadian cyclists had somehow woken up six hours away in São Paulo. She knew the after-parties were a thing of legend, but walking into one was a whole other experience. Arlo, because he was Arlo, had already befriended a few athletes. They'd invited him to a party happening in the huge apartment block occupied by Team Australia and said he could bring a plus one. As they walked up the path they heard loud, intoxicating noughties pop music pouring out of the windows. Olivia reaffirmed her vow to keep saying yes. Arlo opened the door, music blasted out and the two of them were pulled into the wildest, most cinematic party Olivia had ever seen.

As the opening beats of 'Lose Control' by Missy Elliott kicked in, Olivia realized that she was stepping into what could only be described as a high-performing athlete rager. There were clusters of people on every floor drinking out of plastic cups. High-energy pop music playing from different speakers up and down the building. And fresh-faced athletes, who'd been on their very best behaviour during the opening ceremony, completely letting loose. People were dancing in the halls, kissing in quiet corners and taking photos of the party with the unspoken agreement that nothing scandalous would ever leave their phones. The athletes all had immaculate reputations to maintain, sponsors to keep happy and home countries to impress. Posting a risky photo of another athlete guaranteed mutually assured destruction, so while they let themselves go at the party, they kept it cute online.

At first, Olivia watched from the sidelines. But then Arlo convinced her to take a round of shots with him and another group of volunteers who'd ended up at the party. If she'd been an intern like she'd planned to be, she would've tried to stay professional. But there was none of that pressure now, so she let herself go. She danced to old Britney songs with the Argentinian volleyball team and bonded over her current favourite TV show, *Call My Agent!*, with some French cyclists.

Then she and Arlo saw a table set up with a laptop and three microphones. They exchanged a knowing glance and then nodded. Sometimes people misunderstood Olivia, thought she was too focused to have a good time. But Olivia loved a good party and, even more than that, Olivia *really* loved karaoke.

15
Zeke

The day of the opening ceremony

In the months leading up to a competition, Zeke was incredibly disciplined. He stuck to a strict sleep schedule, carefully planned out his dietitian-approved meals and did everything he could to make sure he was at the very top of his game. But there was something about the opening ceremony that made him, and all the other athletes, want to let loose. As soon as the ceremony was over and the final pieces of confetti had fallen to the ground, they let go of their inhibitions.

Zeke watched as everyone around him got their phones out, texting and calling back and forth to decide which after-party to go to. Well, which after-party to go to *first*. Fionn, the captain of the Irish hockey team, sent Zeke a message saying they had ordered kegs. Then Kwabena, one of his friends on the Ghanaian boxing team, invited him to a house party that was guaranteed to have the best music of the night. But Zeke's plans were decided when Haruki found him in the crowd. He ran over and threw an arm around Zeke's shoulder.

'I had a vision,' said Haruki.

'You did?' said Zeke. Nothing good ever came from Haruki's visions.

'It came to me while the choir was singing, divine intervention, I think,' Haruki said with the kind of grin that always ended in chaos.

'What was the vision?' Zeke asked, not entirely sure he wanted to know.

'Australia . . .'

'Absolutely not,' said Zeke. The Australian team was known for having the wildest parties in the Olympic Village and Zeke had training first thing the next morning.

'Ezekiel,' said Haruki, using the fake strict voice he used whenever he was about to convince Zeke to do something he shouldn't. They were as close as brothers and, like brothers, they were really good at getting each other into trouble. 'This is THE opening ceremony night. We've got to go big or go home, and Australia is the biggest party of the night.'

So, an hour later, they'd let themselves be pulled into the joyful recklessness of the first night in the Village. Music bounced off the walls, spontaneous dance floors popped up wherever they turned and a whole delegation of athletes from around the world spread out across all ten floors of the building to party with the Australians. Zeke was playing a particularly energetic game of beer pong with the Colombian weightlifting team when he saw *her*. Olivia.

At first, he wasn't sure if he was actually seeing who he thought he was. Rationally, Zeke knew that if she'd been in the Village the day before, she was probably here for a reason and likely to stay for the whole Games. But he hadn't expected to see her again so soon . . . or at a place like this, for that matter. From their interaction yesterday, he wouldn't have guessed her to be the party type. But there she was, climbing on to a table on the other side of the kitchen.

She wasn't wearing that sexy green suit this time. Instead, she was wearing a blue-and-yellow volunteer top tucked into a denim skirt. Her hair wasn't in a tight ponytail any more; her braids were flowing freely past her shoulders and down her back. But it wasn't her outfit that made her seem so different, it was the expression on her face. In place of the scowl and righteous anger he'd seen on her yesterday was a look of pure joy. She was grinning at something the guy next to her was saying. Zeke knew he was up next in the game of beer pong, but he couldn't tear his eyes away from her. And a moment later, nobody could. Because Olivia wasn't just standing on the table for kicks. The lights in the room dimmed, a projector was positioned on a kitchen cupboard and a crowd formed around the table. The words were projected on to the wall and Olivia put the microphone to her mouth with absolutely zero self-consciousness.

'And I was like, why are you so obsessed with me?' she said. The opening beats of 'Obsessed' by Mariah Carey spilled out of all the speakers on that floor of the party. *Olivia – karaoke?* Zeke was completely transfixed. Olivia wasn't a good singer, like *at all*. In fact, she was really, really bad. But she was giving a *performance*. Dancing on the table and pulling facial expressions that matched each line of the song. Singing the lyrics with such passion that it was as if she'd written them herself. And the crowd was eating it up. The Australian swim team were clapping along to the beat, a group of Venezuelan boxers were dancing and two Tanzanian runners were singing the backing vocals like they were in the audience of a concert.

'You're delusional, boy, you're losing your mind,' she sang, her eyes closed as if singing a hymn. Zeke couldn't help but laugh. He realized that the Olivia he'd met the day before was a completely different version to the one who was making a stage of the kitchen table. As she opened her eyes to sing the chorus, she looked out at her adoring crowd and danced to cheers from all around the room. She had them in the palm of her hand.

Zeke couldn't look away and maybe she could feel him watching because, when she got to the next verse, they locked eyes. She looked startled at first, as if she hadn't expected to see him there either. He raised his plastic cup to her and, in response, she shook her head and went back to her performance. He was completely enthralled. Once she finished her song, the whole room applauded. She bowed and then jumped off the table before disappearing into the crowd.

Zeke led his beer pong team to victory and let them convince him to take a celebratory round of shots. But, like everyone kept reminding him, he was *so close* to winning his first gold, and really couldn't afford to be hung-over during training the next morning. So as the Australian rugby team started chanting a drinking song, he decided it was time to go home.

He scanned the room, looking for Haruki. But, instead, he found Olivia. She was sitting on a kitchen stool gazing out at the party and nodding along to an old Aaliyah song. She looked completely relaxed, like this was exactly where she belonged. She mouthed the lyrics to the song, absent-mindedly twirling her straw around her red cup. Then she caught his eye. This time she didn't look surprised to see him. As he walked over to tell her that he'd found her notebook, he noticed afresh just how pretty she was. Getting closer, he could smell the vanilla on her skin.

'What are you going to sing?' she asked as if they were just two people talking at a party, not two strangers who'd had a full-blown argument about a cup of green juice only yesterday. Maybe she'd forgotten.

'Or are you just going to stand by the drinks table waiting to throw a cup of juice and ruin another innocent bystander's outfit?' she said, taking a sip of her drink. No, she definitely hadn't forgotten.

'I don't sing,' Zeke said, ignoring her second question.

Olivia looked at him like he'd just said he liked watching puppies get run over by motorcycles.

'Everyone sings,' she said, shaking her head. 'You don't have to be good to do karaoke.'

'Oh, you made that *very* clear,' he joked.

'I'm confident in everything I do, Ezekiel, even the things I'm not good at.'

'Everything?'

'Everything.' She didn't hesitate or break eye contact with him. 'But *you*, you're too shy to sing?' She tilted her head, casting him a judging glance, but there was a glint in her eyes, a flicker of mischief in her voice.

'I don't do karaoke.'

'Oh, so you're boring? Okay, good to know,' she nodded as she got off her stool and began to walk away.

'Wait, I'm not boring,' he called out, turning around.

'Then prove it,' she said, challenging him. Zeke looked at the crowd, the karaoke table, and then back at Olivia. He rarely felt self-conscious but the thought of singing in front of other people made him incredibly uncomfortable. Somehow, she'd found the one weak spot in his armour.

'I . . .' he started, trying to come up with an excuse.

'It's all right, you can be boring and spend the whole night standing by the wall while the rest of us have fun. Or . . .'

'Or?' Zeke asked.

Olivia put her straw in her mouth and looked up like she was thinking about it. 'I dare you to get up on that table, sing a song of *my choice* and give it your all,' she said.

'And what's in it for me?'

'You get to defend your honour,' she said with a shrug. 'It's either sing or know for the rest of your life that you chose to be boring on the first night.'

Zeke was many things, but he wasn't boring. So, before he knew it, he was walking over to the other side of the kitchen and taking the microphone.

It wasn't until Olivia and her friends had persuaded him to take a round of shots with them and he was halfway through his performance of 'Pony' by Ginuwine – Olivia's choice, not his – that he realized she'd set him up.

She didn't know anybody here; so she didn't have a reputation to damage. Whereas Zeke was staring out at a crowd of athletes he was going to see for the rest of his life.

Olivia was looking up at him in delight; he'd played right into her hands. There wasn't a scoreboard, yet they both knew Olivia was winning.

But Zeke wasn't one to back down in the face of a challenge, so as he sang the final chorus he looked into the crowd and caught her eye. She nodded and so did he. The games had begun.

16

Olivia

Day one of the 2024 Olympics

Olivia was in love. It happened unexpectedly, caught her off guard and completely swept her off her feet. Sending her into the kind of ecstasy that forced her to close her eyes to experience it fully. All the sounds around her grew more vivid and, for a moment, she forgot everything that she was worried about and every way she'd ever felt slighted.

Because Olivia was falling in love with a Koulouri Thessalonikis. The most perfect piece of bread she'd ever eaten. It was ring-shaped and covered with toasted sesame seeds, crunchy on the outside with a mouth-wateringly soft, chewy centre. She hadn't expected it, and she knew she would never be the same.

'Try it with this,' said Aditi as she slid a plate of feta and tomatoes over the table. Olivia broke off a chunk of her koulouri, sliced it and then added the feta and tomato. She took a bite. It was so good that she could have wept.

'I think I should move to Greece,' Olivia said, looking at her koulouri with such reverence that you'd never have guessed it was just the Greek equivalent of a bagel.

That morning Olivia had woken up with a pounding headache and an embarrassingly clear memory of the previous night. But before she could bury her head back in her pillow, Aditi dragged her out of bed to say that she 'absolutely, non-negotiably' had to go and try a new cafe with her.

Olivia put on her volunteer uniform then helped Aditi carry her camera bag and tripod across Athens into a quieter area of the city to visit the Mnisikleous Street Stairs – a set of old steps lined with cafes, restaurants and beautiful stone houses. As Aditi took photos, Olivia looked up to see bright-green leaves and red bougainvillea flowers growing all around them. Kalopsia was a family-owned cafe with climbing grapevines on its walls and picturesque blue doors and shutters. The two of them ordered small portions of everything they served for breakfast, two huge glasses of fruit juice and, for Aditi, a cup of every single type of coffee on the menu. They spent a solid ten minutes rearranging plates and finding the perfect angles so Aditi could take the photos and videos she needed before they settled down to eat breakfast.

Olivia thought she'd done a pretty good job of tiptoeing back into the apartment last night and that Aditi hadn't noticed how hoarse her voice was from singing. But nothing escaped her best friend.

'So, I'm guessing Summer Olivia made an appearance last night?'

'I have no idea what you're talking about,' Olivia said, but it was a hopeless battle.

'I mean, this,' Aditi said, sliding her phone over to show a video of Olivia sitting on a table in between two Bulgarian weightlifters, singing 'Fantasy' by Mariah Carey.

'Ah, Svetlana and Viktor,' Olivia said. She'd gone from

dancing with Arlo to being introduced to the Bulgarian weightlifting team, to convincing them to do another round of shots and karaoke with her. She watched herself, remembering how much fun she'd had, but then realized there was absolutely no reason for Aditi to have that video. Thanks to her rapidly growing following of devoted iced coffee enthusiasts, Aditi had been invited to an influencer watch party hosted by an athleisure/decaf coffee company.

'Where did you get this?' Olivia asked.

'Well, you tagged this guy named Arlo in a photo of you in your uniform last night, so I went to his profile and watched his story. Then I saw that he'd tagged a Danish sailor. So, I went to her story. She'd posted a selfie with a volunteer, who'd posted a carousel of photos from the opening ceremony. That led me to a story posted by a Bulgarian weightlifter, Svetlana, which led me to this video of you,' Aditi confessed.

'Aditi, I think we need to talk about your deep-stalking skills,' Olivia said.

'You can't distract me with an intervention. What happened last night?' Aditi was single-minded at the chance of a Summer Olivia resurgence. So, Olivia told her about the after-party and the interaction she'd had with Zeke.

'I can't decide whether you hate him or kind of fancy him,' Aditi said wistfully.

'Aditi? I told you he spilled juice all over me, told me to be *nice* and then insinuated that I was a bad singer. What is there to like?' Olivia said.

'Your voice,' Aditi said as if she could see right through her. 'Your voice does the same thing when you're talking about someone you hate as it does when you're talking about someone you like.'

'No, it doesn't,' said Olivia, stabbing her fruit salad and eating a whole forkful in one go.

'Oh yeah, it definitely does. There's always a thin line between you hating a guy and really just fancying them. When we were kids, you used to be mean to boys you liked in the playground and find something to dislike about them so you could—' Aditi began, but Olivia was not going to have that conversation.

'I don't like him. And if everything goes according to plan, I'm never going to see him again unless it's on the TV,' she said decisively.

'Whatever you say,' Aditi replied in a sing-song voice.

'And even if I did like him, or anybody I met in the Village, nothing would happen. I don't do summer flings—'

'Except that one time,' Aditi said.

'Which is *never* going to happen again,' Olivia said. 'Summer is dangerous. So, the only guy I'm going to think about for the next two weeks is Noah in HR, because I still need to find a way to get a real job at the Olympics.' Aditi couldn't argue with that.

'Wait, I haven't even told you the most devastating thing that happened yesterday – I went to lost property but still couldn't find my notebook!' Olivia said, disappointed. The iridescent *Cool Runnings*-inspired I AM FEELING VERY OLYMPIC TODAY notebook had been a congratulations gift from Aditi. Her best friend knew how much she loved the movie, and how much she liked organizing her life out into lists, and so she'd given her the special personalized iridescent notebook in a ribbon-tied box as soon as they'd arrived in Athens. Olivia loved it on sight and had laughed out loud when she saw the note Aditi had written her on the first page. But when she'd gone to repack her work bag, she'd realized it was missing. She'd searched the whole apartment to try and find it, to no avail.

'I remember holding it before I went to Olympic prison, but I can't remember opening it again,' she said with a sigh, trying to retrace her steps across the Village to narrow her search. But before she could whittle it down, her phone started ringing. She glanced down at the caller ID and then immediately looked away.

'Aren't you going to answer?' Aditi asked as they both looked at the phone. The caller ID was Olivia's mum.

'No,' Olivia said, taking another bite of her koulouri. Aditi gave her a quizzical look.

'You haven't told them yet? Liv!' said Aditi, but instead of answering, Olivia declined the call and quickly typed out a text telling her mum that she was so busy getting ready for the third day of her internship that she would have to call her back later on that night.

No, Olivia hadn't told her parents that she wasn't doing the internship she'd flown to Athens for. And she had absolutely no intention of telling them until she fixed it. Her parents wanted her to do well, but they weren't the overbearing type. Still, she'd aced school, got a first-class degree and stacked up her CV with the kinds of things that made them proud.

Olivia knew they wouldn't be disappointed in her if she told them the truth. But she knew they would be disappointed *for her*, which was somehow worse. She was the one who was supposed to overcome and achieve everything their generation hadn't been able to. So, she told them a white lie to protect their feelings, promised Aditi that she'd keep saying yes to everything that sounded like fun, and then she hopped on the shuttle to the other side of Athens to begin her third day in the Village. And track down her iridescent notebook.

17
Zeke

Day one of the 2024 Olympics

Zeke woke up the next morning feeling like he'd been dragged through the streets of Athens, beaten up and then tossed around by a mechanical bull. His head was pounding, his eyes were burning and his stomach was threatening to spill itself out on to the ground.

'Here we go. Look who didn't take my advice,' said Coach Adam, shaking his head as Zeke and his teammates walked into the gym the next morning.

'I told you, party or no party, training starts at six a.m.,' Coach said as Zeke, who was wearing sunglasses to shield himself from the gym lights, slowly walked towards a treadmill. Things had taken a left turn after karaoke. And despite his better judgement, he'd allowed himself to get swept up in the recklessness of the party. But hangover or no hangover, he and the rest of the team had a competition to train for.

There were fifteen other runners on the men's team and each of them was on their own specific training regimen. But they always worked out together at the beginning of the Games. So that morning, they spread out across the gym on treadmills, skipping ropes and ellipticals. They lifted weights and stretched themselves out, did leg curls and hundreds of push-ups.

The workout was soundtracked to Coach Adam's favourite playlist of '70s funk music. At first, it was grating: the music was too bright and cheerful for a team fighting their worst hangovers of the year. But a few litres of water and a two-hour workout later, Zeke started to feel more human. Once they'd finished, half of the team went to breakfast and the other half split off to sit in different parts of the gym so they could have one-on-one sessions with their respective coaches. Coach Adam had been working with Zeke ever since he'd joined Team GB, so they sat down and went over their strategy to get Zeke to the other side of the finish line in record time.

'It's just about improving your technique. Your stamina is great, your speed is better than ever, but you need to make your strides more precise,' said Coach Adam. He replayed the last five seconds of a video he'd filmed of Zeke's last practice run and he leaned over to watch. Zeke loved second-by-second analysis. He combed through each frame to dissect his every move and watched it back by the millisecond to see it from different perspectives. That was the only way he could be sure that he'd truly done everything in his power to be his very best. So, they sat and analysed his run, made a list of things he needed to work on before their next one-on-one training session and then Zeke got ready to leave.

'Team Jamaica has the track booked for the rest of the morning, so we'll practise at twelve p.m., okay?'

'Nothing like watching the competition go first to motivate me, right?' said Zeke. The race to get the 100-metre gold was always a fierce battle between the athletes in Team Jamaica and Team USA. So, everyone had been surprised when he'd won silver at the last Olympics.

'Exactly – a healthy amount of fear always makes you run faster,' joked Coach Adam, 'and don't forget the BBC shoot.'

'Have I ever let you down, Coach?' said Zeke. But then he remembered all the times he had. 'Don't worry, I'll be on time.' He grabbed his training bag and headed over to the canteen to have breakfast. His body wanted a greasy full English breakfast with a big cup of coffee and a whole plate of bacon to soak up his hangover. But that morning his dietitian assigned him . . . a bowl of oatmeal, a banana and a boiled egg.

When Zeke got to the table where his teammates were sitting, he saw an exhausted-looking Haruki sipping a detox juice as he ate breakfast on the other side of the canteen with the rest of the Japanese swimmers. Haruki gave him a tired wave and mouthed 'Help' with a hand over his heart.

'All right, team. Last night, where did you go, who did you meet and what stories am I going to have to swear to never tell a single soul?' asked Anwar as he approached their table.

'I did one round of shots with the Korean archery girls, then spent the night dancing in Nigeria house,' said Camille.

'I ended up in a really intense poker game with a bunch of marathon runners,' said Anwar.

'I woke up in Sweden,' said Frankie.

'Zeke? You're awfully quiet today,' said Camille.

'I partied with the Australians,' Zeke said, knowing that

was enough for them to understand exactly how his night had gone.

'Oh, that explains why you're wearing sunglasses inside,' said Camille.

'And the two jugs of water,' said Anwar.

'I heard there was a . . . cross-Atlantic meeting?' said Frankie, raising an eyebrow, and the whole table 'ooohed' conspiratorially. Gossip spread like wildfire in the Village. Somehow his tragic attempt at karaoke hadn't left the party, but his two-minute interaction with Valentina was part of that morning's gossip train.

'So, does that mean that you and Valentina are getting back together?' asked Camille with a grin. She leaned forward. Camille was the one who'd introduced Zeke to Valentina in Tokyo and, after Haruki, she was the most fervent supporter of their relationship.

'I told you Zekentina was endgame,' she said, nudging Frankie.

Frankie shrugged. 'I still prefer Valenkiel.'

'Valenkiel sounds like a foot ointment,' she retorted. As the two of them went back and forth, Zeke remembered what had happened immediately after his karaoke performance. Olivia had clapped along with the rest of the crowd, but before he could find her again to tell her that he'd found her notebook, she had disappeared into thin air. Then, Valentina had walked into the kitchen. And everyone in the room had been stealing glances.

'Hey, Z,' Valentina had said, pulling him into a hug, either unaware or unaffected by the fact that all eyes were on them. Zeke was aware, but he hadn't cared. He was just happy to see her.

'I'm so glad you're here,' he'd said, hugging her back. He genuinely meant it. They called and texted pretty regularly since the break-up, but this was the first time they'd seen each other in person, and it felt . . . nice.

It was strange, Zeke thought, that he could stand in front of someone who knew the very best and worst of him. But somehow slip into a casual conversation like they were *just* old friends. It had been a year since their break-up, but it was the most amicable break-up of Zeke's life. And when it came to a romantic relationship, they were fundamentally incompatible. So when she'd flown to London to have 'the talk' and explained her reasons, he'd accepted it and understood. They broke up, but stayed friends.

Before Valentina, Zeke had never imagined there could be heartbreak without resentment, or separation without a perpetual feeling of loss. He was his mother's child, after all. The love he felt for the people who'd come into his life never went away. But as he talked to Valentina in the kitchen at the party, he realized that his love for her had found a way to take on a new form.

'So, you two, that's happening again?' asked Anwar curiously, back in the canteen.

'We're just friends,' Zeke said with a shrug.

'All right,' said Camille, rolling her eyes. 'I'll pretend you're *just friends*, but when you both come to your senses and decide to get married, I'm going to be the maid of honour.'

Zeke glanced over at his phone. He'd put it on silent that morning to stop himself from getting distracted during training. But now there were seven missed calls and a rapidly growing list of text messages from Coach Adam.

That much phone activity could only mean one thing. Something terrible had happened to someone he loved, or Zeke was in big trouble. It was almost always the latter, so he winced and called back.

'Hey, Coach,' Zeke said, grimacing at the rest of the team, who instantly recognized the face of someone who was about to get told off.

'Ezekiel Moyo,' Coach said, sounding exasperated. 'Why do you never answer your phone?' Coach Adam had two teenage daughters, so whenever he got annoyed, he switched to dad mode.

'Coach, have I ever told you how much I appreciate you?' Zeke began, but it was useless. Coach Adam couldn't be sweet-talked out of irritation.

'Ezekiel, I put this in your calendar months ago. But it's ten-oh-seven and you're not here yet.'

Zeke closed his eyes as he remembered what Coach was talking about. The BBC interviews. *Damn.* The video shoot was supposed to start at ten a.m. It would take him twenty-five minutes to walk to the venue and he was already seven minutes late. Zeke needed something that would get him to the other side of the Village, and he needed it fast.

He swiped through his phone, opened the golf buggy app and booked a ride. 'I'll be right there, Coach.'

18

Olivia

Day one of the 2024 Olympics

When Olivia arrived at the Village for her third day, she marched over to Olympic prison – or the OOT Office as some people liked to call it – to make a deal with Noah from HR. She told him that she was going to spend the next two weeks doing such a good job that he would have no choice but to write her a glowing reference and consider her for one of their autumn graduate programmes.

But her resolution to say yes to everything and excel at every walkie-talkie request hit its first stumbling block when the equestrian team called for help with 'clean-up'. When Olivia spoke to the stable master on her walkie-talkie, she tried her very best not to think about what he actually meant by 'clean-up'. But as soon as she arrived at the stable, Friedrich, the German head stable keeper, handed her a pair of overalls and led her out to the dressage field. She smelt the horse poo before she saw it.

'How long have you been doing this?' she asked Friedrich, trying to distract herself from the smell by getting him talking.

'Picking up horse shit? An hour. Stable keeping? Thirty years. Longer than you've been alive,' he said with a grin.

'Do you enjoy it?' she asked, curious.

'Working with horses? Best job in the world,' he said, before telling her his favourite horse stories with such genuine joy that he made her smile in spite of the horse poo on her brand-new trainers. She decided that if she was going to spend time picking up horse poo, she was going to be the best horse poo picker-upper that Friedrich had ever seen and do such an efficient job of it that Friedrich would write her a reference too. In fact, she decided she was going to get one from as many of the Olympic staff and volunteers she interacted with as possible. After clean-up, she had a shower, changed her uniform and bought a mini body spray from the Village pharmacy to make sure she didn't smell like a horse stable. She grimaced at the notification on her phone telling her that with each new purchase she was getting closer and closer to her credit-card limit. But she didn't have time to dwell or freak out about how long it would take her to get out of debt, because it was time for her next walkie-talkie call.

As it took around forty minutes to walk from one side of the Village to the other, athletes were allowed to book buggy rides to drive them to training sessions and competitions. Olivia had undertaken a two-hour golf buggy driving lesson during her training day. And, since the transport team was short on drivers, Olivia was called in as back-up. There had been a surprise summer storm last night, and while it now looked like a perfect summer's day, there were still a few big puddles scattered across the Village. So, Olivia was extra careful and drove a gnarly fifteen miles an hour to the athletes' apartments to pick up her first two passengers. She'd made a mental list of questions and conversation topics in her quest to get to know more people. She asked a group of Congolese boxers about the opening ceremony and their journey to the Games. A pair of Chilean swimmers told her about the best places they'd gone open-water swimming. And she learned the Swedish words for 'hello' (*hallå*), 'thank you' (*tack*) and 'it's too hot' (*det är för varmt*) from two archers on their way back from the gym.

After an hour, Olivia had driven around the Village and studied her map well enough to stop needing the buggy app to give her directions. And, to her surprise, she was really enjoying buggy patrol. Her new role allowed her to drive around to almost every part of the Village and meet so many interesting people that she'd forgotten this wasn't the summer she'd planned for. But then things went downhill. Literally.

On her way back to the Hub she took a right turn and found herself hurtling down a particularly long and steep slope. She reflexively put her foot down on the brakes, but they didn't respond. She pressed down harder to no avail. She shouted, 'Look out!' to a group of Bolivian divers, who ran away before she could accidentally commit vehicular manslaughter. But the buggy just kept on rolling. She thought about putting her leg out to stop it, but it would be *so* inconvenient to break her leg. Would her travel insurance cover it? Would she need to pay for the plaster and cast? How much would it cost to go to the hospital in a foreign country? She couldn't afford to spend the last of her credit card on a trip to the hospital. So, she lifted her foot, made one last attempt at pressing down on the brakes and then let the buggy decide her fate. This time the brakes did respond, but they responded at the exact moment she rolled into a wet ditch at the bottom of the slope. She came to a sharp stop and a whole bucket's worth of mud flew up from the ground and splattered all over her, soaking her uniform with a thick layer of dirt.

Olivia closed her eyes and willed every single one of Aditi's inspirational quotes to come and give her strength. She wanted to drive back to the Hub to make her second uniform change of the day. But before she could, her Village phone flashed with a new message, forcing her to shake herself off and move on. Passenger #137 had booked a buggy ride.

So, instead of driving straight back to the office, she shook herself off and drove to her next pick-up. There were quite a few athletes lined up outside the canteen so after a few minutes of waiting to be found, Olivia decided to call out the number on her screen.

'Number one three seven,' she said, then realized that nobody was going to hear her if she used her inside voice.

'Number one three seven!' she said again, this time a little bit louder, trying to channel the energy of a market-stall seller. A few athletes glanced over at her mud-splattered buggy and at least three people actively avoided making eye contact with her after seeing the splotchy brown stains on her shirt. But nobody walked towards her. So she shouted to try and find the athlete who had booked her.

'Number One! Three! Seven!' she called out, noticing the way a few people looked over like there was something wrong with her. But she didn't have time to be self-conscious, she had a graduate job to secure by becoming the best volunteer in the Village, after all.

'Number one three seven? That's me,' said a voice she recognized.

There was a whole crowd of athletes from different countries lined up outside the canteen, but one towered above the crowd, Zeke Moyo. He looked at her mud-soaked buggy, then the stain on her shirt, and opened his mouth as if to make a joke of the situation. But instead, he locked eyes with her. The contact sent a shiver down her spine. Then he shook his head and visibly held in his laughter. She tried her best to remind herself of all her reasons to dislike him. The green juice-stained suit, his borderline arrogant banter and the fact that he probably spent his spare time hanging around with Lars Lindberg. But as he strode towards her with his broad shoulders, perfectly formed face and amused smile, she realized that Aditi was right. When it came to Zeke, Olivia was walking a *very* thin line.

19
Zeke

Day one of the 2024 Olympics

'Are you going to serenade me today?' Zeke asked as soon as he was in the buggy.

'Are you going to do such a painful performance that I have to give you a pity clap like everyone at the party did?' Olivia said without missing a beat.

'Was it that bad?' He remembered his mortifying karaoke performance.

'Let's just say that it lacked self-belief,' she said as she scanned the Village map, planned her route and started driving.

'That's a pretty diplomatic response. I wasn't sure you were capable of one,' he said.

'I'm the most diplomatic person I know,' Olivia said indignantly, and then paused. 'Okay, in the top ten most diplomatic people I know.'

'That lacked self-belief, Olivia,' Zeke said and, to his surprise, she started laughing. It was a warm laugh, the kind that would make strangers want to turn around just so they could be in on the joke. He wanted to keep making her laugh.

'So did you trick me into doing bad karaoke to avenge your suit?' he asked.

'I didn't trick you, you just fell into my trap,' she said, sounding delighted.

'Well, for the record, the only thing I'm bad at is singing,' he said.

'And walking in straight lines,' she said.

'I win medals when I run in them.'

'*And* being humble,' she said.

'That makes two of us,' he said.

She shrugged. 'And you're really bad at apologizing. Because I'm still waiting on that apology, Moyo,' she said.

'You're never going to let that go, are you?'

'No! I loved that suit,' she said, though she didn't actually seem that annoyed at him any more.

'Okay.' He took a breath. 'I could tell your suit was new and you looked like you were having a bad day, so I'm sorry for spilling juice all over it.' Zeke should've stopped there but he couldn't help but tease her. 'However, while some part of me feels bad about ruining your suit, it looks like having things spilt all over you is a regular occurrence. So, it was probably going to happen anyway—'

'Don't start,' interrupted Olivia, putting her right hand up in mock annoyance.

'I'm just pointing out the elephant-sized stain in the room,' said Zeke, thrilled as he watched Olivia's lips curve up despite her best attempts at hiding her amusement.

'You have the personality of a seventeen-year-old boy.'

'You have the comebacks of an angsty teenage girl,' he said as Olivia revved up the engine. 'And the driving skills.'

'Oh, what a surprise.' She shook her head. 'An insult about a woman's driving.'

'Wait, that's not what I meant—'

'But that's what you said.'

'Okay, so how long *have* you been in the golf buggy driving business?' Zeke asked.

'I learned how to drive it yesterday,' said Olivia.

'That makes me feel *really* safe,' said Zeke, prompting Olivia to dramatically press down on the accelerator. The buggy went at full speed and she made a quick, unnecessarily sharp turn.

'Well, you're about to feel *a lot* safer,' said Olivia in a sing-song voice as she drove at the maximum Village speed limit.

He held on to his seat, but he didn't want to let her see him sweat. She was twisting and turning with enough precision for him to know that she was in complete control of the buggy, but it still didn't feel comfortable. She stopped sharply, making Zeke's heart jump out of his chest. Then immediately revved the engine up again, catapulting the buggy back out on to the road. He could see the glint in her eye as she noticed Zeke's iron grip on the overhead handle.

'I'm a *great* driver,' she said, enjoying the power she had behind the wheel way too much. 'I have a car driving licence, a motorcycle licence *and* a lorry licence.'

'A lorry licence?' Zeke glanced over at her to try to figure out if she was bluffing.

'I could drive a heavy goods vehicle for three days across mainland Europe if I needed to.'

'Of course, women can do whatever they want, and I believe in HGV equality . . .' Zeke said.

'Look, I'm working right now, Ezekiel. I don't need your try-hard "men can be feminists too" spiel,' she said sceptically.

'Well, they can, and I am,' he said. She rolled her eyes exactly as he'd predicted she would. 'But, if it's not too impolite to ask, why do you have a lorry driving licence?'

'Partly to prove a point . . . but mostly out of spite,' she said, her eyes twinkling at the memory of her grudge-based upskilling. He couldn't figure out if he was impressed or terrified. But then he looked over at her and the answer was clear. Her expression was a mixture of mischief and delight.

'Is that something you do a lot? Take on complicated tasks just to prove a point?' he asked.

'Oh yeah, my grudges are like seeds in the orchard of my life. I like to water, feed and nurture them,' she said with a grin. He found himself glancing down at her lips.

'You strike me as the type to hold a lot of grudges.'

'*The type?* You've known me for like, what, *three minutes?*' she said. This time he knew from the bite of her lip that she wasn't annoyed at him. Olivia was flirting with him; she just had a strange way of doing it. Zeke leaned towards her, hyper-aware of the ease between them. Every line was a challenge, asking him if he was game enough to play. He was.

'Yeah, and in those three minutes, you've driven recklessly to scare me *and* thrown me to the ground,' he said.

'First of all, I didn't *throw* you to the ground.'

'Sorry, no, you're right – you didn't throw me to the ground, you *pinned* me to the ground,' he said with a smirk.

'If I'd wanted to *pin* you to the ground, you would have known it, and I wouldn't have done it like that.'

'How *would* you have done it, then?' he said as he raised an eyebrow, challenging her.

'Well, first of all I would've . . .' Her voice trailed off as she thought about it. She glanced over at Zeke, and they locked eyes for a fraction of a second. For a moment the heat in Athens felt a little bit hotter. But Olivia tore her eyes away from him before the atmosphere could get any more charged than it already was. She returned her focus back to the road. The slightly flustered look on her face confirmed that she'd felt that sharp pulse of attraction too.

'I would feel a lot safer if you slowed down, I don't want to die like this,' he said after a pause.

'I don't know, *Olympic athlete killed in freak golf buggy accident* kind of feels like a pretty good headline to go out on.'

'The fact that you're smiling as you're saying that . . . terrifies me,' he said as he looked over at her, less terrified by her driving and more alarmed by just how quickly he could feel himself starting to like her.

'That's kind of the effect I was going for,' she said with a gleam in her eyes.

For a few moments, they just sat in comfortable silence. Zeke hadn't really got the chance to walk around the Village – he'd spent most of his time in Athens so far at the gym or in practice sessions. But as Olivia drove them, he looked up at all the different venues and training facilities, noting the similarities between this Village and the ones he'd got to know in Tokyo and Rio. Then, once he was sure she was too focused on the road ahead to pay attention to him, he looked over at Olivia. She seemed completely at ease behind the wheel. She had an air of effortless confidence about her. And despite the fact that she was covered in mud and wearing a garishly bright volunteer uniform, she was still as pretty as the very first time he'd seen her. Her lips were glazed with a dewy layer of gloss that glimmered in the sunlight as she smiled into the distance. Her long, intricate braids were pulled back into a ponytail. One curl was threatening to break loose, but it gave him an unobstructed view of the delicate way her lashes framed her warm-brown determined eyes. She was gently tapping the steering wheel as if playing along to a song he couldn't hear and, while her expression was far away, the smile on her lips made it clear she was happy wherever she was in her imagination. Then she took a sharp turn to avoid a puddle on the ground and almost drove them both into the Karate Centre.

'It's not me, it's the buggy,' she muttered as she pressed down on the brakes and then started driving again. 'And the rain last night,' she added.

'Is that why you're covered in mud?' he teased.

'If you're not careful, next time I *will* drive you into a puddle,' she warned.

'Killing a national hero wouldn't look *great* on your CV, Olivia,' he joked.

'No, it probably wouldn't. And your fan club of teenage girls and middle-aged men would probably dox me too,' she nodded.

'Oh, they'd do way more than just that. They'd make true crime podcasts and write fanfiction about how you started plotting this the second we met,' he said.

'And then you'd have no choice but to come back to earth as a ghost to read fanfiction about your own murder,' she said. 'But you already do that, don't you, Zeke? Read fanfiction about yourself.'

They were both silent for a second as Zeke opened and closed his mouth.

'I knew it,' she laughed as she glanced over at him.

'In my defence, the fanfic writers know how to tell a good story,' he said, shrugging off his embarrassment. He'd accidentally stumbled across a link to a website called AO3 while reading through his mentions and found a whole trove of dubiously written but gripping fanfiction about him. He knew he probably shouldn't, but whenever he got bored, he read through new posts tagged with his name and found himself engrossed in spelling-mistake-littered epics about fictional versions of himself in increasingly imaginative scenarios.

'Why can I imagine you just sitting in bed, reading erotica about yourself while giggling and kicking your feet—' she teased.

'*Giggling and kicking my feet?* Stop it,' he said, rubbing the side of his head. He was mortified.

'Waiting up late *every single night* to see if a new chapter has been added to one of those smutty one-hundred-and-thirty-chapter fanfiction series.' She clearly loved watching him squirm.

'You're ridiculous,' he said, trying not to let his face betray him.

'What's your favourite genre?' she said wickedly. 'Do you like fluffy fic where you're the dream boyfriend? Or are you more into those mafia stories? Do you like the ones where you're not famous or are you more of a *plot? what plot?* kind of guy?' she asked, delighted to have found something to hold over him. Zeke should never have booked a buggy. Walking for half an hour and being late would have been much less stressful than this ordeal of a journey.

'First of all, I don't know what any of those things are.

Secondly, isn't it a little bit misogynistic to make fun of a genre mostly written by young women, Olivia?'

'I'm not making fun of them, I'm making fun of you,' she said. 'And remember, I'm doing you a favour. I could leave you stranded at any—' But before she could finish her sentence, the golf buggy hurtled down another hill, skidded into a puddle and sent a huge splash of mud and water into the air. They came to a sharp stop as he and Olivia threw their arms up in fear.

Olivia turned the buggy off, took the keys out and looked over at him in shock. He didn't need a mirror to know what she was staring at. Zeke's red-white-and-blue uniform was completely soaked. He could feel the splatters all over his face and, as he reached up to touch the top of his head, he felt sticky mud beginning to seep into his brand-new trim. Olivia, on the other hand, had somehow managed to escape this puddle unscathed because of the angle they'd crashed at.

Zeke was supposed to be at the stadium for a big-time TV interview with the BBC. He was already twenty minutes late and now his outfit was completely ruined. He jumped out of the buggy and tried to shake the mud off his shirt, but his running shoes plunged straight into a puddle and came out coated in a perfectly thick layer of mud.

Zeke looked at Olivia and then Olivia looked at Zeke. He tilted his head to the side and she bit her lip. He saw a wave of emotions cross over her face. Shock and then guilt and then worry and then her lips started to tremble. She covered her mouth with her hands and her eyes began to water. He was about to tell her that it was okay and he wasn't upset with her, but he was completely misguided. Olivia wasn't about to cry.

She did everything she could to try to hold back, but the impulse was too strong. So she let out a belly-aching, shoulder-shaking, full-body laugh. Her eyes scrunched up and the laughter poured out of her like a warm bright light. The joy on her face was infectious and soon enough he was laughing too. An uncontrollable laugh that left tears on his face and his whole body feeling a little lighter.

'I'm glad *you're* having a good time,' said Zeke, shaking his head.

'I am . . . so . . . sorry . . . I . . . mean . . . it,' she said between breaths of laughter. Zeke tried to squeeze the muddy water out of his shirt.

'If this was your payback for the green juice . . .' he said, wiping his eyes.

'I would never!' said Olivia, pausing her laughter. 'If I wanted revenge, I'd *have* to be creative with it,' she said as if she was defending her honour. Zeke noticed the way the sun-kissed glow of her deep-brown skin glistened under the light of the bright Greek morning.

'I'd expect nothing less than expert-level revenge from you,' said Zeke.

'Don't worry, I can pay for your dry-cleaning,' said Olivia. 'I'll get it all pressed and folded too. My treat.'

Zeke was wet, muddy and about to get into so much trouble with Coach Adam. But when he looked at Olivia, he realized that he'd end up soaked to the skin with mud every day if it meant he'd get to see her again.

20

Olivia

Day two of the 2024 Olympics

'I don't think we're supposed to be here,' said Olivia.

'We're definitely not supposed to be here,' said Arlo.

'We should go,' said Olivia, looking at the sea of athletes milling around them. She still hated feeling out of place.

'Olivia, trust me. Nobody will ask you questions if you act like you're supposed to be here. People think you belong somewhere until you give them reason to think you don't,' he said, confidently striding into the athletes' canteen and towards the lunch line.

The athletes' canteen in the Olympic Village wasn't your average canteen. Every once in a while, an athlete did an interview and talked about just how magical it was. Olivia had spent years reading about how it included a menu of foods from all around the world and she'd heard stories of athletes from different countries becoming friends while sitting at these tables. So, when she mentioned wanting to see what it looked like inside, Arlo snuck her in.

As soon as she walked through the shiny glass doors, she was immediately hit by the smell of the most amazing food she'd ever seen. There were rows and rows of tables filled with appetizing dishes, shelves stocked high with delicious-looking snacks and a series of long curved counters serving food from all around the world. The Olympics was an international event and the menu was too. Each athlete and sport followed a very different nutritional regime and so they couldn't just walk in and eat anything. There were big bulky athletes loading up on carbs, lean athletes whose plates included only meat, athletes who'd just popped in, grabbed a smoothie and left, and athletes in line for pre-portioned meals planned out by their team's nutritionist.

Arlo was on a mission to try out as many Greek foods as he could and Olivia decided to join him, so they headed over to the Greek counter and loaded their trays with mezze, mini gyros, courgette balls called kolokythokeftedes and a plate of baked moussaka. They found a quiet table on the outskirts of the canteen and then went back and forth trying each other's food as Arlo told Olivia about all the countries he'd travelled to over the past four years, and Olivia told him about all the internships she'd done over the same timeframe.

After Olivia talked him through the list of jobs she was planning on applying for when she got home that night, Arlo asked, 'Have you ever thought about just letting go and seeing where life takes you at the end of the summer?'

'Not really. I like having a plan, it grounds me,' she said. What she didn't say was that the uncertainty of not having a plan made her feel like she was opening herself up to every worst-case scenario. Her parents had made perfect, seemingly foolproof plans, but they'd still had to start again when they moved to the UK. So, she'd trained herself to be consistently overprepared. It was more practical to be driven by the fear that at any moment the bottom could fall out. At least that way she knew she'd always have a fire beneath her feet.

'What about taking a year off and going travelling while you're still young?' Arlo asked.

She liked the way he saw the world; it just wasn't the way she could. 'I've thought about it, but I don't have enough money in my savings and I can't really relax when I don't know when my next pay cheque is coming,' she said, not mentioning the fact that it would probably take her years to get out of the debt she'd plunged herself into by self-funding one too many unpaid internships.

'I went on a silent retreat for a week and it really helped me to figure things out. You should try it.' Arlo bit into a gyro.

'That would mean sitting alone with my thoughts for a week,' she joked.

'Gotta keep the existential thoughts at bay,' he said with a knowing smile and then changed the conversation. 'What do you think yellow shirt over there does?' He nodded in the direction of a tall athlete who was walking past them wearing headphones and a bright-yellow shirt.

Arlo liked guessing the sport of each athlete who passed them. And Olivia, who had a near-encyclopaedic knowledge of Olympic athletes, could almost always tell him what they actually did.

'He's got to be a hockey player, right? It's in the arms.'

'Nope, he's a cyclist on Team Ecuador,' said Olivia.

'That explains the tight shorts,' said Arlo. 'Okay, how about her over there? I'm thinking equestrian.' They watched a brunette girl in a blue-and-green jacket walk past them.

'She's a Croatian water polo player, but the ponytail does look very horse-esque,' Olivia said, nodding. 'Do you ever wonder what sport people would think you played if they looked at you?'

'I'd like to think surfer, but in reality it's probably golf. You?'

'Someone once said I have the energy of a lacrosse girl,' Olivia said with a sigh.

Arlo whistled. 'That's low.'

'Right?' she said indignantly. 'Like, yeah, I get passionate and maybe I would feel more powerful with a net and stick—'

Arlo started laughing.

'Oh no, I do have the energy of a lacrosse girl!' Olivia covered her face with her hands.

While Arlo tried to figure out if the six-foot guy who'd just walked past them played basketball or tennis, Olivia glanced up and saw an athlete she immediately recognized. *Everyone* knew who Haruki Endō was. When Arlo spotted him, his eyes widened in recognition.

'Hey! We met the day before the opening ceremony, right?' Haruki asked as he came over towards them.

'Yeah, we did,' Olivia said enthusiastically, happy to see him again.

'Is this table big enough for the three of us?' Haruki asked, smiling over at Arlo.

'The more the merrier,' said Arlo, not able to hide the excitement in his voice as Olivia internally screamed at the fact that Haruki Endō was having lunch with them. Olivia didn't get starstruck easily, but Haruki was one of her favourite athletes in the world. She'd watched him compete at the World Aquatics Championship last year and she'd been mesmerized by how easily he'd beaten his own 200-metre butterfly record. He was one of those one-in-a-generation athletes, and now, because Arlo had dragged her into the canteen, they were having a meal with him.

'What are you having for lunch?' Olivia asked. She knew all the athletes had different diets, but she was always surprised to see just how much the swimmers ate to balance out all the energy they needed to swim.

'I've got a big race later, so I've got to load up with some eggs, noodles, soup and vegetables,' he said. 'Want a taste?' He held his fork up in her direction. It smelt incredible so she did have a taste. It was delicious.

So was that whole mealtime. She and Arlo sat in the canteen with Haruki for the rest of lunch. He answered all of their excited questions about what it was actually like to be an Olympic swimmer, debated the best sports film and then asked Olivia and Arlo about what led them to the Village. Olivia knew that Haruki was friends with Zeke Moyo, but they were so different. While Zeke was annoyingly hot, dripping with charm and raw star power, Haruki had a warm boy-next-door vibe. Zeke brought out the impulsive, unpredictable side of Olivia, her quick tongue and her sometimes scalding wit. Whereas Haruki was the walking personification of 'Do meet your heroes'. She knew that if she'd gone to university with him, they would have been firm friends. Haruki had the best personality of any athlete she'd met so far.

Olivia left lunch in such a good mood that for the rest of the afternoon she was sure nothing could bother her. When she was called to the referees' offices to do an in-depth inventory of clipboards and whistles, she distracted herself from the boredom by listening to a podcast about what it was like behind the scenes of the anti-doping department. When she was called to pick up plungers and drain unblockers to help a plumber fix a blocked toilet in New Zealand House, she distracted herself from how gross it was by listening to the plumber tell her stories about some of the most high-profile athletes he'd unblocked toilets for. But then she got a call from one of the 'Village experience' managers in the facilities department.

'Olivia, we need a little bit of help down in the canteen,' he said.

'Sure, what kind of help?' she asked.

'We have a code one-oh-five in the East Canteen but we're short-staffed, so could you resolve the situation?' he asked.

When she arrived, code 105 was even worse than she could have imagined. Olivia was equipped with a whole trolley of cleaning supplies, but nothing could have prepared her for the floor of shellfish-filled vomit. Though when the nauseous Norwegian boxer apologized to her, she assured her that everything was going to be all right. Once the floor was clean and smelt like lemon soap instead of bodily fluids, Olivia ran to the staff bathroom, showered and doused herself in perfume. The smell had lodged itself so deep into her consciousness that she couldn't shake it off. But the second she got on to her phone, she was hit with an even more sickening sight: Lars Lindberg's post on Instagram.

She'd resolved to enjoy the rest of the Games and not dwell on the summer she'd imagined having. But she'd forgotten to unfollow Lars and, in some sick twist of fate, his was the first face that popped up. Olivia couldn't look away as she saw just how differently his day was going compared to hers. He'd started the morning at a fancy team breakfast and then he'd gone to the velodrome to watch cyclists race with the free tickets he and the other interns were given. Tickets that Olivia should have been given.

He was living out the Olympic summer that Olivia had spent her whole life working towards. And to top it all off, he'd just posted a photo captioned: 'So excited to be celebrating the launch of Zeus Athletics' latest collaboration tonight with my friend the Olympic medal-winning Zeke Moyo!'

Olivia let out a quiet groan as she clicked on the Zeus Athletics page and saw that Zeke *was* in fact being interviewed at an event that evening being hosted by Lars. Remembering that he was sponsored by Zeus Athletics was a bit jarring. After all, the Lindberg family business had just been the subject of a long investigation into a years-long sweatshop scandal. Some part of her knew that it wasn't fair to judge Zeke for being friends with Lars. Zeke was also friends with Haruki, who was kind and down-to-earth. Olivia knew better than anyone that sometimes you had to get along with people you didn't necessarily like to get to where you wanted to go. But she couldn't reconcile the idea of the funny, charming, slightly cocky guy she'd spoken to that morning being friends with a guy like Lars. So rather than trying to find excuses for him or separating the two very different sides of Zeke that his friendships suggested he could be, she resolved to take him at face value. And she decided to unfollow Lars.

If there was one thing that her last summer fling had taught her, it was just how easily she could cast aside her better judgement when faced with a guy she maybe kind of liked. But she couldn't get sidetracked again. So, she vowed not to let herself get pulled in by Zeke's charm. Or his smile. Or how outrageously hot he was. Because day-dreaming about him would be irresponsible, wouldn't it? Letting him flirt with her and flirting back would be a poor decision, right? Zeke Moyo was a bad idea. But that didn't stop Olivia from wondering when she'd see him again.

21

Zeke

Day two of the 2024 Olympics

Zeke had been in the game long enough to know how to play it. Of all the kids of corporate executives and heirs of billion-dollar companies, Lars Lindberg was far from the worst. Yes, he was a bit rude to service workers and he posted photos with everyone he met with overfamiliar captions to make it seem like they were friends. But compared to the other super-rich kids Zeke knew, Lars wasn't that bad. And he was definitely going to take over the company when his father retired. So, Zeke made small talk and shook hands with Lars, the son of the CEO whose hefty sponsorship money funded Zeke's athletics career.

'We're so glad to have you here with us today, aren't we?' said Lars, once the two of them were on stage for the press launch of Zeke's latest collaboration with Zeus Athletics. The whole room erupted into applause. Zeke flashed them a smile and sat up straighter in his seat.

Zeke hadn't done as well as he usually did in morning training because he'd woken up with a familiar, unplaceable sense of anxiety. Running usually made him feel better; the simple act of putting one foot in front of the other was the easiest way to distract himself from his thoughts. But that day, he'd left the gym feeling worse than he'd felt when he'd walked in. His anxiety only got worse that evening when his Zeus Athletics interview began.

'First of all, Zeke, tell me, what's your favourite thing about Zeus Athletics?' Lars asked.

Zeke was drinking water out of a Zeus Athletics cup while wearing a Zeus Athletics tracksuit in front of a Zeus Athletics backdrop on a Zeus Athletics stage in the middle of a Zeus Athletics venue filled with Zeus Athletics executives. It felt like overkill to talk about how much he loved working with his brand sponsor . . . Zeus Athletics. But that's what he was there for.

Walking out on to the stage wearing the logo-covered outfit that the PR team had given him made Zeke feel like a bit of a sell-out. Especially since, thanks to his extremely socially conscious cousin Rumbi, he knew there were whole decades of Zeus Athletics' history conveniently removed from their 'about' page. But sponsorships like this funded his career, so he answered Lars's questions and watched as the audience applauded every single thing he said.

'You've got to tell me about that moment in Tokyo, Zeke. How did it feel?' Lars asked as several people in the audience nodded.

'Honestly, it was an out-of-body experience,' said Zeke, smiling as he remembered the day he'd won his silver Olympic medal. But then he felt his smile falter as he remembered the night he'd endured afterwards.

In Tokyo, he'd got off to a bad start at the 100-metre final. He'd started running a few milliseconds later than he should have and began the race way behind his competitors. But something happened in the third second. It was like a part of him he didn't even know existed kicked in. He'd taken a stride much larger than he usually did, and then another, and then another, at a faster pace than he'd ever run before. It happened so quickly that he didn't have time to doubt himself. So seamlessly, that it felt like he was flying. He'd zoomed ahead of his competitors and crossed the finish line in second place, in shock as his teammates crowded around him cheering, screaming and holding him tight. It was the best moment of his life. But as soon as he'd gone back to his room after celebrating the whole evening . . . the anxiety had begun. A wave of nervousness, a rush of restlessness and the unshakeable sense of impending doom. It had got so bad that he'd begun to worry he was having a heart attack. That his body was about to fail him as a consequence of pushing it too far. After a panicked call, Coach Adam found him in the middle of a full-blown anxiety attack. Deep in a pit of despair just hours after winning his first Olympic medal. But he didn't tell *that* part of the story on stage.

'And next week's race? Back home, people have already started calling you the golden boy. How are you feeling ahead of it?' Lars asked.

While the people online and in the sports world thought he was going to win gold in the 100-metre final and run faster than ever before, Zeke wasn't quite as sure. He'd come first place in the last World Athletics sprint, making him the fastest man in the world. But Hasely, Team Trinidad and Tobago's legendary sprinter, outran him within a couple of months. The Jamaican athletics team dominated at pretty much every Olympics. And Jesse, from Team USA, had already broken the world record that year. The competition was tougher than ever and the last Team GB sprinter to bring a 100-metre gold home was Linford Christie all the way back in 1992, eight years before Zeke had been born. If he was honest with himself, the pressure of all that expectation was beginning to weigh down on him. But everyone was here to see an interview with Zeke Moyo, the fastest man in Britain. The '(almost) golden boy' who was his country's surest hope for an Olympic gold medal. Nobody wanted to hear about his self-doubt, so he didn't let his facade slip.

'I feel confident,' he lied. 'I think you have to when you're competing at this level. But I guess we'll see on the track.' He was trying to move the conversation along.

'And what does it feel like to represent Britain?' Lars asked.

This, Zeke answered truthfully. 'It's such an honour. I don't think there's any greater privilege than knowing you're going to help inspire the next generation of athletes. When I was a kid, I used to stare up at the TV screen and watch the greats like Linford Christie, Mo Farah and Kelly Holmes. So, I hope there's some kid out there who watches my races and thinks that, with hard work and determination, they'll break my records.'

'You think someone is going to break your record?' asked Lars.

'Not before I do it first!' Zeke said to laughter from around the room. 'But it's only a matter of time before someone does break my record. Eventually someone's going to break all of our records.' He knew that he was going off-script, but he couldn't seem to stop. 'Everyone gets triumphed over and replaced eventually . . . and that's what makes each race so exciting.'

It wasn't the idea of being replaced that worried Zeke, it was the question of legacy. While he could name a dozen achievements his sporting heroes had made off the track, he couldn't name anything he'd done outside of running that would leave a lasting impact on the world. When his records were inevitably broken and he became one of the *former* best runners in the world, he didn't know what would really be left of him. Whether he'd have any real legacy beyond the medals that hung above his mother's fireplace.

There wasn't a single day since his dad died where he hadn't questioned whether or not he was doing the right thing. His mind always wandered back to their car-time conversations when he was growing up. To his dad's dream of Zeke using his success to help other kids with funding and scholarships. How he could give back to the community and create opportunities for the kids who hadn't grown up with the same running tracks, coaches and resources as him. But Zeke had got so caught up in climbing up the ranks and winning medals that he was yet to see any of those promises through. The more he thought about it, the more uneasy he began to feel.

'This is your *third* Olympics, not everybody gets this far,' said Lars. Zeke knew he meant it as a compliment, but Zeke's body responded to it like a threat. And each question Lars asked made it worse. Zeke was beginning to feel the way he did that night in Tokyo. How he'd felt after the World Championships, the Commonwealth Games and the Diamond League. The anxiety always started in his shoulders – it was a tension that he couldn't train himself out of no matter how much he rolled his shoulders or stretched out his legs. He was starting to feel hot under his shirt. The material of his trousers was itchy. The lighting was too bright.

'Can you imagine yourself back in this seat competing for Team GB in four years?' Lars asked.

'Athletics is the only job where people start to ask you about retirement before you've even turned twenty-five,' Zeke said.

'No, I didn't mean—' said Lars, looking nervous.

'It's okay,' said Zeke, reassuring him. 'I like to take it one run at a time. Don't get me wrong, I'm ridiculously ambitious. I don't know a single athlete who doesn't want to be the very best in the world at what they do . . . and luckily, right now, I am.' The audience laughed long enough for him to catch his now-shallow breath. 'But at the moment, my head is completely focused on my race next week.'

He wanted it to be true, he wanted to feel like his head *was* completely focused on next week's race. But, in reality, it was taking everything in him not to get up, walk off the stage and out of the tent, and hide in bed for the rest of the day. He stretched his neck from side to side and tapped his foot to try to help him focus on the interview instead of the thoughts that were swirling around his mind. But he just couldn't make them stop. As he sat on stage, hearing the quiet click of a camera, he felt himself fading into history. The guilt of unfulfilled promises mingled with the familiar anxiety that crept back into his life every couple of days. He could feel the tension in his muscles, feel the ache in his neck and feel his heart beating a little faster. So, as soon as the Zeus Athletics event was over, he made a beeline for the door and stepped back out into the fresh air. He needed to go back to the apartment, go for a run or just do anything to get him out of his head before he got too deep into his thoughts.

As he walked towards GB House, he realized that he'd left his keys in his room that morning. His housemates were both out training and Coach Adam was probably busy on the track. But he needed to get back into the apartment. The only way to get into his room would be to try the Hub. They must have spare keys, right? So, Zeke walked across the square, down the path and through the door to the Athletes' Hub. Behind the desk, a tall, cheerful-looking guy wearing a blue-and-yellow volunteers' uniform was talking emphatically to a girl who was facing away from the desk, obscuring Zeke's view of her.

'Hey,' said Zeke as he reached the desk. The guy behind the desk gave him a warm, friendly smile and then Olivia turned around, raising her eyebrow as she caught his gaze. Her dark, deep-brown eyes seemed to glimmer in the evening sunlight pouring through the window. Her hair was loose, her braids down her back, and she was wearing delicate gold earrings that brought out the warmth in her face. Zeke knew that he was supposed to be focusing all of his attention on training, and avoiding anything that could take his mind off the goal. But he couldn't help but get distracted whenever he looked into Olivia's eyes. He was in trouble, and he was already too far gone to change his mind.

22

Olivia

Day two of the 2024 Olympics

When Zeke wasn't in the room, Olivia could focus on what she didn't like about him. Because it was much easier to look past his perfect face and clearly ripped body when he wasn't standing right in front of her. But her resolve not to get pulled into his orbit came crashing down with an embarrassing speed as soon as he walked into the Hub.

Why? Because Zeke Moyo was annoyingly hot. Like, infuriatingly good-looking.

Olivia hated to admit it, and she'd never known herself to be fickle. But Zeke had a disarming smile, the kind that made her want to lay down her weapons and let down her guard.

'Olivia,' he said, smiling at her. His voice was low and the sound of her name on his lips was almost too much to bear. She told the weak-kneed part of herself to stand up. Because as tantalizing as the thought of Zeke was, Olivia didn't have time to get sidetracked by a crush on a superstar athlete. She was supposed to be getting her life back on track.

'Ezekiel. To what do I owe the displeasure?' She meant to say it like she wanted to get the conversation over and done with. But even she could hear the playfulness in her voice.

'Olivia, where's your Village spirit?' he said, leaning against the desk until he was just a few centimetres away from her. *It should be illegal*, she thought, *for him to smell that good.*

'Zeke, shouldn't you be in practice instead of stalking me?'

'I thought volunteers were supposed to be upbeat and friendly,' he said.

'I'm a goddamn delight, and I'm also very busy,' she said even though she and Arlo had just spent the last thirty minutes debating whether they loved or loathed the final season of *Ted Lasso*.

'I'm guessing now would be a bad time to ask for a favour?'

'What do you need, someone to buggy you? A babysitter to guide you around the Village?'

'Only if you're the one driving.' His eye contact made her want to twirl her hair. She could feel herself beginning to fold. She *had* to reinforce her defences.

'So, what's this favour you're looking for and, more importantly, how are you going to try and convince *me* to help *you*?' she asked, desperately seeking more stable ground.

'Okay, so I might have locked myself out of my apartment,' Zeke said with a grimace.

Olivia faked a sharp intake of breath. 'Oh, that *is* a tricky one. Village keys are like gold . . . I'm not sure I can help you there,' she said, enjoying the temporary power she held over him.

'I could drive the buggy there, be your chauffeur. You'd

just have to let me in one time and then I *promise* I'll leave you alone.'

'Ah, but that would mean having to find the key . . . and then going through security to make sure you are who you say you are . . . and then I'd have to sign you out . . .' She sighed, pretending to be annoyed, even though she knew the whole process would take less than five minutes.

'What if I gave you something in return?' He leaned back against the desk until they were just centimetres away from each other again.

'Ezekiel,' she said. Her voice quietened to an almost threatening whisper. But instead of stepping back, he leaned closer.

'Olivia,' he said, glancing down at her lips, biting his and then looking back up at her eyes. She could feel the tension hanging in the air between them. The possibility that lingered whenever they stood face to face. She kept her voice quiet and low.

'If you offer to pay for my dry-cleaning again, I'll break protocol, deactivate your pass and completely exile you from the Village,' she whispered.

'You can do that?' he said, whispering back.

His lips looked really soft. She wondered what they would feel like against hers, how easily one of them could close the distance between them.

'I can do a lot of things.'

'I knew it.'

'Knew what?' she asked, tilting her head to the side. They were so close that she could feel his breath against her cheek.

'That you're the kind of person who gets drunk off

power,' he said, looking right at her. She held his gaze and then stood back up, breaking the spell.

'Everyone needs a kingdom.' She shrugged, a little dizzy from being so close to him. 'This desk is my castle and that cabinet of keys over there is my crown.'

'Well, what if I said I have something that belongs to you?' he said.

'What do you have?'

'Ohh, you see, I can only give it to you if you help me get back into my apartment.'

'Keeping your bargaining cards close to your chest, smart,' she said, nodding. 'Seems like something I would do.'

'I'm just trying to be like you, Liv.'

'It's Olivia, Ezekiel.'

'I prefer Zeke, Olivia.' He paused and they locked eyes. For a moment it was like some sort of force was stopping them from noticing anything but each other. Like they were playing a game of chess, looking down at the board, trying to predict each other's next move. Olivia could almost see the sparks of electricity humming between them. For once, *she* was the one to look away; she couldn't let him see the destabilizing effect he was having on her.

'What of mine did you say you have again?' Olivia asked, feeling like she'd just wakened from a trance.

'I'll only give it to you if you promise to let me into my apartment,' Zeke said.

'I promise, I guess,' she said, non-committal.

'I guess?' he asked, raising an eyebrow.

'Okay, I'll let you back into your apartment,' she said.

He looked at her, took his backpack off and undid the zip.

'You dropped it on the day we met, then walked away before I could give it to you,' he said as he rummaged through his backpack and pulled out her iridescent I AM FEELING VERY OLYMPIC TODAY notebook. The one she had lost on her first day in the Village. She'd been determined to find it, but then she'd got so busy running around the Village that she'd completely forgotten about it. Usually, she couldn't live without a notebook in her back pocket. Her lists and plans felt like such a fundamental part of who she was that she always needed paper handy to map things out. However, she could already feel the sun getting to her head. She could feel herself slipping into the carelessness of Summer Olivia, and the boy with her notebook in his hands wasn't making it any easier to regain her focus.

'Here you go,' he said. She put her hand out to take it, but Zeke hadn't let go yet. 'Only if I get the keys,' he said, looking directly into her eyes as they both held the notebook. The notebook was big enough that there was no need to touch, but still, his fingers gently grazed hers. She felt a tingle spread across her body. A glimmer of something dangerous, something intoxicating. Standing in front of him made her cheeks warm and her mouth dry. Looking into his eyes made her want to walk around to the other side of the desk and lean forward until they were too close not to touch. Feeling the soft, sharp graze of his skin against hers brought what she wanted into sharp focus. But, after a moment, he let go. Then she heard someone clear their throat.

'Ahem, I look after the keys,' said Arlo. He'd been standing behind the desk with her all along.

'Here you are,' he added as he gave Zeke a new set of keys.

'Same time tomorrow, Olivia?' Zeke said.

'There's nothing I want less than to see you again,' said Olivia as he fixed her with a gaze so intense it made her feel dizzy.

They both knew she was a bad liar.

23

Zeke

Day three of the 2024 Olympics

Every competition at the Games unfolded before an audience of energetic fans from around the world. But that year's athletics crowd was more fervent than ever, because watching sprinters in Athens felt like watching history unfold in real time. In fact, because running was one of the first sports in the Ancient Olympic Games, the main stadium in the centre of the Village had been built in honour of athletics. The exterior walls of the stadium were covered with a mural of some of the most legendary athletes in history. Majestic gold-lined silhouettes of sprinters and marathon runners in motion. As Zeke walked into the stadium that morning, he was awed by the magnitude of it all.

It was the day of the 100-metre heats, the races that decided who made it to the quarter-finals of the Olympic sprint, so Zeke had woken up early that morning to do his pre-run rituals. He'd jogged around the perimeter of the park, journaled for fifteen minutes, eaten breakfast with the rest of the GB athletics team and then headed over to the stadium. Usually, he went into a race day with a completely clear mind. He tried not to think about anything other than his run and how to get to the other side of the finish line as fast as he could. But Zeke's mind was filled with thoughts of Olivia.

'All right, lads, I know it's just the heats and you've all got further than this before, but you have to apply everything you've learned in training and treat today like it's the final, okay?' said Coach Adam to the changing room full of athletes getting ready to go out on to the track. 'There's no final without getting through the heats. So don't fall into the bad habit of saving your best performance for a bigger race, because the race you're about to run is *always* the most important race, all right?' A few of the athletes nodded in agreement. 'All right?' he said again, louder, and this time the whole room echoed him. They slowly started to get pumped up as Coach put on his signature playlist and went around giving all the athletes one final piece of advice. Zeke did one last round of stretches and tried to shift his focus away from Olivia and on to the race he was about to run.

'Ezekiel,' said Coach Adam, coming his way.

'Coach,' said Zeke. He still felt bad about embarrassing Coach in front of the BBC video crew in his mud-stained uniform.

'I'm going to put Mudgate behind us because, frankly, I don't have time for that. But your last run? It was sloppy.' Coach was referring to Zeke's practice run the day before. Zeke already knew that, so he just nodded his head in agreement.

'I want you to improve your form because your kick-off yesterday was a bit poor,' began Coach Adam before giving Zeke an in-depth explanation of how he could improve. Once they were done, Zeke and the rest of his teammates left the changing room and walked down the tunnel until they could hear the sound of the audience eagerly anticipating the competition ahead.

Zeke had already been in the main stadium a few times. He'd seen it lit up with colour and costumes during the opening ceremony and run laps around it when it was completely empty during training sessions. But walking into the stadium on the first day of the athletics heats was a whole different experience. People were excitedly milling around, collecting their snacks and finding their seats. Officials were pacing around the track making sure all the equipment was set up and ready for the day ahead. Athletes in multicoloured uniforms were warming up around the field. The perimeter was filled with production crew members adjusting their cameras and microphones to get ready to capture it all and beam it out across the world.

As Zeke walked on to the track, he looked over at the other sprinters getting ready to take their places. In the outside world, there was this idea that athletes only saw each other as competition. When it came to team sports like football and one-on-one matches like tennis, it often *was* like that. Fierce rivalries often made for even better results. But it wasn't quite the same when it came to sprinting. It was the kind of sport where you set yourself up to fail the minute you took your focus off your own lane to see what someone else was doing. So, there weren't the same intense rivalries on the track as people would expect. Zeke knew all of the other runners because they'd spent the whole year competing at the same international races. While they were all intensely competitive, they were pretty friendly with each other too. He nodded at Jesse, the American sprinter who he'd seen at the opening ceremony after-party. Smiled at Hasely, the Trinidadian sprinter who'd sent him a handwritten card after his silver-medal win in Tokyo. And said hi to Arthur, the Jamaican sprinter he'd met at his first World Athletics competition. Sprinting could be quite a solitary sport, so they looked out for each other. But once they were in the stadium, it was every man for himself.

Zeke got into his lane, focused on his track and tried to clear his mind of everything except for the race ahead of him. He could feel the adrenaline pumping through his veins, the excitement at the tip of his toes and the fear beating inside his chest. There was nothing more thrilling or terrifying than a race. Running had started out as a way to feel the wind blowing against his face and see the world moving in fast motion. As he'd grown up and begun doing it competitively, the hope of a medal, fear of a loss and question of what came next had clouded the purity of it. But when he put his foot on the starting line, heard 'On your marks' and then the loud bang of the starting gun, all of that disappeared.

He lifted one foot from the ground, kicked off with a level of precision that would make Coach Adam proud and ran as if it was the most important race of his life.

Some runners sprinted with an absolutely clear mind, too high on the adrenaline of the race to think about anything except moving forward. Others repeated affirmations and sang the lyrics to their favourite songs. But Zeke's mind was always flooded with thoughts, images and ideas. His family, his friends, his favourite runs and feelings he couldn't quite capture.

Everyone was either running towards or away from

something. And while the images he saw when he was running didn't always hold the deeper meanings that dreams did, they always propelled him forward. Whether he was running towards the idea of the joy they evoked or away from the idea of the fear they triggered. As he ran that morning, he remembered one of the last international competitions his father had taken him to as a child. Then he remembered the feeling of walking into his first Olympic Village. And for a fraction of a second, he thought about how easy it would be to trip and fall. But, luckily, the last thought didn't come to pass.

He ran along the track and sped past the competition, finishing in second place by just a fraction of a second. As he heard the sound of the audience's applause, he tried not to think too much about his memories of his father. Or the fact that he would never be there to watch Zeke cross the finish line again. He tried to focus on the fact that he'd secured his place in the quarter-finals instead of dwelling on the low-level sense of dread he'd been feeling after all of his races lately.

Once he'd said goodbye to his teammates, Zeke walked out of the changing room and through the hallways of the stadium. He congratulated a few athletes who'd just qualified and watched playbacks of his teammates' competitions as they were shown on the screens around the stadium. Then he did a double-take as he walked towards the reception and saw a face he immediately recognized, but hadn't seen for years.

'Coach Chikepe!' said Zeke. The man turned around and smiled in recognition.

'Ezekiel, it's so good to see you,' said Coach Chikepe,

the head coach of Team Zimbabwe Athletics. Zeke pulled him into a handshake and then a hug. Coach Chikepe was one of the many coaches who Zeke's dad had befriended while they travelled around the world for competitions. Zeke and Coach Chikepe caught up and started talking about Zeke's progress since the last time they'd seen each other. The World Athletics medals he'd won (five), the world records he'd broken (three) and the height he'd added (twelve inches . . . well, at least a solid ten).

'I knew you when you couldn't get on funfair rides and now you're so tall I have to look up,' Coach Chikepe said.

Zeke was never going to be a kid going to the funfair with his dad again. As he saw Coach Chikepe's wrinkles and grey hairs, he realized just how much time had passed since they'd last seen each other at his dad's funeral. Zeke's expression faltered for a second. Coach Chikepe must have seen it because he patted Zeke on the shoulder.

'Your father would be so proud of you, Ezekiel,' he said.

'Yeah,' said Zeke, feeling that low but constant grief rise up again.

'Truly. We used to sit around and talk for hours as we watched you kids run. Imagined all of the things you could do, and now look – you're doing it! Above and beyond, we thank God,' said Coach Chikepe, radiating pride.

Zeke wasn't sure his dad would be *entirely* proud of him, but he brushed those thoughts aside. He took a photo with Coach Chikepe and then sent it to his family group chat to an almost immediate response from his mother telling him to invite Coach Chikepe to dinner the next time he was in London. As Zeke walked across the Village, he bumped into another familiar face, Valentina Ross-Rodriguez. But this time it was a twenty-foot photo of her mid-leap. He smiled, took a picture of her photograph and then texted it to her.

Zeke: we've got to stop meeting like this.

She replied straight away.

Valentina: guess who I'm celebrating your heats win with?

A photo came in of her and Haruki posing with that year's Olympic mascot.

Valentina: we're strategizing how I can use my 12% English ancestry to get British citizenship and become your team captain.

Zeke: well I have 0.1% English ancestry so you're already further ahead than me

Valentina: will send over a draft of my hostile takeover plan tomorrow

Valentina: but more importantly, you're definitely coming to my competition tomorrow night, right?

24

Olivia

Day four of the 2024 Olympics

'Olivia, I am in distress,' Arlo said from the other side of the call.

'Arlo, why are you in distress?' Olivia asked. She was now well accustomed to the dramatic start to all of Arlo's walkie-talkie calls.

'My art class is falling apart,' he said.

The athletes were all so busy with practice and competitions that sometimes it was hard for them to get out of their heads enough to relax at the end of the day. So, the Village hosted a series of mindfulness activities in the Culture Hub every evening. One of the activities Arlo had helped organize was a life art class. He'd spent that afternoon working meticulously to create a beautiful set filled with fresh fruit and ornate jugs, and then formed a circle of canvases and chairs. But at the very last minute, just an hour before the workshop, the model Arlo had booked had called him up in tears saying that he'd been infected with a pretty explosive stomach bug and could no longer make it to the art class that night.

'I think I'm going to have to do it.'

'Can't you book another model?' Olivia asked.

'No. They'd have to go through the whole weeks-long Village screening and security process to even step through the gates,' said Arlo, defeated.

'I can do it for you,' said Olivia, trying to bring the kind of enthusiasm to the situation that Arlo usually brought. 'I'd just have to stand there while they draw me, right?'

Arlo groaned. 'It's a *traditional* life drawing class,' he said.

Olivia tilted her head to the side, not fully understanding what he meant by that.

'Traditional life . . . in the nude – well, mostly in the nude,' he said nervously.

So, instead, Olivia drove a buggy to the other side of the Village and went along with Arlo to the art class for moral support. She spent the entire walk to the Culture Hub trying to hype him up.

'Arlo, you're an objectively handsome man,' she said as they power-walked.

'In a Village of men that look like literal Greek gods,' Arlo said, trying not to panic as he opened the door.

'You're an incredibly fit surfer, even your hair looks sea-swept,' she said. They ran up the stairs.

'That's true, but I'm not used to having thirty people staring at it,' he said, rushing into the shower as Olivia searched the staff cupboards for a spare towel.

'Think of it as a character-building moment, and a really good story to tell at parties.'

'Well, my boyfriend is going to get a good kick out of this when I tell him why I missed dinner.'

'Exactly, and I'm going to go home with a one-of-a-kind drawing of you,' Olivia said as he walked out of the shower and tightened the belt around his robe. 'But you don't have to do this, Arlo, not if you don't want to,' she reminded him. 'They can just draw the water jugs and fruits, and you can keep the robe on.'

'I promised the full life-drawing-class experience,' said Arlo dramatically as he walked into the room filled with athletes sitting patiently in front of their canvases, 'and that's what I'm going to deliver.'

Which is how Olivia ended up in a room with thirty of the world's best athletes, listening to traditional Greek music and painting a nude portrait of a co-worker she'd only met three days before.

When Olivia was a child, she'd spent the whole school week excitedly anticipating art class. Back then, all that really mattered on Thursday afternoons was her paints and paper and the way they made the rest of the world melt away. Painting hadn't felt like an escape for her, it was a way of seeing the world more vividly than she saw it with her own eyes. Art made her more aware of the curves and contours that made someone's face beautiful, more alert to the way the streets reflected sunlight in the moments after rainfall. But she hadn't painted in years.

'You're really good at this,' came a voice from behind her. Olivia turned around to find its source.

'Hey!' she said, pleasantly surprised to see that Haruki was painting on one of the easels behind her. Haruki had one of those kind faces that instantly made Olivia feel at ease.

'The Village is huge, but we keep bumping into each other. It's got to be fate, right?' He seemed genuinely happy to see her too.

'Right? I feel like the universe is trying to tell us something,' she said.

'Yeah, actually, I was thinking about you the other day. The Village has an outdoor cinema that screens sports movies every night and I was wondering if you wanted to come and watch one with me some time,' he said. He sounded kind of nervous, and for a split-second Olivia wondered if he was asking her out on a date. But it was *Haruki Endō*. She had seen the celeb gossip account stories about him and his dating history consisted almost entirely of supermodels and gold-medal-winning athletes. She was pretty confident in herself, but it felt incredibly unlikely that Haruki was asking her out, so she brushed the thought aside.

'They're screening *Bend It Like Beckham* on Sunday?' he continued.

'As in *Bend It Like Beckham*, the singular best British sports film of the twenty-first century?' she grinned, delighted that she and Haruki shared another favourite film in common. She knew they were going to become fast friends.

'Yeah, it would be fun, right?' he said cheerfully. If he was asking her on a date, he would have attempted to flirt, but he just looked really excited to watch the film, so Olivia nodded her head in agreement and said yes.

'Oh, and my best friend, Aditi, loves that film. I promised I'd spend the weekend with her, so I'll bring her along,' Olivia said enthusiastically. The outdoor cinema was on the spectator side of the Village, open to any member of the public who'd bought a ticket, so she was thrilled to have a reason to finally get Aditi on Village grounds.

'That would be great,' Haruki said.

She saw his smile falter for a second and then reappear

so she didn't think anything of it. She got him to phone her so that she had his number and said that she would text him to set a time for the three of them to meet up. Then she went back to her canvas.

'What paint are you using? The colours look so vibrant,' Haruki said, coming closer.

'It's gouache paint,' she said as she made another brush stroke. Her painting of Arlo was turning out much better than she'd thought it would. But when she stepped back to look at Haruki's canvas she saw that his drawing was truly mesmerizing.

While Olivia was painting a bright portrait that blurred colours and light, Haruki was working on an incredibly detailed, almost photorealistic pencil drawing that looked like it should have taken days to create.

'I used to take art classes when I was younger but then I got distracted by swimming and put it to the side,' Haruki said.

Olivia nodded. She wondered how often pursuing greatness got in the way of pursuing the other things you loved.

'I'll let you get back to your painting,' Haruki said, nodding before he returned to his easel and she went back to hers.

As Olivia had approached her late teen years, painting wasn't the only thing that she'd found herself gradually letting go of. Slowly, whole parts of her life had begun to fade away. She'd told herself that if she didn't intend to become great at something, it wasn't worth wasting time or money on. But as she looked at her canvas, she couldn't help but feel a certain kind of loss for the time in her life when just enjoying something was a good enough reason to do it.

She'd spent years trying to avoid slipping back into Summer Olivia, but the summer that birthed the name had been a carefree one. She'd gone out to the beach in the mornings and soaked in the sun, taken her sketchbook out and drawn the landscape. As distracting and unfocused as that summer was, it had felt like coming home to herself. Maybe this summer could feel that way too. She just needed to decide how much she was willing to let go.

25
Zeke

Day four of the 2024 Olympics

Zeke was sitting in a soft leather armchair drinking a glass of water and evading questions.

'Are we doing small talk for an hour today or do you want to talk?' asked Fiona.

Fiona was the Team GB therapist he'd been assigned to ever since his first panic attack back in Tokyo. She was a forty-year-old Welsh woman who had a way of saying things that coming from anybody else would have sounded passive-aggressive, but from her just sounded refreshingly straight to the point.

'The weather in Athens is great, isn't it?' said Zeke.

She smiled at him, but it was the kind of smile primary school teachers gave you as they readied themselves to explain something they'd already spent a week trying to teach you.

'Zeke, I have to remind you these sessions aren't compulsory. If you don't enjoy talking in this setting you won't get into trouble for not showing up,' Fiona said.

'Are you saying you don't love our sessions? I thought I was your favourite athlete. You're breaking my heart, Fi,' Zeke joked.

'Zeke, this is session number . . . twenty-three. I can rank your favourite colours, list every TV show you've watched over the past three years and remember all of your favourite running stories. But I'm not sure we're actually making progress . . . If you don't enjoy therapy, what motivates you to keep coming?' she asked.

He sighed. 'Honestly, I just come so Coach and the rest of the team don't worry about me,' he said with a shrug. 'If I stop going to my therapy sessions, they'll start pulling me aside for heart-to-hearts. And I don't really want to go through the constant "How are you *really* doing, kid?" routine again,' he said, imitating Coach Adam.

'How *are* you really doing, kid?'

'Great,' Zeke said.

'As always.'

'Exactly.'

'Have you spoken to your family much since you've been here?' she asked.

'Every day,' he said, already tired of the conversation.

'I know times like this can sometimes feel a little bitter-sweet—' Fiona began, but Zeke cut her off.

'I feel absolutely fine, Fi, no need to worry,' he said. He knew he couldn't hide his feelings from her, but that didn't mean he had to engage in a conversation about them.

Zeke was always the first to check in on his friends, but he didn't like talking about *his* feelings because he didn't like people worrying about him. His mother had been so worried about him after his dad died that she'd booked him in for a four-week series of counselling sessions. Zeke had hated them. At fourteen, he'd just wanted to move on with his life, to make everything go back to normal again.

He didn't want to fall apart all the time like his mum did or spend all his time reminiscing like his brothers did. But each time he'd spoken to a counsellor, they'd asked him questions that threatened to reopen the wounds he'd been trying so hard to heal. So, he'd disengaged and convinced his mother to stop the sessions.

But when Coach Adam had found him in the middle of a panic attack on the other side of the world during his last Olympics, Zeke had agreed to regular meetings with the Team GB therapist . . . despite his aversion to the whole thing. All of his friends who went to therapy said they left feeling lighter. Like talking about what they'd been holding in took a weight off their daily lives. But for Zeke, there was something about sitting face-to-face with someone whose job it was to make him open up that felt suffocating. He felt like if he did start talking, she'd find something in his words that would worry her. Or worse, that if he talked for long enough, he'd find something in his words that would worry *him*.

Once you opened a locked door in your brain, it was impossible to close it without walking away from the room a different person. If he truly allowed himself to crack open, it would lead him down a path that would eventually force him to make changes. But Zeke liked his life and who he was; he didn't want to put that in jeopardy.

'Zeke?' said Fiona.

'Hmm,' said Zeke, his mind still wandering. 'Sorry, Fiona, what were you asking me?'

'I said, have you been sleeping well? You have bags under your eyes.'

Zeke hadn't been sleeping well but he'd made the

decision to blame it on the jet lag, even though Athens was only two hours ahead of London.

'I'll take that as a no,' said Fiona as if she could see right through him. Usually, he tried to hide what he was thinking, but for once, Zeke wanted to tell her everything.

He was almost twenty-five now and, while that was young by most people's standards, he knew that he was at the start of his peak in the athletics world. If he kept training, looked after his body and avoided any major injuries, he was pretty sure that he'd make it to at least two more Olympic Games. But he wasn't sure if he wanted to.

It's not that he'd fallen out of love with running; it was still his favourite thing to do. And being an athlete was so wrapped up in his identity that he couldn't even imagine who he would be if he wasn't competing. But, lately, something about it had started to feel a bit empty. He felt a low-level sense of foreboding before he went to practice each day and qualifying for the quarter-finals hadn't filled him with the same sense of accomplishment that it usually did. So, the answer to Fiona's questions was yes – he did have something on his mind, and no – he wasn't sleeping very well. But before he could convince himself to open up, their time was over. As he left her office, his phone rang.

'Zeke, I'm not kidding you when I tell you that I really do think I've found the love of my life,' said Haruki.

'Again? Who is it this time? A Dominican weightlifter, an Italian fencer?' asked Zeke.

'No! The girl I told you about last time. The one I took a photo of on the first day and ate lunch with. I just saw her again,' said Haruki.

Zeke could hear the smile in his voice. 'So, I should start

planning my best man speech?' he said with a chuckle as he walked down the hallway.

'I got her number and made plans to see her, I think it's going to work out,' said Haruki.

'You asked her out? Okay, Endō – I see you,' Zeke said, impressed that his friend had finally taken the plunge.

'Yeah, we're going to see a movie. She said that she was going to bring her best friend along, but—'

'She's bringing her best friend . . . on a date?' asked Zeke.

'Yeah . . . that's not a good sign, is it?' said Haruki, sighing.

'Maybe she just wants to bring her wingwoman?' said Zeke, trying to reassure him.

'Well, that's actually why I was calling you. I thought I should bring someone too . . . So, what are your thoughts on a double date this weekend?' he said, trying and failing to sound nonchalant. Whoever the mystery girl was, Haruki was in deep.

'If you need me to come, I'll be there,' said Zeke.

26

Olivia

Day four of the 2024 Olympics

Olivia wanted to catch the 8.15 p.m. shuttle back into Athens. She needed to write new cover letters for some of the jobs she wanted to apply for. So, as she got into the lift after Arlo's art class, she began to make a to-do list on her phone. When the doors opened on the seventh floor, she was so preoccupied that she didn't even realize there was someone standing in the doorway.

'Olivia,' the voice at the door said. It was low and warm, and sent a shiver down her spine. Ezekiel Moyo kept popping up when she expected him the least.

'Zeke,' she said. The lift suddenly felt smaller, and a lot hotter.

'Now I don't mean to be forward,' Zeke began, glancing down at her hands, 'but is there a reason you're carrying a canvas drawing of a naked man . . . that looks a lot like the guy you work with at the Hub?'

'I . . . I don't have a good explanation for that, to be honest,' Olivia said. She looked down at the canvas, seeing it through the eyes of someone with no context of the last three hours of her life. But when she looked back up, his eyes were slowly sweeping over her. He was *definitely* checking her out and seemed startled when their eyes met again.

'And you? Is there a reason you're still standing in the doorway or are you just too *mesmerized* by the sight of me that you can't look away?' she asked.

He opened his mouth to reply, shut it, opened it again and then just shook his head, to her amusement.

Instead of the athletics kit or Team GB uniform the athletes usually wore, Zeke was wearing a loose, slightly unbuttoned white shirt. They were standing on separate sides of the lift, but they may as well have been shoulder to shoulder because Olivia had never been more aware of another person than she was of Zeke. He was looking straight ahead of him, so she let herself look over at the sharp curve of his jawline, the gentle crease around his eyes and the big muscular arms unfortunately covered up by his shirt. He was built enough to pick her up with ease, strong enough to hold her with one hand. But before she could let her thoughts get ahead of her, he glanced over at her for a second and she looked away.

Olivia took on a sudden interest in the different ways the word 'welcome' was translated into the different languages represented at the Olympics. She became fascinated by the brightly coloured Village map and the floor number buttons. She looked at absolutely everything in the lift except for Zeke. Worried that if she did, she wouldn't be able to control the unruly part of her that was hyper-fixated on his smile.

'It's a really good painting,' Zeke said, breaking the silence. 'Running in heels, reckless buggy driving accidents, nude paintings . . . is there anything you're not good at?'

'Carrying trays,' she answered without hesitation.

'Carrying trays?' he asked, amused.

'Yeah, I worked at this Italian restaurant when I was seventeen and I dropped a tray every single shift.'

'And they didn't fire you?'

'I was bad at trays but good at everything else.'

'*Of course* you were good at everything else,' he said with a firm nod.

'You're catching on,' she said and winked. Why was she winking? She'd never winked at anyone in her life. It was definitely too warm in this lift.

'I guess it's only a matter of time before you're running this place too,' he said, gesturing around them.

'The Village? Think bigger, Zeke. Head of the Olympic Organizing Commission, then Secretary-General of the United Nations, then I'll use my powerful international connections to become a billionaire, retire to a beach town in Australia and open a combination bookshop, plant shop and cafe.'

'Why do I feel like you sat and wrote that down when you were, like, eleven?' he said, laughing that warm deep laugh that made Olivia melt.

'I was actually nine,' she said with a nod. 'Oh, and obviously I'll make sure to give away all the money before I die because nobody actually needs to be a billionaire.'

'But you want to be one?' he asked.

'Just to prove I can,' she said, shrugging. 'Are billionaires unethical? Yes. Does that stop me from wanting to make that *Forbes* list? No.'

'At least you're honest.'

'Thank you,' she said, putting her hand to her heart. 'And you, what's the grand plan?'

'Just vague world domination, you know?' he said.

'I do know,' she said with a smile.

'Have we moved?' he asked, suddenly noticing the stillness around them. It definitely didn't take this long for a lift to go down seven floors. Olivia pressed the ground-floor button again, but the lift didn't move. Zeke pressed the open-doors button, but the doors didn't shift. Olivia pressed the buttons for floors 1, 2 and 3 but nothing happened. Zeke went back and did the same, but their lift stayed completely stationary.

Zeke went to the lift doors to try, and fail, to pull them apart. He knocked on the doors and crouched on the floor to yell for help, but there was no response.

'I don't know if I'm going to be able to get us out,' Zeke said as he turned around. But Olivia was already speaking to the lift technician through an intercom on the wall.

'How did you do that?' Zeke asked in surprise.

'I took a course on lift escapes,' Olivia said with a solemn nod, then pointed at the big red button on the wall that said PRESS IN CASE OF EMERGENCY. She raised her eyebrows and went back to her conversation with the lift technician.

'Okay . . .' she said to the technician, 'thank you . . . No, I don't think either of us is claustrophobic . . .' she replied. 'Yes, I'll practise some deep breathing.' She nodded. 'I don't need anything else . . . no worries . . . I think we both have music on our phones so no need to turn on any elevator music, but thank you, Giannis, I appreciate the offer . . . Okay, thank you . . . All right, speak later . . . Thank you, bye.'

She turned to Zeke. 'Well, Giannis the lift technician is

a lovely man who reminds me of my Year Eleven history teacher,' she said, 'but he's on the other side of the Village so it'll be thirty minutes before he can help us get out.'

'Well, if it's any consolation, I'm great company,' said Zeke, flashing her a smile, which prompted Olivia to quite literally slide down the wall and sit on the floor.

'Am I that bad, Olivia?' he said as she tried to ignore the way hearing her name on his lips made her feel.

Olivia looked over at him and then closed her eyes. No, he wasn't that bad. He wasn't bad at all. But the way his eyes lit up and the skin around them crinkled when he smiled was that bad. The way he was looking down at her with an equal measure of amusement and curiosity was that bad. And the way her pesky heart fluttered a little when he slid down the wall and sat next to her on the floor was that bad. Olivia was trying everything she could not to get distracted by Zeke Moyo, but her resolve was beginning to melt away. Dissolving into something much more difficult to hold on to.

27
Zeke

Day four of the 2024 Olympics

As Zeke sat next to Olivia, he realized that whatever it was that he'd started to feel for her, he was already too far gone to shut it down. The sight of her when he'd walked into the lift had quite literally stopped him mid-step. He'd never reacted to anyone like that before. It had taken him a real moment to shake off. She wasn't wearing her volunteer uniform; he could see it poking out of the bag on her shoulder. Instead, she was wearing a pair of denim shorts and a white linen shirt with a few specks of brightly coloured paint on the sleeve. When she'd slid down the wall, he'd joined her. But now that they were just a few centimetres apart, he wondered if he'd made the wrong decision. Because while he'd been able to keep the conversation going when they were standing up, now they were sitting so close together he couldn't ignore the almost magnetic pull she seemed to have on him. Or how nervous he got around her.

'You're not claustrophobic, are you?' Olivia asked, looking over at him. 'I just assumed when I was speaking to the technician.'

He held her gaze for a second too long. And then tried

to act more confident than he felt. 'The opposite actually,' he said.

'So, you like being squeezed tightly into small spaces?' she asked, raising an eyebrow. That perfectly arched eyebrow would be the death of him. 'If that's what you're into, no judgement. This is a safe space,' she went on, shrugging her shoulders as she teased him.

He glanced down at her lips, noticed the deep-red lipstick she was wearing and then quickly glanced away. He needed to get better at maintaining his composure.

'What I meant is that I don't get claustrophobic because I've been trained not to.'

'Oh, now I need to know the full story.'

'Do you remember that football player who disappeared in the middle of the World Cup a few years ago?' he asked, grateful for a topic of conversation that would steady him. 'So, the official story was that he got lost in the host city, but the truth is he got kidnapped.'

'Really?' said Olivia, her eyes widening.

'Really. Luckily, they were pretty amateur kidnappers – unlike you, who I know would excel at kidnapping,' he joked.

'It's a given,' she said with the warm, bright, infectious laugh he was always trying to get out of her.

'So, the footballer was able to escape and the kidnappers were caught. But then every international sporting organization sent their athletes on a mandatory kidnapping prevention and survival course.'

'That sounds like something from a movie,' she said.

'Right? It felt like it. We all did self-defence training, an actual real-life escape room class, learned how to hold our breath, and . . .' he gestured to the lift.

'Learned how not to get claustrophobic in small spaces,' she finished with a nod.

'Exactly,' he said.

As Olivia moved around to get more comfortable on the floor, a waft of the perfume she was wearing mixed with the paint and vanilla drifting his way. She smelt so good he had to hold his breath to stop himself from leaning towards her.

'So, I was painting Arlo in the nude, but why were you in the building?' Olivia asked.

'*So, I was painting Arlo in the nude,*' Zeke mimicked, 'is a great way to start a sentence.' He paused. 'I was in therapy . . . and I hate therapy.'

'Hate it?' Her face and tone were gentle.

'Truly hate it. Don't get me wrong, I can talk about my feelings,' he said – though he never had to Fiona – 'but there's just something about talking to someone knowing that they're going to analyse everything I say that makes me close off.'

Olivia nodded. 'I get that, it doesn't really feel like a natural conversation.'

'Yeah, it feels like a weird treasure hunt. Like, *what trauma, insecurity or anxiety can we uncover today?*'

'An emotional treasure hunt? Sounds like my idea of a good time,' she said, making him laugh a little. 'I love talking about things.'

'Really?' he asked.

'Yeah, the more I talk about something, the clearer my thoughts on it become,' she said.

'Oh, I'd rather sit in silence and come to my own conclusions,' he said.

'You like sitting alone with your thoughts?' she asked. 'Sounds like my personal idea of hell.'

'It's the best. You can just sit there and eventually, if you wait around long enough, you clear away everyone else's opinions and the things you think you're supposed to think until all that's left is what you truly want and feel,' he said. Plus, coming to his own conclusions meant he could avoid hearing questions he wasn't sure he wanted to know the answers to.

'But then I'd have to actually listen to what I really want, not what I've told myself I want,' Olivia said with a nervous laugh. 'And truly knowing myself terrifies me.'

'And having someone question the things I tell myself to make life easier? That terrifies *me*,' he said, looking at her with a self-conscious laugh.

After a few moments, they both went quiet. As if worried they'd revealed too much. The silence grew louder until all Zeke could hear was the gentle hum of the lift.

He looked over at Olivia and whispered, 'Is this the silence you hear in your nightmares?'

Olivia shook her head and smiled. 'Careful, go long enough without speaking and I'll start asking you questions about the meaning of life.'

Zeke faked a shudder and they both laughed. Thirty minutes passed as the two of them talked about all the weird but wonderful things they'd seen so far in the Village. Olivia told Zeke about some of the strangest walkie-talkie calls she'd had, and Zeke told Olivia about some of the wildest training accidents he'd seen. Giannis the lift technician called to tell them it was going to take another thirty minutes for him to reach them. So they took it in turns to put their phones on shuffle and see who could guess the song first until they reached a draw. Then, Zeke showed Olivia the photos he'd taken of the exclusive athlete-only areas of the Village. After that, they played a game where they took turns saying random dates and scrolled through their camera rolls to see where they'd been and what they'd been doing.

'March twenty-ninth?' asked Zeke as they both scrolled.

'My cousin's twenty-first birthday party,' said Olivia, turning her phone to face Zeke, who nodded and then turned his to face her.

'Camping,' he said, showing her a photo of him camping with Anwar and Frankie on a rainy day in the middle of Wales. 'June seventh?' he asked as they both scrolled.

'My master's graduation.'

'You look good in a cap and gown,' he said. He could hear the flirtation in his tone.

'That's what my grandad said before trying to convince me to do a PhD,' she said jokingly. 'How about you?'

'June seventh . . . a photo shoot.' He looked away, quickly scrolling past the pictures.

'Is that what you look like when you're embarrassed?' she said with amusement.

'I'm not embarrassed.'

'Yes, you are. See, now I want to see the photos.'

'Nope,' he said, feeling a sudden wave of self-consciousness.

'Zeke!' she said, her eyes widening. 'You can't tell me you were doing a photo shoot and then not show me the photos.' She leaned towards him mischievously. He was finding it harder and harder to say no to her.

'All right, all right,' said Zeke as he gave her his phone to look at the photos. As she scrolled through he tried to guess what she was thinking, but her face was impossible to read.

'What's the verdict?'

She looked at the photos, and then back up at him.

'You look good,' she said matter-of-factly. 'Did you get your eyebrows done for it?'

'Yeah, I did, but I think they've started to grow back now. Look,' he said, pointing up at his eyebrow to show Olivia the short thin hairs growing back outside of the lines the stylist on the photo shoot had shaped them into.

'Zeke, you know how I'm good at a lot of things . . .' She rummaged through her bag.

'I don't know if I like where this is going,' Zeke said, half in terror and half in amusement as he watched her take out a make-up bag and bottle of hand sanitizer.

'Trust me,' she said, excitedly pulling out a pair of tweezers.

'You are way too enthusiastic for me to trust you,' said Zeke, looking at the tweezers and then the delighted, to the point of maniacal, smile on Olivia's face.

'Okay, this might hurt a little bit,' she said.

'I did kidnap training, remember? I'm familiar with torture.'

Olivia rolled her eyes and leaned over to place her hands on the side of his head. They were warm, soft and smelt like vanilla. The gentleness caught him by surprise.

Maybe it was the fact that she was hovering right above his face or maybe it was the fact that they'd been talking to each other for almost an entire hour now, but he felt like something was shifting between them. Like he'd known her longer than just the past few days. He felt so at ease with her that it made him nervous. Zeke could feel himself getting gently pulled in. Their faces were just centimetres apart, so close that he could smell the perfume on her skin.

'If I didn't know better, I'd think you were trying to make a move on me,' he whispered.

'If you're not careful I might end up *accidentally* over-plucking you,' she whispered as she leaned so close to him there was barely any separation between their bodies. Taking the lift was the best decision Zeke had made all week.

28

Olivia

Day four of the 2024 Olympics

That was how Olivia found herself hovering just a couple of centimetres away from Zeke's face for ten minutes. Taking her time as she plucked his eyebrows hair by hair until they started to resemble the form they'd been shaped into for his magazine cover shoot. She kept looking back down at the photo as a reference image and each time it was a relief to be able to look at something that wasn't his actual face. Somehow the photo captured Zeke exactly as he was up close, so handsome that Olivia couldn't look at him for too long without wanting to touch his beautiful eyelashes or kiss his absurdly gorgeous lips. She caught a glimpse of the hair-thin necklace that had slipped under his shirt, the gentle ripples of fabric accentuating all the hours he clearly spent in the gym. His cologne was warm and musky.

'How's it going up there?' he whispered after a few moments of silence.

'Just thinking about how you talk a *big* game for some-one whose eyes started watering two seconds into this,' Olivia said. She gently stroked the skin around his eyebrow, absent-mindedly tracing a line around it. His skin was soft and smooth.

'My eyes aren't watering, it's . . . it's just the light and the angle,' he said unconvincingly. She shook her head, smiling to herself.

'All right, I'm done,' she said softly, sitting back to check that his eyebrows were completely symmetrical.

'How do I look, Olivia?' he asked.

She loved hearing her name on his lips. 'Good,' she said. For some reason, she didn't feel the need to follow it up with a joke or fill in the silence. While she'd moved back a little bit, their faces were still just a few centimetres away from each other. Everything in her wanted to lean nearer and close the distance between them. And, it turned out, he felt the same.

Zeke moved a little bit closer and so did Olivia. They leaned closer, and then closer again, like they *needed* to be together. Like this was inevitable. As Olivia breathed in, she felt Zeke's nose gently touch hers. Her heartbeat quickened. He placed his hand on the side of her face and softly cupped it to bring her closer still. Without thinking, she gripped his shoulder to bring him forward. Zeke brushed a strand of hair out of her face and traced his finger from the top of her head, down over her cheek and then across her lips . . . so achingly slowly that Olivia could feel herself trembling.

'Zeke,' she whispered, her voice shaking at his touch.

'Hmm?' he said, his nose grazing her chin as his hot breath swept up across her neck, leaving each inch of her skin feeling like it had been set alight. She was going to lose her mind if he didn't just hurry up and kiss her.

'Zeke,' she said again, her voice strained. They were so close now that they could feel each other's breath and hear each other's heartbeat. All that separated them was a sliver of distance so delicate she could almost taste it. She *really* wanted to taste it. And then their lips crashed straight into each other. Olivia's breath hitched at the contact. His lips were soft and the kiss was hot and urgent. She wrapped her arms around the curve of his neck, and he snaked his hand around her waist to pull her closer. The sides of her shirt had lifted a little and the sensation of his firm hands against her sensitive skin sent a trickle of pleasure down her spine. She deepened the kiss, tilting her head and gently biting his bottom lip, smiling into his mouth as she heard his quiet moan. Her self-control weakened as she felt the slide of his tongue inside her mouth. She was melting at her core.

In one effortless swoop, Zeke lifted her up from the floor and placed her firmly on his lap, his hands gripping her thighs. She wrapped her legs around his waist, realizing how thin her shorts were when she felt him beneath her. She wanted to get closer. There couldn't be any space between them. She was intoxicated by the sensation of her body against his. She laid hot, breathless kisses on his lips and his hands tangled up in her hair. She traced circles on the firm, soft skin underneath his shirt. She gently began to lift it up and then retreated as he kissed her with such passion and urgency that she began to feel light-headed. He ran his hands down the sides of her body, creating a need so visceral she felt it crackling under her skin. They were both getting so lost in the blinding intensity of the moment that it would only take a few more seconds to tip over the point of no return.

'Is that your phone?' said Zeke. Olivia opened her eyes,

came to her senses and climbed off Zeke's lap. She was flushed and a little disorientated. Zeke's shirt was rumpled and his mouth was covered with her lipstick. His face was still wearing an expression of heady, breathless desire. And she was the cause.

29
Olivia

Day four of the 2024 Olympics

Olivia shuffled away from Zeke and glanced down at her phone to check the caller ID.

'It's my best friend,' said Olivia. A part of her wanted to let the phone ring out and slide back over to the other side of the lift. But she and Aditi were both in a foreign country. What if it was an emergency and she actually needed to reach her?

'Hey, are you okay?' Olivia asked as she answered the video call.

'Are *you* okay?' said Aditi from the other side of the phone. 'You usually text me every three minutes when you're on your way home. I hope the radio silence is because you're having fun, not because you're in a dark room somewhere staring at your screen applying for jobs and muttering about how much you hate . . . Wait, where are you?' Aditi was peering at the screen.

'I'm in a lift, I'm stuck in a lift,' Olivia said.

'Oh no, are you with someone? How are you getting phone service? Do you need me to call Village Security?' Aditi asked. She said it like she was concerned, but Olivia could see the delight in her eyes. This was exactly the kind of thing that happened in the K-Dramas they watched on Friday nights.

'I'm fine,' Olivia said.

'The technician should be here in, like, five minutes, right?' said Zeke. But before Olivia could reply she saw the look of glee on Aditi's face.

'Wait, is that a boy? Are you stuck in the lift with a boy?'

Olivia closed her eyes in embarrassment. Zeke looked amused; Olivia bit her lip to maintain her composure.

'Olivia, pass the phone over to whoever you're with right now. I need to warn them about how intense you get when you have to deal with a situation you can't control for more than ten minutes,' said Aditi.

Zeke shuffled closer, and Olivia shook her head in defeat as the side of his face came into frame. Aditi's eyes and mouth widened.

'Zeke Moyo? Oh my God,' said Aditi. 'Wait, Olivia *hates* you.'

Olivia tried to silence Aditi with just her eyes, but it didn't work.

'Oh, I already know,' Zeke said. 'She quite literally slid down the wall when she realized she was going to be stuck in here with me.' Nobly, he failed to mention that she'd also just climbed on top of him so she could kiss him from a better angle.

'Well, I think you might have a smudge of something on your lips, Zeke. Something red?' Aditi said, not so subtly pointing out the lipstick stains around Zeke's mouth.

'I'm hanging up now,' said Olivia.

'Thin lines, right?' Aditi said with a wicked smile.

'Bye, Aditi,' said Olivia as she ended the call. She put

her phone in her pocket and looked anywhere but at Zeke.

'Thin lines?' Zeke asked.

Olivia had no intention of giving him an answer. And, luckily, the emergency intercom in the lift buzzed before he could ask again.

'Hey, Giannis . . . yep, I'm here,' she said, trying to make her voice sound upbeat and casual to distract herself from the fact that her whole body was drawing her back to Zeke, to finish what they'd started. She could still remember the feeling of Zeke's hands running up and down her sides, the dizzying effect of his lips and just how breathless she'd been when they'd let go. The tension between them was still lingering in the air. Olivia knew that if the lift doors stayed closed, there would be no stopping what they'd put into motion.

But she didn't have to test the limits of her self-control because the lift was moving again; Giannis had reached the building and re-set the system. The lift was finally at the ground floor, the doors opening. Olivia was so relieved to breathe fresh air again that she immediately stood up and began to walk out.

'Forgetting something?' Zeke asked as he pointed at the painting of Arlo. She'd almost left it in her rush to escape the complicated feelings she could sense herself beginning to form towards Zeke. Who was she kidding? The complicated feelings she'd been forming ever since they'd fallen on to the ground together that first day.

It was blue hour when Olivia and Zeke stepped out of the building. The sky was a haze and the bright-yellow street lights that were beginning to turn on made it feel like they were floating in an other-worldly window between day and night. The air was thick with a heady sense of possibility. They could so easily get swept away.

'That's my turning,' she said, breaking the silence as they reached the bend in the path that would take her to the shuttle bus.

'Okay, will you be all right getting back? There's just one shuttle an hour, right?' he asked. Both of them were looking everywhere but at each other.

'Yeah, the next one is in fifteen minutes,' she said, checking her phone.

'Text me when you get home?' he said with a gentleness that startled her.

'I don't have . . .' She trailed off. He put his hand out and she gave him her phone, then he gave her his. They saved numbers and swapped their phones back, fingers gently grazing as they made their returns.

But as soon as she took her first step towards the other path, he reached for her hand. It was gentle but firm. Her heartbeat began to quicken. His hand was a question, and whatever she did next would be the answer.

If Olivia had taken the stairs instead of the lift, she would have gone straight home in time to catch Aditi watching a rerun of that afternoon's Olympic beach volleyball game. If Zeke had taken the stairs instead of the lift, he probably would have put his trainers on and gone straight out for a run.

If the lift hadn't got stuck somewhere between the seventh floor and the ground floor, they would have just exchanged a few words and then walked back out into the Village, too busy with their own lives and worries to spend time thinking about the person they kept bumping into. But that's not how it had played out.

The thing with magnets was that as much as they tried to resist each other, hold back their power, face opposite directions and try to stay apart, the force of attraction would always win. They could both feel the gravitational pull.

Olivia turned around and looked at Zeke. Zeke pulled her closer to him. Their lips felt hot against each other like they were two forces colliding in the most magnetic, passionate chemical reaction. As if their lips were specifically designed to meld together. But this kiss was different. He kissed her softly, like she was something precious. Gently stroking her hair and holding her close as if what stood between them was too delicate to rush. She kissed him slowly, savouring each moment. Lightly running her hands up and down his back, pulling him closer and placing delicate kisses on his lips with a tender intimacy that surprised her. She was as comfortable with him as if she'd known him all her life, but with each touch, kiss and sigh her body felt completely electrified.

The energy between them inside the lift had been so intense that she'd almost been able to convince herself it was just a physical thing, a natural human response to being stuck in an enclosed space with someone she was attracted to. After all, Zeke was ridiculously hot, an insanely good kisser, and she was an adult woman with wants and desires. But as they kissed under a lamp post, she realized that it wasn't just lust. Lust was easy, lust had a clear solution. No, as she gently kissed the soft area around his mouth, she knew her feelings for Zeke were much more complicated than that. Olivia *liked* Zeke Moyo. And that realization kind of terrified her. As he planted tender kisses on her cheek, held her close and looked down at her with a kind of startled adoration, she realized that he might feel the same way too. Which terrified her even more. So, she gently disentangled herself from him and let go. She looked at Zeke and the lipstick stain she'd left on his lips. The creases on his shirt and the buttons at the top she was pretty sure she'd unbuttoned. They stood in silence for a moment. And then she reached down, put her bag on her shoulder and placed the canvas back in her hands.

'The shuttle,' she said. Her heart threatened to run out of her chest.

'Only once an hour,' he said breathlessly, still brushing a hand against his lips.

She turned around and walked down the path towards the shuttle bus, fighting the urge to turn back and look at him one more time.

Olivia could still taste him on her lips.

30
Zeke

Day five of the 2024 Olympics

Zeke was supposed to be focusing on training, but his mind kept replaying the night before. That earth-shattering, head-dizzying kiss. Remembering the way he'd wrapped his arms around her and how fiercely she'd pushed herself up against his body, her thin shirt and maddeningly soft shorts brushing against him. They'd kissed with such an urgency that it had taken everything in him to let go. It wasn't the kind of kiss that he could walk away from and remain the same. Olivia wasn't the kind of girl he could meet and then just go back to his normal life. And he could feel it in his performance that morning. It was the day of the quarter-finals, but he kept on making silly mistakes.

'Too late off the finish line, Moyo,' said Coach Adam, shaking his head after yet another sub-standard run.

'Sorry, Coach, just feeling a little distracted,' said Zeke.

'Well, un-distract yourself.'

Zeke walked back to the other side of the track to try again. But when he got into his starting position, he remembered the way Olivia had gasped when he'd lifted her off the floor and the way she'd whispered his name as he'd planted hot, impatient kisses against the side of her neck.

'Zeke!' shouted Coach Adam. Zeke looked around and realized that Coach had blown the whistle to signal the start of his practice sprint, but he was still stationary. He'd never missed the start of a run before. Coach Adam looked at him with a mixture of worry and disbelief. Zeke couldn't believe himself either.

'I don't know where your head is at, kid,' said Coach Adam, with a look of pure incredulity, 'but you need to get it together.'

'Yes, Coach,' said Zeke, nodding.

By the time he walked into the stadium for the quarter-finals, Zeke had shut off almost all of his distractions. He'd listened to music that helped him focus, watched videos of his old races to study his technique and spent the hour leading up to the race alone so that he couldn't get distracted by other people's conversations.

Zeke had been watching his Team GB teammates' competitions all week. He'd cheered wildly as he'd watched the rowers win their semi-final. Nearly bitten his fingers off as he'd watched the intense boxing quarter-final. And he'd stared up at the screen in the Team GB common room in awe as he and his teammates watched the synchronized swimmers do their first routine. Camille had sprained her wrist during practice, so the team physio had prescribed her two days of rest before she trained again. Frankie had made it to the semi-finals of the 5,000-metre run, but Anwar missed out on qualifying for the next round of the javelin throw by just a couple of centimetres. There were mixed emotions in GB House as some athletes celebrated their first medals while others hid away in their rooms, packing their suitcases to go home early. Each time Zeke saw one of his teammates reach their goal or miss out at the last hurdle, the pressure and the stakes went up.

As he entered the stadium, the energy of the crowd was on a whole other level. Because while the athletes channelled the intensity of the occasion into their performance, the audience did it by filling the stadium with the excitement and energy of a festival. There were adults with flags painted on their cheeks and kids sporting brightly coloured wigs. Families who'd travelled across the world in matching DIY shirts and groups of friends singing and chanting the words to unofficial national anthems. There was music pouring out of the speakers and a wave rippling across the stadium. But when the 100-metre sprint was announced, a hush descended on the spectators.

Zeke shook hands with each of his competitors, reminded himself that the most important sprinter was the one in his lane, and got ready to run.

When the starting gun blew, Zeke got off to a clean, confident start. As he felt the wind in his face, distractions melted away and all he could think about was the sound of his shoes as they hit the track. He was doing what he'd been put on this earth to do, and he was doing an excellent job of it. But then, as he approached the end, his foot slid. It was only for a fraction of a second but enough to skew his balance. Before he knew it, he was falling. Everything after that happened in slow motion. He threw his hands out to brace for impact. The colours and lights in the stadium began to blur and the world turned sideways as he fell. When his hands landed on the hard red ground of the running track, everything went silent for a second.

Zeke felt an overwhelming sense of terror at the

realization that he'd fallen in the middle of his race. His immediate worry should have been about whether he was injured, the possibility of not qualifying for the semi-finals or the real threat of missing out on his chance to win gold. But, instead, he thought about his father. What if this summer was his last chance to become the great athlete they'd dreamed he could become? What if this was actually a career-ending moment?

Zeke opened his eyes and pushed himself up from the ground as the other runners thundered past and reunited with their coaches. The race was over. He could feel himself beginning to panic.

But then the whole stadium began cheering for him. His heart sank; he'd heard cheers like this before: *It's okay, you tried your best* cheers. His face fell. Then he was surrounded by his Team GB teammates. Anwar and Frankie jumped on him and the rest of the team ran to hug him, pounding his back and yelling until their voices were hoarse.

'You did it!' shouted Anwar, who'd decided to stay in Athens until the Games ended.

'What?' said Zeke, still confused.

'Got into the semi-finals!' said Frankie. Zeke looked around in disbelief. His teammates and the crowd were still going wild. He looked up at the big screen to watch the replay and finally connected the dots. Yes, he'd lost his balance while he was still on the track, but he'd been in the lead for the whole race. He'd fallen just a fraction of a second after both of his feet had passed the finish line. If he'd fallen just half a second earlier, he would have gone home empty-handed. But now he was through to the semi-finals. It was such a breath-taking near loss that it felt even more spectacular.

Zeke gaped in astonishment. Coach Adam hugged him and shook his head in shock.

'You were *this close*,' said Coach Adam.

'This close,' said Zeke, his eyes widening with an equal amount of terror and relief as the gravity of it all began to settle in. He could feel his knees stinging and, when he looked down, he could see blood in the places he'd scraped them on the ground. But besides a few cuts and bruises that would heal in a matter of days, he had escaped the fall without an injury or any serious pain.

'There's got to be someone up there looking out for you,' said Coach Adam. Zeke believed there was.

The older he got, the more he tried to treat each win as cause for celebration. And he immediately knew how he was going to celebrate his skin-of-the-teeth victory.

But first, he had to find Olivia.

Zeke

Day five of the 2024 Olympics

Zeke's phone had been burning a hole in his pocket ever since he'd given Olivia his number. He'd been agonizing over what to text her and trying to come up with something cool and witty to make her laugh. But the more he thought about it, the more he realized that he didn't want to text Olivia, he wanted to see her. Face to face. So, he found an excuse to go to the Hub.

'I already know what you're going to say,' Zeke said, throwing his hands up in defence.

'It's giving stalker,' Olivia said as she tilted her head. Zeke tried to ignore the effect that her head-tilt had on him. It was the same way she'd tilted her head right before she'd kissed him. All he wanted to do was walk over to the other side of the desk, lift her up on to the counter and kiss her again. Feel her soft, perfect lips against his and wrap his arms around her. But despite everything last night, and the fact that he knew without a doubt that he liked her, he didn't want to scare her off by coming on too strong.

'You work at the Athletes' Hub, and I am an athlete, it's inevitable that we're going to keep crossing paths,' he said.

'This isn't the only Athletes' Hub in the Village, though, is it?'

'It's the closest one to my apartment,' he said.

'I think you were just looking for an opportunity to see me,' she said, her gaze unwavering.

'You're right,' he said, 'I wasn't satisfied with yesterday.' Olivia's eyes widened for a moment. He knew she thought he was talking about the kiss. And if he was honest, he kind of was. He'd spent the whole night wondering what would have happened if her phone hadn't rung. If they'd gone straight from the lift to his apartment and let the night take the lead.

It had felt like a game of sorts; the two of them going back and forth. Taking and exchanging power. Kissing like it was both a duel and a dance. But, this time, they were on the same team.

'What . . . what weren't you satisfied with?' Olivia said, looking vulnerable for the first time since Zeke had met her. She ran her fingers through her hair. Zeke looked at her in pleasant surprise; he hadn't realized he was capable of making her nervous.

'The song game we played in the lift where we had to guess the song? I wasn't satisfied with how it ended,' said Zeke. 'It ended in a draw, and I'm an athlete. A draw is the same as losing.' He watched in amusement as relief flooded her face.

'Zeke, I've got to deliver five thousand biodegradable paper planes to the production team in ten minutes. So do you actually need help with something or are you just here to flirt?' Olivia asked, her head to one side. They both knew the real answer to that question. Which made *his* next question tilt the room off balance for a moment.

'So, one of my friends is competing in the gymnastics competition tonight.'

'And is that *friend* Valentina Ross-Rodriguez?' Olivia asked. Zeke noticed the emphasis she put on the word 'friend' but also the fact that the expression on her face didn't waver. He wondered if she'd read all the headlines about his and Valentina's break-up and all the subsequent times the press had incorrectly reported that they were back together.

'Yeah, it's my *friend* Valentina's competition,' he said, putting an extra emphasis on the word 'friend' as well to make it clear that was all they were. He noticed a small flicker of what looked like relief on her face.

'I wanted to support her, *as a friend*,' he said. He knew saying 'friend' again was probably a little bit overkill, but he didn't want Olivia to worry. Because he was telling the truth. He and Valentina were just friends now; it was completely platonic.

'But I forgot to request tickets,' he said. 'So, I was wondering if you'd be able to check if there are any spare athlete VIP envelopes?'

'Oh, that is a big favour. A *lot* of people want tickets for tonight,' she said, turning her back and looking through the filing cabinet. 'It's not looking good, Moyo,' she said, shaking her head and whistling. She sifted through every single folder of the cabinet . . . despite the fact that they could both see the drawer beside her that was clearly marked ATHLETE TICKETS in bright-red Sharpie.

Zeke watched her in amusement. 'You love this, don't you?'

'Love what?' she said, still pretending to look through the folders.

'Having the power to dictate how the rest of my night goes.'

'I just love power generally,' she said nonchalantly. There was that unflinching confidence that made her so attractive. 'It doesn't have to be over anyone in particular. It's just the *feeling* of having it.'

'I like that about you,' he said.

'That I'm power hungry?'

'Yes. And that you're not afraid to admit it,' he said. It was the thing he kept coming back to, the way she seemed to be completely certain of herself. It pulled him in.

'Why lie?' she shrugged.

'A lot of people hide their ambition and act like the good things in their life happened by chance,' he said, leaning against the desk, his voice getting lower. 'But the reality is, people like us plot it all out and work really hard for what we want.'

'People act like "strategic" is a dirty word, like calling someone "calculated" is an insult, but I like being in control,' she said honestly.

His mind flashed back to last night. To the way she'd held on to his shoulders, the way she'd bitten his lip, the way she'd wordlessly asked for what she wanted, and how each kiss sunk him deeper and deeper into what he already knew he was falling into.

'If you know what you want, you make it happen . . . right?' he said. Everything he was thinking lingered in that pause. The intensity of feeling was so persistent that it made him feel light-headed.

'So, do you know what you want, Zeke?' she asked, pinning him with a gaze he couldn't turn away from. The way she was looking at him made him want to take a long cold shower.

'I think I do.' His mouth was dry.

'And what's that?' she asked, challenging him.

They locked eyes and for a moment it felt like time stood still. Like once again they were the only two people in the room, the Village, the city. Zeke knew that he was late for Valentina's competition, but the only person on his mind was Olivia. He could feel himself becoming infatuated with her quick wit, sharp sense of humour and wicked smile. Starting to fall for the light in her eyes and the soft curve of her lips. As Zeke looked at her, he forgot about the questions nagging away at him; about the fact that he'd fallen in the middle of a race and that, now he was through to the semi-finals, the pressure to win and take home a gold medal was stronger than ever. His worries melted away, because in that moment, all that mattered was Olivia. It was intoxicating and it was terrifying. They were only a few inches away from each other. It wouldn't take much to close the distance.

'You should probably leave,' she said, pulling him out of the gaze he'd been so intently locked into.

'Why?' he asked. He wanted to lean forward and kiss her, but Olivia's expression had changed, the moment had passed.

'Your *friend's* competition?' she said, handing him an envelope with two tickets to Valentina's final. Olivia's expression faltered for a moment before she plastered on a smile. It didn't quite reach her eyes.

'Bye, Zeke,' she said, before turning around and going back to her paper planes. He wanted to stay, but she was right. If he didn't leave now he would be late, and the stadium ushers wouldn't let him in once the competition had begun. So he nodded, and reluctantly opened the door of the Hub to leave.

'Hey, did you get the tickets?' asked Haruki, who'd been standing just outside. Zeke nodded and held the envelope up in victory.

'We're about to have the best night,' said Haruki as the two of them walked back out into the Village.

Zeke knew that they probably would have a good time. But he couldn't help but wonder how the night would have turned out if he'd given Olivia the answer to her question by putting her on the desk and kissing her the way he'd wanted to.

'Wait, was that . . .' said Haruki, turning around.

'We're gonna be late,' called Zeke as his best friend walked back to the Hub, glanced inside and then ran back towards him.

'Zeke! It's her!' Haruki said with a grin.

'Who?' asked Zeke, coming out of the haze his moment with Olivia had swept him up into.

'The girl!' said Haruki, as if he was talking about something completely obvious.

'What girl?' said Zeke in confusion.

'The future love of my life! The one I bumped into outside the Village, the one I'm going to the outdoor cinema with. Her!' said Haruki, smiling from ear to ear.

'Where is she?' asked Zeke in amusement.

'In the Hub! Should I say something? Ask her if she's

still on for Sunday? I should definitely say something,' said Haruki, seeming uncharacteristically flustered. But Zeke was lost; there wasn't anybody else in the Hub. He was sure this time. The only person in the room, when he'd walked in to get tickets, was . . .

'Olivia?' asked Zeke in confusion.

'Olivia . . . yes, of course, that's her name!' Haruki said as if he'd just found the missing piece to a puzzle. But then he looked over at Zeke, perplexed. 'Wait, how do you know her name? I never told you her name.'

Zeke closed his eyes for a moment then looked at his best friend. His hopeful, lovestruck best friend. Luckily, Haruki didn't seem to think there was anything suspicious about the fact that Zeke knew her name, so he said nothing.

'Okay, I'm going to go back to the Hub and talk to her tomorrow, but we're going to be late, Zeke, let's go,' said Haruki, walking cheerfully off.

Zeke felt his heart sink.

The girl Haruki had been talking about had been Olivia all along. Zeke was completely and thoroughly screwed.

32

Olivia

Day five of the 2024 Olympics

Olivia usually hopped on to the first shuttle bus out of the Village when her shift ended. She and Aditi were renting in the centre of Athens and Olivia had slipped into a nightly routine of going home and sitting in bed writing out job applications until Aditi convinced her to leave her room. Because, while she was having a better summer than she'd expected to have when she'd found out about the lost internship, September was just three weeks away and she knew that she needed to have an idea of what came after she caught her flight back home. But that evening, instead of worrying about jobs, Olivia decided to take the long way home.

Athens was still bathed in sunlight. As she wandered through the busy streets, she stopped to listen to the sound of a Greek folk band playing music in the middle of a square of busy restaurants. She wandered down a road lined with lemon trees and followed the sound of cheers that led her past a bar where a whole group of people were gathered to watch an Olympic sailing race. Then she took a left turn, and walked down a quiet street until she reached her destination: *Meraki* – a tiny hole-in-the-wall shop. It was a legendary art shop that Olivia had read about while planning her trip. It had been open for over a century and Olivia could feel the history as soon as she walked through the door. She heard the bell tinkle above her and was immediately immersed in a room that smelt like old books, sweet tea and paint. She greeted the kind older woman at the counter then filled her bag to bursting with everything that caught her eye. She definitely didn't have the money, and she knew she should probably be saving for whatever September held, but she'd decided to let herself do one thing that was just for her. For her present-day self, not some idealized future.

'Olivia, I haven't seen you painting in years,' said Aditi when she came home to find the kitchen table covered with paper, paintbrushes and colourful glasses of water.

'I shouldn't have stopped,' Olivia said as she put the final touch to the postcard-sized portrait she'd been working on and handed it over to Aditi. It was a painting of Aditi drinking coffee outside Cafe Kalopsia. Aditi stilled for a moment as tears pricked her eyes.

'Liv, you made me look so happy.' She squeezed Olivia's shoulder. 'I almost forgot how talented you are at this,' she said, taking a seat on the other side of the table.

'I was supposed to be doing that,' said Olivia, pointing at the laptop filled with incomplete job applications. 'And I should probably get back to it.'

'But it's summer,' said Aditi knowingly.

'It's summer,' said Olivia.

'And Summer Olivia has decided to join us this year?' Aditi said, a quick smile appearing on her face.

Olivia knew where the conversation was going. The

night before, Aditi had cornered her at the front door and convinced her to divulge every single detail.

'Your skin is glowing, you're wearing cute little dresses, you're painting? I know Summer Olivia when I see her,' said Aditi.

'It has nothing to do with Zeke,' Olivia said, sounding a little more defensive than she'd meant to. 'Okay, it has a teeny bit to do with him,' she conceded, throwing her hands up in defeat. 'But it's more about summer.'

'And is *summer* a code word for hot athletes? Just checking we're on the same page.' Aditi hadn't got any less excitable in the almost twenty years they'd known each other.

'No, I mean actual summer. It wasn't the boy last time and it's not the boy this time, it's the way I feel when the sun comes out.' Olivia put her paintbrush down.

Aditi went to the fridge, cut up a bowl of mango and placed it in the middle of the table. They always got the fruit out when they needed to have a long conversation.

'Do you remember how fearless we were when we were kids?' Olivia asked.

'Like the time I jumped into that pond and broke my leg?' Aditi said. 'Or the time you convinced me to go to that abandoned warehouse party when we were fifteen?'

'Yeah, they were dumb decisions, but we didn't think about the consequences of everything so much back then. We just did what sounded fun and figured out the details later.'

'So – what I'm hearing is that you want to go to a party tonight and jump into a random pool? Because if that's it, I'm so down,' said Aditi.

While that sounded like fun, Olivia was talking about the fearless way they used to dream when they were teenagers.

How the two of them had sat on Olivia's bedroom floor drafting out big-eyed plans for the women they wanted to become when they grew up. Aditi had written out her dream of owning her own iced coffee business and Olivia had written out her dream of working at the Olympics. But ever since arriving in the Village, she'd been wondering at what point her childhood dream had become such a firmly mapped-out plan. How something she'd excitedly aspired to had become the gauge she measured the success of her whole life against. Her five-year plan had gone from being the goal that woke her up in the morning to a source of rigidity and dread, with no space for distractions.

'That summer in Lisbon . . .' Olivia started.

'Tiago?' Aditi asked, referring to Olivia's Portuguese summer fling.

'Kind of. I don't think I fell in love with Tiago,' she said out loud for the first time. Aditi nodded. 'I think I fell in love with the way that summer made me feel.'

'It was the best,' said Aditi. 'Remember? We would go swimming every day and dream up our futures at night, walk through the streets with no destination in mind.'

'It was perfect. But because of how it ended, I kind of put the ways I changed when I got home down to heartbreak, but I don't think that's what it was,' said Olivia. 'I feel like that summer was the last time I actually just enjoyed myself. The last time a part of me still felt like a kid.'

'Well, it was our last year of being teenagers, so it kind of was,' said Aditi, a hint of wistfulness in her voice.

It had been five years since that summer, but so much had happened. They'd both finished university, stepped into the working world and grown up.

She'd mistaken falling in love with the summer for falling in love with the boy. For a few brief, heady days she'd thought about staying in Portugal until the end of the year, deferring her studies and seeing where the summer could take her. But when she'd found out that Tiago had a girlfriend, she'd realized that her epic summer romance had been nothing more than just a fling to entertain him while his girlfriend was away. The experience crushed her, so she'd panicked and booked the next flight back to the UK.

It had been devastating, and as much as she hated to admit it, she'd gone into every romantic encounter ever since feeling a little bit guarded, a little less quick to trust. But it wasn't just the discovery that he wasn't who he'd said he was that left her heartbroken. It had been her last care-free, teenage summer and, after Tiago, she'd gone home and realized she had no choice but to grow up.

Her teenage self could have made careless decisions like moving country for some guy she barely knew. But her adult self had to set out a clear path for what she was going to do after graduation. Her teenage self could ignore signs and take a boy at his word, but her adult self had to be much more discerning than that. Her nineteen-year-old summer self could be reckless and figure things out as she went along. But her nineteen-year-old autumn self had understood that her life wasn't just her own.

She'd landed in the UK on a random Saturday and, when she'd opened her front door, there was no one at home. It was a rare, perfect summer weekend, but her parents were both at work.

It wasn't term time, but her mum was at the secondary

school she taught at, manning the free summer lunches programme. It was her dad's day off, but he was at the social services office, stepping in to advocate for one of the vulnerable adults he worked with. There were never enough social workers or council budget for her dad to have a real weekend and there were never enough school resources or government funding for her mum to stop thinking about her students. Yet Olivia had just wasted hundreds of pounds and a whole summer . . . having fun.

She had unpacked her dresses, looked around at the small two-bedroom flat they lived in and thought about how much money she'd spent on cocktails and fun nights out in Lisbon. She'd thought about how many hours her parents worked every week and shook her head in guilt as she thought about how much time she'd wasted at the beach.

How could she have forgotten that there was more to life than just having a good time? What if she never got to do her dream job? What if she never got to buy her parents the house they'd always wanted? What if she never lived up to her potential?

If she was ever going to achieve her goals, make her parents proud and build a better life, she was going to have to get a lot more focused. So, she'd written out the plan.

After that summer, she'd become fiercely regimented. She spent every night studying. Every university break doing an internship. Every spare moment trying to build her future. In short – everything in her life became an assignment she was too scared to fail.

The truth was that the only thing that stopped her from reverting to the carefree spontaneity of that summer was guilt. But it was easier to blame it on heartbreak than admit that adulthood had taken a youthfulness from her that she wasn't sure she could ever get back.

'I obviously still loathe Lars Lindberg,' she said.

'With a burning passion,' Aditi nodded.

'And that internship was mine,' she said.

'You were completely robbed,' Aditi said.

'But I think if I'd got the internship, I probably would have sped through that too, spent all my time trying to make contacts and prove myself . . . wait, no. I take that back,' she said, remembering who she was. 'I would have probably had so much fun doing that. It's what I've wanted my whole life. I'm not going to spin this into some anti-ambition lesson. And what I'm *not* going to take away from this summer is that I should be okay with second best,' she added.

'We are *not* big city girls who accidentally ended up in one of those summer beach reads, where the takeaway is that you have to sacrifice your career for happiness!' said Aditi, despite currently having three of those exact kind of books on her bedside table.

'Ambition is a brilliant thing! I still want every single thing on that list. And I *will* get them. But I want success because I love it. Not because the fear of not achieving my goals is the thing that gets me out of bed in the morning.'

'And while Mai Nkomo and Baba Nkomo are proud of everything you're doing, it's not your responsibility to live for them,' Aditi said softly.

Olivia nodded. She knew that, but it didn't stop her from feeling that way.

'Sometimes I can just do things for me, because I want to,' she said.

'Exactly,' Aditi said, hitting the table to reinforce her agreement.

'And today, I want to just sit at home and paint instead of applying for jobs.'

'Because it's summer,' said Aditi, repeating her favourite mantra.

'And I'm fun in the summer,' Olivia said, cutting the final mango chunk in half and giving Aditi the bigger piece.

'Liv,' Aditi said, suddenly serious. 'You know the Summer Olivia thing is just a nickname, right? Summer Olivia is just who you are when you let yourself be the truest version of yourself. Which comes out all year round.' Aditi went to put her bowl in the kitchen.

Olivia stayed seated at the table for a moment, sending a silent wish to the universe that they'd stay best friends for the rest of their lives.

'Remember the rule?' Aditi said as she picked up her phone and connected it to the kitchen speaker.

'What rule?' said Olivia, but then she heard the song Aditi was playing. 'Wait, the rule only applies to random moments, you can't just put on a Ciara song and insist on the rule.'

'I didn't make the rule, I just reinforce it,' said Aditi. She began to dance around the kitchen. Olivia shimmied across the room to join her. They'd been friends since they were five years old and seen the very best and worst of each other. Their friendship didn't have any rules. Except that if a Ciara song came on, they had to dance. So, Olivia danced.

Sometimes she forgot who she was. But Aditi was always there to remind her. Maybe that's what love was, she thought as she spun around in the early evening light.

Maybe it was just the feeling of being around someone who made her remember who she was. Who brought out the parts of her that she'd forgotten. Or the parts she sometimes got too self-conscious to show. She felt it when she was around her parents, even when she was hiding things from them to protect their feelings. She felt it when she was with Aditi, talking about everything and nothing and knowing they'd never get bored. And she realized that she'd been feeling more and more like herself ever since she'd walked across the Village in that green juice-stained suit.

But that didn't matter, because in the Hub that afternoon she'd been reminded of something that she'd been doing her best to try to forget. Like everyone else in the world, Olivia knew about Zeke's on-again off-again relationship with Valentina Ross-Rodriguez, the star gymnast of Team USA. Yes, she and Zeke had kissed, and she was pretty sure he felt that spark too. But as confident as she was in who she was, Olivia knew that his ex was basically sporting royalty. She rarely got insecure but when it came to her and Valentina, there wasn't really any competition. Because Valentina was one of the greatest athletes in the world. She was talented, accomplished and incredibly beautiful. She was the kind of girl you either wanted to be or you wanted to be with.

Olivia had seen dozens of photos of Zeke and Valentina on red carpets, in stadiums and at A-list parties. They were the internet's favourite couple. And she found it hard to truly believe that Zeke, who'd specifically hunted down tickets to watch his ex-girlfriend compete, didn't still have feelings for her.

But while that summer five years ago had changed her, the one thing she'd resolved not to let it change was her ability to hope.

She didn't want to go through her life distrusting everyone she met because one boy lied to her. And while she wasn't the same carefree, nineteen-year-old girl she'd been, she could still let her mind wander back to those hot, perfect, sun-fuelled kisses, right?

Allow herself to live in the joy and uncertainty of a crush.

Enjoy the quiet thrill of starting something having no idea when, or if, it would end.

Olivia planned and mapped her way through every area of her life. But love was too complicated to try to control. So, she shook her head, resolved to just let the summer unfold and channelled all her energy into swaying around the kitchen with her best friend as the sun set.

33
Zeke

Day five of the 2024 Olympics

Whenever Zeke and Haruki walked into a room together, everybody looked in their direction. They were two of the most famous athletes in the world and they had four Olympic medals between them, Zeke's silver and Haruki's bronze, silver and gold. So, when they entered the stadium that night and took their seats in the 'friends and family' section of the gymnastics arena, the camera panned over to them and the whole audience roared. But this time it was for a slightly different reason.

'Do you think the shirts might have been overkill?' Zeke asked Haruki as they made eye contact with the camera and waved.

'Nah, we look good, and she's going to love it,' said Haruki. He threw his hands up in the air and the crowd cheered even louder.

Showing up at Valentina's final wearing pink, bejewelled 'Team Ross-Rodriguez' shirts with her face on them definitely made a statement. All of her friends and family were wearing them. But Zeke was Valentina's equally world-famous ex-boyfriend so all eyes were on him. When news of their break-up had got out, the blogs and gossip accounts had immediately jumped to speculate about what had happened, and then they'd taken the handful of times they'd been spotted in public together since as a sign that they were either on again or off again.

Their friendship was layered in the way that any friendship with someone you've once been in love with was. But they were just as supportive of each other as they had been when they were together. Which was why there'd been personalized 'Team Ross-Rodriguez' T-shirts waiting for Zeke and Haruki when they arrived.

'So have the two of you hung out much since the opening ceremony?' Haruki asked.

'Haruki, we're not getting back together,' said Zeke. Haruki didn't know the real reason behind their break-up, and Zeke had absolutely no intention of telling him until Valentina did. It wasn't his story to tell. But sometimes having to explain himself all the time did get a little bit exhausting. The strange thing about having had a relationship under the spotlight was that everyone around him seemed to be invested in it like they were characters, not people. Zeke tried not to let it bother him, or let the attention affect the way he approached new relationships too much. But he couldn't help but wonder what Olivia would think of it all.

'Don't give up on love,' Haruki said wistfully. There was nobody Zeke knew who earnestly believed in true love and soulmates more than Haruki. Which was why the revelation that the girl Haruki had spent the entire week talking about was, in fact, Olivia worried Zeke so much.

His best friend fell easily. It never lasted long, and he usually got distracted by something or someone else pretty quickly. But if he really did like Olivia, Zeke had essentially spent the last couple of days thinking about, flirting with and kissing the person that his best friend was infatuated with.

He knew that the right thing was to tell Haruki that he'd kissed her. Haruki would be disappointed, but telling him now would stop him from finding out on the odd double date he was planning. Zeke didn't want his friend to get even more invested in Olivia than he already was only to find out that Zeke was withholding such a vital piece of information. Haruki would feel doubly betrayed.

Zeke hated talking about his love life in normal circumstances. And telling his best friend that he'd kissed and was maybe starting to fall for the same girl he liked sounded like a conversation from hell. So, he decided to put it off until tomorrow and just enjoy the final.

'Ladies and gentlemen, welcome to the 2024 Athens Olympic Games Women's Gymnastics Final!' said the announcer. The whole audience roared and waved their flags. It was one of the most anticipated finals of the Games. Zeke had been watching all of the competitions leading up to this one with his teammates in the common room of GB House. But seeing it in person was so much better. Ever since he'd arrived, he'd been so focused on running that he hadn't watched anything live. But now he was part of the energy, atmosphere and excitement of the audience. Looking up at them from the competition grounds always pushed him forward, but sitting in the stands with them made him feel like he was a part of something bigger than himself. He took a mental picture to come back to whenever he walked out on to the track feeling lost.

When it was finally Valentina's turn to do her floor routine, Zeke could barely sit still. He was excited to see her do what she did best, but he also felt that familiar fear at the pit of his stomach. Because for as long as he'd known her, Valentina had been pushing herself to do the riskiest and most extravagant stunts she possibly could.

The whole stadium hushed as Valentina walked out on to the stage wearing a sparkly blue leotard. Her long brown hair was swooped up into a ponytail. She had a look of pure focus. The only thing she could see was the performance floor and the only thing she could hear was the music. She made her way to the centre, where she stood with her arms out and head pointed to the sky. She pulled her face into a smile, heard the first beat of her song and began.

Zeke held his breath. She leaped and flipped and ran with a delicate light-footedness that hid the fact that she possessed more sheer strength and skill than most athletics teams combined. Each stunt, flip and trick was majestic. But it was all so incredibly dangerous. He knew that all it would take was one second of mid-air hesitation for her to make the kind of catastrophic mistake that could leave her with a life-changing, career-ending injury. But she didn't make a single mistake. When she landed her final flip and took a bow, the whole stadium roared with applause. He didn't need to hear the score to know she'd won.

The audience cheered as they watched the gymnastics team return to the stage in their Team USA tracksuits and Valentina was given her gold medal. Nothing made Zeke happier than seeing his brilliant, hardworking, fearless friends win. So, he clapped until his hands hurt. Watching in awe as the national anthem played and Valentina took her final bow. Then, it was time to celebrate.

34

Zeke

Day five of the 2024 Olympics

By 11.45 p.m. Zeke, Haruki and Valentina were heading towards their third club of the night. They were meandering down one of the main roads by the city square when they walked past a building that radiated a pulsing energy they could feel from outside. The windows were lit up with warm lanterns and they could see people dancing and moving along to the music that was spilling out into the street. It was a small bar with an unassuming sign, but something about it drew them in. So, they opened the door to Club Cassiopeia and walked inside.

It was like walking into a movie scene. Everybody in the club was singing, dancing or in the midst of an animated conversation. The DJ was playing a selection of songs from all around the world, and everyone was up on their feet. The clubs in Athens opened late so even though it was almost midnight, in the city centre, the party had only just begun.

'This is so much better than the last place,' said Valentina.

'And what would our favourite multi-gold-medal-winning legendary gymnast like to drink?' Haruki asked.

'If you two were drinking, trust me, it would be tequila

shots,' she laughed, 'but since you're not, can I get a mojito?' They'd decided to take a sneaky night off to celebrate Valentina's gold medal win, but Zeke and Haruki were too close to their races to drink anything stronger than a protein shake.

'And you, Zeke? Non-alcoholic Espresso Martini?' Haruki said, smiling at Zeke's new-found passion for the mocktail menu and the fact that he always needed caffeine to get him through a night out.

'I can get it,' he said, taking out his wallet.

'Bro, one of us just signed an eight-figure Louis Vuitton campaign, and it wasn't you. Drinks are on me tonight,' said Haruki as he went off to the bar.

'Did he just . . .' said Zeke, standing with his mouth open.

'Call you broke? Yes, he did.' They both started laughing.

'I can't keep up with high-fashion Haruki,' Zeke said, relieved to have something to laugh about to stop him obsessing over the conversation he knew he needed to have with his best friend the next morning. Or his own semi-final. In fact, he'd spent the whole evening grateful to have a night to take his mind off things.

After Valentina's coaches took her out for a celebratory dinner at six p.m., they'd gone home to catch an early night ahead of their final competitions the next day. So, at nine p.m. Zeke and Haruki had picked Valentina up and taken her out into town to really celebrate.

They'd started out at a glamorous high-end bar. It was filled with extremely wealthy people who'd travelled from all around the world for the Olympics. The whole bar clapped for Valentina as soon as she walked in. Then someone anonymously sent a bottle of the most expensive champagne to toast Valentina's third Olympic gold medal. The bar was decadent and beautiful, but the atmosphere was a lot more elegant and reserved than the three of them were feeling. So, they went out into town to find the next spot.

A short walk led them to one of those super-exclusive clubs filled with celebrities and high-profile athletes. But everyone in there had been a little bit *too* eager to talk to them and the three of them made a swift exit. They were thinking of just getting some takeout, heading back to the Village and calling it a night when they'd stumbled across Cassiopeia and, now that they were inside, Zeke knew it was the right decision. Everyone in the room was too focused on dancing to pay attention to them, and Haruki was having a great time making friends with the bartenders and getting recommendations for the best souvlaki in the city.

'I heard Haruki's in love,' said Valentina, turning towards Zeke. His stomach dropped. So much for a night out to take his mind off things.

'You did?' said Zeke. He hoped his voice didn't give his disappointment away.

'Oh yeah. He called me to tell me that he'd taken a photo of a girl by the Olympic rings and that ever since – and I'm quoting him here – "the universe has been conspiring to bring them together". So, I think he's in deep.'

'Well, you can't question fate, can you?' said Zeke, the guilt beginning to set in. If he'd been paying more attention to Haruki, maybe he would have done a better job of putting the pieces together. The thought that he'd been so caught up in his own life that he'd missed the details of his friend's felt like a punch to the gut. But he felt even worse as he realized that, despite Haruki's revelation, his feelings for Olivia hadn't wavered. He still wanted to text her, to see her, to kiss her. Zeke had never thought of himself as a bad friend.

As he talked to Valentina, he found out that Haruki had asked her for advice on what to do if he saw Olivia again. That the outdoor cinema date was her idea, and that Haruki had called her just that morning for advice on what to send as his first text. As Valentina explained it all, Zeke could see just how invested Haruki was in this. And if he'd been talking about anyone but Olivia, Zeke would have been really happy for him.

But it *was* Olivia.

He wanted his best friend to be happy, but not with the girl that he had feelings for. It was selfish, he knew that. But the more he thought about the very real prospect of Olivia liking Haruki back, the worse he felt.

'He gets so excited every time he talks about her,' said Zeke, realizing that he was either going to have to tell Haruki the truth or break things off with Olivia before they'd even begun.

'How about you?' she asked gently as she took a sip of her drink. 'Are you seeing anyone?'

While he and Valentina stayed friends after the break-up and hung out with each other whenever they were in the same city, they were only just reaching the point in their friendship where they talked to each other about their newly separate romantic lives.

'I'm . . . not *seeing* anyone,' said Zeke. It was hard to

know how to explain Olivia. He rarely talked to his friends about his relationships, but he wanted to tell Valentina about Olivia. About the fact that he hadn't stopped thinking about her all week and that, ever since they'd swapped numbers, he'd spent hours trying to think of something good to say. He could see them all getting on. But Haruki's revelation had complicated things, so Zeke bit his tongue and turned the conversation away from him.

'How about you?' he asked, knowing that the question held more weight when he asked her than when she asked him.

Valentina paused for a moment and then her face broke out into a smile that told him everything he needed to know. Being happy for her was an easy feeling. If he'd told his twenty-one-year-old self that in two years Valentina would break up with him and that a year later he'd be standing in a bar with her talking about how she was seeing someone new, he wouldn't have been able to understand it. But that night in Athens he was just glad to hear that she was happy.

'How did you meet?'

'At a party, it was really . . . natural. You know when you meet someone and instantly get that sense that they're going to become a really important part of your life?' Valentina asked. Zeke nodded. He'd felt something very similar when he'd looked at Olivia in the lift.

'It was like that,' Valentina said, looking at a bracelet on her arm with a smile.

He'd noticed the screensaver on Valentina's phone earlier in the evening. A photo of Valentina smiling as a girl he didn't know kissed her on the cheek.

'Her name is Leila. She's an English teacher from Chicago. She's met my friends and most of my family, and I really really like her. No, I love her.' She flipped through her phone and showed him photos of them.

'I feel like I've spent so much of my life trying to make sure that the rest of the world approves of me, you know? Never saying anything political so I don't offend people on either side of the spectrum, hearing from a whole committee of advisers before I make even the smallest of business decisions and getting every single thing I post screened by at least ten people to make sure I don't become the subject of a social media firestorm.'

Zeke nodded. He did the same thing.

'But I wish I didn't have to do that with my personal life too. I just want to post a cute picture of me and my girl-friend at my cousin's wedding without it being a big deal. I don't want to be an activist or feel like I have to speak on behalf of every single queer athlete in the world. But I know that once that part of me is out there, there's no going back,' she said, looking burdened.

'It's special and it yours, just yours. You don't owe the world an explanation or announcement,' he said, trying to be helpful. 'And you don't have to post it if you're not ready.'

'But I don't think I'll ever really be ready, not for all of those opinions. I'm terrified of the headlines and the trolls the pundits are going to fire up and send my way. But the love I have for her outweighs the fear.' She showed Zeke another photo on her phone. It had been taken in low light and you couldn't see all the details of their faces, but you could see their dresses, their arms intertwined and the look of love on Valentina's face as they held each other close.

'When you're ready,' he said, squeezing her hand.

'When I'm ready,' she agreed, squeezing his back.

35
Zeke

Early hours of the morning,
day six of the 2024 Olympics

'Look at you two, reconciling, planning your future together,' said Haruki, returning with a mojito for Valentina and two icy glasses of water for him and Zeke. Zeke shook his head and Valentina dragged them both to the centre of the dance floor. Moving their bodies in time to the music amidst a group of people they didn't know, but who were just as happy to be there as they were. The room was dimly lit by brightly coloured lanterns hanging from the ceiling. Everyone looked beautiful, the way that people did when their faces were filled with joy. Their bodies appeared golden under the warm lights of the dance floor and Zeke felt a lightness that he hadn't experienced in a long time. Zeke was easy-going, but he was far from carefree. There was always something on his mind, whether it was thinking about the past or trying to predict the future. But as they danced that night, all that mattered to him was his friends and the music.

However, something shifted in the air as soon as a stranger came over to ask Haruki for a picture. The bars and clubs they'd been to earlier on in the night were boring in the way that clubs that were exclusive with their guest lists were. They'd been surrounded by people who were used to being in the same room as celebrities. And while exclusive places like that were dull, the people who spent their nights there knew what it was like to feel hunted and so they never pulled their cameras out. Cassiopeia, on the other hand, was a small under-the-radar spot filled with normal Athenians. But the thing about partying in normal places was that it was only a matter of time before someone took a photo and caused a scene.

It was Valentina who noticed it first, looking startled as a bunch of new people suddenly walked into the club. Haruki's face clouded over as he asked a random guy to stop recording a video of him in the middle of the dance floor. Zeke grimaced when a group of people began asking him about what life was like in the Village. The three of them grabbed each other and tried to subtly leave. But they were greeted by a small crowd of photographers who immediately started asking questions and taking photos. So, they ran back into the club and sweet-talked the bartender into letting them use the back door. They fled into the closest alleyway to hide from the paparazzi who had descended on Athens at the start of the summer and were now trying to find them.

It was a long dark alleyway, lit only by the faint glow of the club windows and a distant lamp post on another road. In the dim light, Zeke saw his friends both as they actually were and as how the world saw them. He saw Haruki, the boyish, enthusiastic, endlessly supportive friend. But he could also see him as the heart-throb swimmer whose topless shoots sent the internet into chaos. He saw Valentina as the thoughtful, deeply compassionate person that she was. But he could also see her as the elegant, other-worldly gymnast who graced magazine covers and made onlookers stop in their tracks. He wanted to stay in that moment because he could feel things changing. They were all in their early twenties but in sports terms they were on their way to retirement. Zeke could feel how close they were getting to not seeing each other every four years in an Olympic Village or at international competitions. He knew they'd stay in touch but, outside of the world they'd found each other in, it wouldn't be the same. He tried his best to just soak in the moment.

'We're going to get in so much trouble,' said Haruki. Valentina tried to call a taxi, but she didn't have service. Haruki tried to send a text to one of his coaches, but he'd spent so much time recording Valentina's competition and taking photos of the three of them that his battery was dead. Zeke's phone was on 4 per cent.

Technically, athletes were allowed to leave the Village. But high-profile athletes weren't supposed to go into the city without one of the official Olympic security guards. The guards weren't just there to look after them and protect them from overenthusiastic fans, they also came with the kind of authority that stopped the paparazzi from taking photos of them. If they'd left the Village with a guard, the guard would have driven them to wherever they wanted to go in a secure armoured vehicle that could pick them up at a moment's notice and stop them from getting stranded in a random alleyway.

The three of them had got into a lot of trouble when they'd gone out to do karaoke during the Tokyo Games.

Not because they weren't allowed to go out, but because the paparazzi had caught them walking out of a club looking incredibly messy just a few days before all three of them were supposed to be taking part in the biggest competitions of their lives. Last time their late-night adventures ended with them being grounded by their coaches for the rest of the Games. They couldn't afford to be put on Village house arrest again.

'This could be my last Olympics,' said Valentina quietly.

'Don't say that,' said Haruki firmly.

'I'm not being pessimistic, I'm being realistic,' said Valentina. 'I'm turning twenty-five. By the time the next Olympics happen I'll be almost twenty-nine, basically geriatric by gymnastics standards.'

'You could still out-jump all those sixteen-year-olds,' said Zeke.

'Without a doubt,' said Valentina, 'but I might not. So, if this is it, there's nowhere I'd rather be than in this gross, smelly alleyway with the two of you. This feels like the pinnacle. Everything else is just an abundance of—' Valentina was a Texan girl from a Mexican Catholic family and so she was always ready to give a speech about gratitude. But before she could finish her sentence, two men with big cameras rounded the corner and started running towards them.

'We have to go, right now!' Zeke pushed his friends ahead of him, running until they reached a quiet, residential street. When they could no longer see or hear the paparazzi, it dawned on Zeke that they were in a foreign city and none of them knew how to get home.

Haruki was in the middle of trying to convince them

to knock on a random door and pray that the people on the other side weren't psychotic serial killers when Zeke had an idea.

'I think I know someone who can help,' he said.

He knew exactly one person who was living in Athens city centre and, even though his phone was about to die, it was worth a shot. He realized it would mean explaining things to Haruki sooner than he'd planned to, but at that point, there was no other choice. So he opened his phone and clicked the call button. It felt like each ring took longer to come around than the last, but just when he was about to give up hope, the person on the other end of the call picked up.

'I know I should've called you sooner, trust me. And I know it's the middle of the night and you're off the clock. But for the third and final time, *I promise*, can I ask you a favour?'

Ten minutes later, he heard the sound of someone humming Dolly Parton's 'Nine to Five' and saw the silhouette of a woman carrying two bags of what smelt like souvlaki. She walked towards them and took off her headphones. Olivia was wearing a yellow sundress with her braids down. There was a glint of curiosity in her eyes.

'I already know what you're going to say,' said Zeke. He held his arms up in surrender.

'You've made up some pretty bad excuses to see me but *Help I'm being chased by the paparazzi and have no way to go home* takes it to a whole new level, Zeke.'

'You're right, I was just looking for an excuse to call you.'

For a moment Zeke felt like they were the only people on that street, the only people in the whole world. They held each other's gaze. He was about to say something else, but then he remembered they weren't alone.

'Hi, I'm Valentina,' his friend said, putting her hand out.

'Hey! I'm Olivia. Congratulations on your big win! Me and my housemate watched it and you were incredible,' said Olivia, smiling excitedly as they shook hands.

'Olivia? Hey!' said Haruki with a grin. He looked at Olivia and then at Zeke, confusion slowly starting to drift across his face. Guilt began to creep up Zeke's body.

'Haruki!' said Olivia, turning to him. She said his name with a casual cheerfulness that Zeke had never witnessed before. In fact, now that he thought about it, she was looking up at Haruki like he was the literal sun.

'I didn't think I was going to see you until *Bend It Like Beckham*,' she said. Zeke looked back and forth between them. They seemed to have such an easy familiarity. Zeke was in distress. He wasn't usually the jealous type but there he was, head spinning at the suddenly very real possibility that Olivia might like Haruki back. The shock must have been evident on his face because Valentina was looking at him strangely. She raised an eyebrow.

'Wait, where was my invite?' Valentina said, joking as the three of them began a conversation of their own. Zeke looked on, but he wasn't focused on the interaction itself; he was focused on Olivia, on how different she was with Haruki and Valentina.

Then the realization hit him. Olivia had the same expression on her face as the people who stopped him in the street to take a picture. Olivia wasn't madly in love with Haruki – at least, he hoped she wasn't. And she wasn't just putting on a whole new persona for Valentina – Olivia was a *fan*. He realized that she was completely starstruck, nervously asking questions and nodding attentively at everything they said.

'Why do I get the sense that you're nice to everyone except for me?' asked Zeke.

'Because nobody else insults my driving or finds new reasons to bother me at my place of work every day,' said Olivia, teasing him without missing a beat.

'I didn't realize you knew each other?' said Haruki, looking back and forth, trying to connect the dots.

'Unfortunately,' said Olivia, the look she gave Zeke betraying her. He wanted to smile back, but then he caught Haruki's eye. This was about to get complicated.

'Okay, well, I really hate to interrupt whatever *this* is, because, honestly, I'm fascinated,' said Valentina, 'but we really need to get out of here.' She nodded over at a small crowd that had followed them out of the club. They seemed harmless, but they had their phones out and Zeke could see that at least one of them had a professional camera. The paparazzi always descended on a city as soon as the Olympics came to town. And a good photo of Zeke and Valentina, while the internet was still speculating about their relationship status, could go viral in minutes. But Zeke and Haruki really couldn't afford to get photographed partying less than a week before their finals. Again.

Olivia looked at the three of them and then over at the man with the camera.

'I live a ten-minute walk away, you can come up if you need somewhere to hide out?' she said.

'Are you just offering so you can have something to hold

over me?' Zeke said, quietly enough that only she could hear him.

'I don't need something to hold over you.' She paused. 'I know you'll keep coming back.'

36
Olivia

Early hours of the morning,
day six of the 2024 Olympics

When Olivia had walked out of the apartment that evening to buy a late-night takeaway, the most exciting thing she'd expected to find was a new item on the menu at her and Aditi's favourite Greek restaurant. What she didn't expect was to get a call from Zeke just after midnight on her way home. But there she was, shepherding three of the world's most famous athletes up seven flights of stairs to her front door.

They were glamorous and out of place in the apartment stairwell. Valentina looked gorgeous in a red dress that hugged her hips, and curls that tumbled down her back. Haruki looked expensive in a fitted vest and impeccably tailored light-blue blazer. And Zeke? Olivia had never seen anyone dressed so simply look that hot. He was wearing a plain white shirt but the way it was fitted to accentuate the muscular contours of his chest triggered something so uninhibited and carnal in her that she had to look away.

Olivia tried her best to be as loud as possible as she walked into the apartment. Aditi was expecting two big bags of Greek food to fulfil their late-night cravings, not three athletes dressed for a night out. Olivia had sent a rushed text message warning her that she was bringing people home. But she didn't know if Aditi had read her message yet. And she knew her best friend had a tendency to fall asleep in the middle of the living room in her pyjamas with a face mask on. So, Olivia jangled her keys in the door longer than she needed to and talked extra loudly as she came in. But she shouldn't have worried, because if there was one lesson Aditi had taken to heart in all the years they'd spent going to Girl Guides together, it was to *always* be prepared.

'Welcome to our humble abode,' said Aditi as soon as they stepped through the door. 'Snacks?' Somehow in the five minutes since she'd received Olivia's text, Aditi had managed to clean the flat and make a whole table's worth of food. Aditi had been trying to convince Olivia to throw a party in their apartment ever since they'd arrived in Athens, and from the looks of it, she'd decided that tonight was the night.

'Oh, that looks incredible. Can I have a taste?' Valentina asked. Aditi passed her the plate of warm pitta and taramasalata. Valentina gratefully dipped the bread and took a bite. 'Do you know how long it's been since I ate something this good? I've been on such a strict diet all year for this competition. But now I can eat *whatever* I want.' Valentina was ecstatic.

'Well, I have enough souvlaki to feed a small country,' said Olivia, enjoying the genuine joy on Valentina's face.

'I could kill for some souvlaki,' said Haruki, 'and swimmers have to eat a lot.'

'I don't *really* think that's how it works,' Valentina said, easy in the way you are with siblings.

As Aditi walked past Olivia, she shot her a wide-eyed look and whispered, 'He's even better in person.' Olivia's mind immediately landed on Zeke, but then she saw Aditi's eyes glance over to Haruki and she smiled. Of course, Aditi fancied Haruki, that was the reason why Olivia had said she would bring her along to Movie Night. But, instead, they were meeting in the apartment, with Zeke and Valentina. Olivia felt like she was having an out-of-body experience.

She'd tried her best to play it cool when she'd noticed that THE Valentina Ross-Rodriguez was standing in the alleyway with Zeke and Haruki. But, like anybody else who'd ever watched one of Valentina's majestic, gold-medal-winning performances, Olivia was in awe of her.

If it wasn't for the fact that Valentina also just happened to be Zeke's very high-profile ex-girlfriend, Olivia probably would have sat across from her and enthusiastically showered her with compliments. But Valentina *was* Zeke's ex-girlfriend.

As she watched the way they interacted in the living room, she saw just how comfortable they were with each other. They had a shorthand that Olivia had only ever had with guys she'd dated and friends she'd known for years.

But Zeke didn't look like he had anything to hide, and he wouldn't have come up to her apartment with his ex-girlfriend if she was currently more than just his ex-girlfriend, would he?

And he'd kissed Olivia. Twice. That meant something, right?

Or maybe it felt special to her, but to him it was just

another kiss while he waited to get back together with Valentina. Olivia was a girl he'd met a few days ago; Valentina was someone he'd been in a relationship with for years. Those feelings didn't just go away. Even if they were definitely broken up, Zeke couldn't be completely over her, could he?

As she watched them chatting to Haruki and Aditi, she felt an unfamiliar sense of self-consciousness mixed with unease. It wasn't jealousy, it was something closer to fear. She hadn't realized just how much she liked him until she was faced with the possibility of his ex-girlfriend still being in the picture. It was unsettling, she couldn't watch them any more. So, she walked to the kitchen to fetch some plates.

'I'll help,' said Zeke. She didn't even notice he was following her. 'Glasses?'

'In the cupboard just next to the window,' she said. From the kitchen, they could hear snippets of the conversation that Aditi was having with Valentina and Haruki.

It was strange having Zeke in her space. When she was in the Village she always felt like a visitor, like she was working in an alternative universe that really belonged to the athletes. They were almost all pretty friendly, and the atmosphere was welcoming, but when she was there, she was a guest in their world. Here in the apartment, she felt the reverse – like she was the one welcoming them into her space. In the apartment, she could just be herself. It was a bit like the way she felt when she was around Zeke.

Back outside in the alleyway, she'd felt her demeanour change. Noticed the way she'd immediately softened when she'd seen Haruki and Valentina. How she'd smiled a little bit longer and stepped into the friendliest, most easy-going version of herself. But in the kitchen with Zeke, she didn't feel like she needed to be anybody but herself.

She heard Valentina laugh at something Aditi had said and saw Zeke look up to catch a glimpse through the door. She studied his face for a moment to see if it would confirm or deny her suspicions. But she couldn't draw a conclusive answer.

She averted her eyes and went back to the cupboard, stacking plates on top of each other. She could feel her walls slowly going back up. Maybe she'd read too much into those lingering looks, Zeke's continual presence at the Hub and those two all-consuming kisses. She wanted an answer. When she looked over, he was staring at her.

'Why are you looking at me like that?' she asked.

'I was just thinking,' he said.

'What were you thinking about?' There it was again, that flutter, that thrill.

'That I think you have a crush on me,' he said, taking a sip from the icy glass of water in his hands.

'You think really highly of yourself, don't you?' Olivia said, trying her best not to fixate on the curve of his lips.

'I do think pretty highly of myself,' Zeke said, 'and I know you think pretty highly of yourself too.'

'Wouldn't you?' she said, not missing a beat.

They were on opposite sides of the kitchen, but it felt like they were standing right next to each other.

'I do. I like you, Olivia,' he said without an ounce of self-consciousness. Like he was stating a fact rather than making a confession. A part of her already knew he liked her, but that didn't stop the butterflies in her stomach from fluttering at hearing it out loud. Nor did it quieten her self-consciousness enough to let her say it back.

'I like me too,' Olivia said.

This time it was Zeke rolling his eyes.

He walked over to her until they were just centimetres apart. She breathed in the faint scent of his cologne. He smelt like summer. It was intoxicating. He moved closer, their cheeks brushing, and she felt the gentle sensation of his breath against her lips. Their friends were just a couple of metres away, but she wanted to lean in, to taste his smile.

Before she knew it, they were pressed up against the kitchen counter kissing like there was no one around. He slid his hands about her waist and a tingle shot down her back. She wrapped her arms around his neck and sighed as he ran his fingers through her hair. He kissed her sweetly. She parted her lips. He slid his tongue in and tightened his grip on her hips. Then he slowly, *torturously* drew his fingers up the front of her legs, circling up to the back of her thighs where he lingered on the soft skin just below the hem of her dress. *Their friends were in the other room.* But still, she found herself reaching down, laying her hand over his and guiding him up past the hemline of her dress until she almost had him where she wanted him.

Then she heard someone get up and move towards the kitchen. Olivia ripped herself away from him and practically leaped back over to the kitchen sink.

'Hey!' said Valentina as she walked in, casual as anything. 'Aditi said you have some olives in the fridge, could I grab some?' If Valentina had seen the end of their kiss, she didn't say anything. If Valentina noticed the lipstick stain on the side of Zeke's mouth or the startled expression on Olivia's face, she didn't call attention to it. And if the unmistakeable tension between Olivia and Zeke bothered Valentina, she was doing a pretty good job of hiding it.

'Yeah, of course.' Olivia opened the fridge, hoping the cold air would stop her from looking as flustered as she felt. 'Olives . . . and we have hummus and chopped-up vegetables too.' She could hear the pitch of her voice go up.

But was kissing Zeke in the kitchen with his ex-girlfriend in the next room something she shouldn't be doing? If Zeke and Valentina really were just friends, there wasn't any harm. And if Valentina seemed completely unbothered by the fact that they'd clearly just been kissing against the kitchen counter, Olivia wasn't breaking some unwritten girl code, right?

Or was she walking into something dangerous with her hands over her eyes? Willingly letting herself be caught up in the chaos of other people's lives? Olivia wasn't that kind of girl. So, she picked up the plates and tried to dissect whether the knowing smile Valentina was giving her was a sign of approval or a subtle threat from America's Sweetheart.

37

Zeke

*Early hours of the morning,
day six of the 2024 Olympics*

Valentina gave him an amused look and whispered, 'Sorry for walking in on your make-out session,' before leaving the kitchen. She definitely knew there was something going on between him and Olivia. And from the look she exchanged with Aditi as the three of them walked back into the living room, Olivia's flatmate was in on it too. But, if Haruki suspected anything, he didn't say a word. Still, Zeke felt guilty about going into the kitchen to kiss a girl his best friend fancied. If he'd known Haruki had been talking about Olivia all along, he wouldn't have gone as far with things without talking to his best friend first. But now they were all sitting together in one room, Zeke knew that it was only a matter of time before the whole situation imploded.

'You have so many games, it's unreal,' said Haruki, who was sitting on the sofa going through the board game collection Olivia and Aditi's Airbnb hosts had left in the living room. A game! That was exactly the kind of distraction Zeke needed to prevent the night from dissolving into chaos.

'Did you say game?' said Zeke, sounding way too eager.

'Immediately, no,' said Valentina. 'I'm never playing a board game with you again.'

'Zeke is crazy competitive,' said Haruki, looking over at Olivia and Aditi. Zeke couldn't tell if Haruki sounded more pointed than normal. But he did notice the way that Haruki held Aditi's eyes for a moment longer than he needed to. Interesting.

'He will play until everyone wants to go home and then win by his sheer ability to still care about winning after five hours of competition,' said Valentina, teasing him.

'One time he convinced people to play Monopoly at a house party and it lasted four whole hours,' said Haruki.

'Everyone enjoyed it,' protested Zeke, remembering the party he'd thrown for his twenty-second.

'Everyone *played along* because it was your birthday,' said Valentina.

'And *let you win* because it was your birthday,' said Haruki, looking him in the eye. Either Zeke's paranoia was distorting Haruki's words or that was definitely a dig.

'I would've won anyway,' said Zeke, and Haruki laughed. Zeke felt a moment of relief. Haruki wasn't mad at him, he was just making a joke – everything was going to be okay. He took a swig of the iced coffee Olivia had given him. But he was so alert to everything going on around him that he didn't need the caffeine to stay awake any more.

Then Valentina made a terrible suggestion.

'Shall we play truth or dare?' she said with the smile of a troublemaker. Zeke opened his mouth to object, but he was immediately outnumbered.

Playing a game of truth or dare with his ex-girlfriend, his best friend, the girl they both liked and her best friend. What could possibly go wrong?

38

Olivia

The five of them were sitting in a circle on the floor around the living-room coffee table. Olivia was between Haruki and Aditi, Zeke was opposite her and Valentina was seated between Aditi and Zeke. The table was covered with gyros, dolmadakia, souvlaki and mezze plates. Olivia was fascinated by the dynamics unfolding before her. She'd interacted with everyone in the room except for Valentina, but seeing them together showed all four of them in a different light. As they ate, she realized that if they'd met in more normal circumstances, they could have easily become a group of friends. Valentina and Aditi matched each other's playful and slightly chaotic energy. And Zeke and Haruki bickered like siblings, with Haruki throwing small barbs at his friend and Zeke either playing along or shrugging it off.

Despite the low but constant worry about her being Zeke's ex, Olivia really liked Valentina, and the two of them kept finding themselves in on the same joke. Aditi was playfully but precisely grilling Zeke for Olivia's sake, and she and Haruki had a sparky energy between them that everyone in the room seemed to notice except for them. There were only five of them but the room had the buzz of a really good party.

'Okay, Valentina – truth or dare?' said Haruki.

'Umm, let's start off tame. Truth,' she said, taking a bite of her souvlaki.

'All right, what's the wildest rumour you've heard about yourself that was actually true?' Haruki asked.

Valentina answered without hesitation. 'That I broke up with someone in a two-line text,' she said with a grimace.

Zeke almost spat the water he was drinking out of his mouth. Looking at Valentina, and then at Olivia, and then at Valentina again. 'Val? Is nothing sacred?' he asked, clearly more embarrassed by the public revelation than he was upset about the memory. Selfishly, Olivia was glad.

'Sorry, I wanted to give you a minute to take it in by yourself before I came to your apartment for *the talk*,' she said with a laugh.

'Okay, Zeke, truth or dare,' said Aditi.

Olivia knew her best friend well, but she could never predict what was going to come out of her mouth.

Zeke was still on a strict pre-competition diet and couldn't indulge in foods beige and beautiful, unlike the rest of them. So, he took a bite of a carrot stick and answered, 'Truth.'

'Boring, but all right,' Aditi said playfully. 'Zeke, who is the last person you hooked up with?' She gave him a mischievous smile.

'Aditi!' said Olivia as they exchanged looks. Olivia was shocked, while Aditi was in her element.

'Well, it wasn't me,' said Haruki, making the others laugh.

'Or me,' said Valentina, 'unless . . . It's been a year, Zeke? I can introduce you to someone if you need me to. Who's going to be a better wingwoman than your ex-girlfriend?' Valentina glanced over at Olivia. Was that a nod of approval? The clarification definitely felt like it was more for her benefit than everything else. So, Olivia took it.

Zeke was squirming opposite her. It was kind of fun to watch him this way. And Olivia was so curious to hear his answer. She wanted to know about Zeke's romantic life so she could gauge whether she was just another number in the Village *before* she got in over her head.

'Um, the last person I hooked up with was a model I met at London Fashion Week,' Zeke said with an air of finality.

'A model? That's kind of basic,' said Valentina.

'I'm a model, I'm not basic,' said Haruki with mock offence.

'You could never be basic,' said Zeke, reassuring him.

'And when was the last time you texted this model? Do you stay in touch?' asked Aditi casually.

Olivia's eyes widened. 'Okay, that's enough now,' she said, nudging Aditi to stop.

Zeke smiled, clearly respecting Aditi's commitment to vetting him.

'Aditi, since you're *so* enthusiastic, truth or dare?' Olivia said, taking a gulp of her drink.

'It's always dare,' said Aditi confidently.

'Okay, I dare you to . . . kiss the most attractive person in the room,' Olivia said.

Aditi looked around. She paused for a moment as if pondering her options. Then she put her hand up, pressed it to her lips and made out with herself.

'Boo!' shouted Valentina.

'Commit to the bit!' said Haruki.

'If I had tomatoes, I'd be throwing them at you right now,' shouted Olivia.

'Wait, so you want me to be dishonest?' said Aditi, taking her hand away from her face as the rest of them laughed.

'All right, kiss the most attractive person in the room . . . who *isn't* you,' said Olivia.

So, Aditi got up, made a show of walking around the circle twice and then went over to Haruki.

'Hi,' she said, her voice thick with charisma.

'Hey,' he smiled.

'I'm Aditi,' she said as she smoothly put her hand out to shake his, 'nice to meet you, again.' There was nothing she loved more than flirting with new people.

'Haruki. The pleasure is all mine,' he said, leaning towards her, all charm. It was a fascinating scene; the energy between them was palpable.

'Okay, I see you improv class meet cute!' laughed Valentina.

'What can I say, I'm a romantic,' said Aditi with a grin.

'Get to the point, Aditi!' Olivia laughed.

'Um, I need consent, Olivia,' she teased. 'Yes, Haruki is a very hot athlete and gorgeous *high fashion* model, but that doesn't mean I can just walk over and kiss him.'

'You *can* kiss me,' Haruki said gamely.

Aditi smiled, leaned over, and then the two of them kissed. For much longer than they needed to for a simple dare.

'Wow,' said Olivia as they parted lips.

Aditi came back to her seat next to Olivia and cast her a 'we have to debrief' look.

'Whose turn is it?' said Valentina, looking around the circle until her eyes landed. 'Olivia, truth or dare?'

'Truth,' Olivia said after weighing up her options.

'Where is the weirdest place you've ever hooked up, or almost hooked up?' Valentina asked.

Olivia surprised herself by responding immediately. 'Almost, a lift,' she said with a shrug to a raucous round of cheers from Aditi and Valentina, who were having entirely too much fun. As Olivia held back a smile and picked her glass up to take a sip, she locked eyes with Zeke.

39
Zeke

Zeke liked to think that he was a pretty smart guy.

His whole career revolved around strategy, looking at a situation, calculating the risks and making bold decisions for a maximum pay-off. When he'd come back from the kitchen earlier, he'd noticed Aditi and Haruki swapping phones as they talked about the outdoor cinema that they and Olivia were planning on going to at the weekend. So, in trying to solve the issue of having to tell Haruki the truth, he made a gamble.

'Haruki, truth or dare?' Zeke asked.

'Uh . . . dare,' Haruki said.

'I dare you to call the last number saved on your phone and . . . ask them out on a date,' Zeke said, certain that person was Aditi. He watched as Haruki picked up his phone, scrolled through his contacts and pressed call. Zeke was proud of his strategy for exactly one second because his gamble immediately revealed itself to have been a mistake.

First, he heard the dial-out sound on Haruki's phone. Then he heard a phone vibrating from somewhere else in the room. But then he heard the ringtone. It was 'Fantasy' by Mariah Carey.

'Oh, plot twist,' said Valentina, putting her head in her hands and watching the scene unfold like she was watching a TV show.

Zeke felt his stomach drop as he watched Olivia get up and walk around the room, hunting for the sound of Mariah's high notes. Olivia picked up the phone as if everything was perfectly fine, and to her, it probably was.

'Hello?' she said, making a pantomime of acting like she hadn't been expecting the call.

'Hey, it's . . . Haruki,' he said, clearly a little bit embarrassed.

'Oh, Haruki from art class?' Olivia said, still playing along.

'Yeah, I was just wondering, do you want to go out on a date or something?' Haruki asked nervously. Zeke could feel the guilt rising up; he should have never postponed telling Haruki the truth. But now it was too late to stop the chaos unfolding before him.

'Well, you've just kissed my best friend,' said Olivia playfully.

'And it looked like a pretty good kiss,' added Valentina.

'What can I say, I'm a natural talent,' said Aditi.

'And I kissed your best friend yesterday,' said Olivia. Zeke held his breath as he and Olivia caught eyes for a second. 'So maybe let's just stick to *Bend It Like Beckham*.' Olivia was casual, completely unaware that, to Haruki, it wasn't just a dare.

Zeke felt like he was watching a car crash in slow motion.

Olivia, Valentina and Aditi were completely oblivious to the parallel, silent conversation in the room. Zeke shuffled around until he was next to Haruki.

To someone who didn't know him, the expression on Haruki's face was blank. But to Zeke, who had known him for eight years, the emotion behind his eyes was crystal clear. Disappointment.

'Right,' said Haruki, as if confirming something he'd long suspected, but finally knew for sure.

'I can expla—' said Zeke, quiet enough for just the two of them to hear.

'No need,' said Haruki flatly.

But before Zeke could say anything else or try to explain, Valentina and Aditi pulled out a pack of Uno and decided to change the game. Zeke could sense the chill coming from his best friend. Haruki quickly went back to being his normal self, with the others. He seemed to be having a good time. But he refused to look at or even interact with Zeke. After two rounds of Uno, Olivia and Zeke both got kicked out for being really bad at the game and way too competitive. So, they got up to go and put the plates and takeaway boxes in the kitchen.

'I feel like our friends have formed an alliance against us,' said Zeke. When Haruki had said, 'Zeke plays to win, he doesn't care about who he'll hurt to get there,' it was definitely a dig, not a joke.

'They could tell that we were going to win,' said Olivia, who was definitely joking around. 'So, they tricked us into playing badly.'

'Did we trick you into playing badly or have you just been bad at card games since we were five years old?' asked

239

Aditi affectionately as she, Haruki and Valentina came into the kitchen with the rest of the cups and plates.

'Maybe I've just been bad at card games since I was five years old,' Olivia laughed.

It was strange seeing her this relaxed, thought Zeke. He'd seen flickers of what Olivia was like when she was having fun or being playful, but here she seemed totally laid-back. Probably because she was with Aditi, who knew her well and loved her fiercely. Her demeanour reminded Zeke of how he felt when he was with his brothers, his teammates and – up until tonight – Haruki. Who was still refusing to make eye contact with him.

'So, one of Aditi's friends is throwing a party tonight,' said Valentina.

'It's going to be so much fun!' said Aditi, nodding along.

'Isn't it, like, two a.m.?' said Zeke, looking up at the clock on the kitchen wall.

'Okay, *grandpa*, the night is still young,' said Valentina, clearly excited about her spontaneous late-night plans. 'And in case you forgot, I just won a gold Olympic medal,' she added as they all whooped for her.

'Thank you, thank you,' she said, taking a bow as they clapped. 'This doesn't happen every day, and I don't have any other competitions to train for this summer. So *I* am going back out to celebrate,' she declared.

'Who's coming with us?' said Aditi, throwing her hand in the air as if leading a crowd into a rally.

'You know I'd love to,' said Haruki, 'but I have training first thing tomorrow morning and I should probably get some sleep.'

'Wise, but boring,' said Valentina. 'Zeke? Olivia?'

'I also have training tomorrow,' said Zeke, 'and a race in the afternoon.' He knew it would be irresponsible to party until the sun came out.

'So we can get a taxi back together? I'll book it,' said Haruki, looking at Zeke for the first time since truth or dare.

But then Olivia glanced over at Zeke and Zeke looked back over at Olivia, a silent question and answer passing between them. The apartment was going to be empty for the rest of the night. And they weren't in the Village.

'I think I'm going to stay in, I'm kind of tired,' said Olivia.

Zeke held his breath. 'I'll stay to . . . finish washing up,' he said. Looking at the sink and pile of dirty dishes.

'Are you sure?' Haruki said. Zeke glanced over at his best friend. He wore an emotionless expression and sounded like his usual self. But Zeke knew that if he studied Haruki for long enough, he'd be forced to do the right thing. So, he didn't look.

'I'm sure,' Zeke said. He could feel the guilt rising up, but he pushed it down.

Valentina and Aditi said goodbye, promised to send Olivia photos of their night and left through the front door, with Haruki trailing behind.

Zeke watched them go. When he turned around, Olivia was on the other side of the room looking out of the window. He walked over to see what she was looking at.

'That's the Village over there,' she said, pointing out into the distance. Zeke looked through the window and saw it too. It was a few miles outside of the city, built in the countryside, but so bright and sprawling that it stood out on the skyline.

'It feels like the centre of the universe when you're in it, but from up here it's just buildings and lights,' he said, pulling his eyes away from her for a moment as he looked at the stadium in awe.

'It is beautiful, though. Everything is from up here,' she said wistfully. 'There's the Acropolis up on that hill.'

The ancient ruins were illuminated with a golden light so majestic that it looked other-worldly. But it was Olivia that really took his breath away. She told him stories of the city with a wide-eyed wonder that made him want to see history through her eyes. Whenever she spoke about something she loved, Olivia was animated and unselfconscious. She told him about places she'd watched documentaries about and still wanted to visit and Zeke could imagine nothing better than exploring with her. He marvelled at the way she saw the world, how he felt whenever he was around her.

Zeke took in the way her face lit up and her eyes crinkled a little at the sides when she smiled. The way softness and edge converged in her facial features to create something that felt too delicate to hold. She had the kind of eyes that made him want to tell her all his secrets. He held her gaze for a moment, feeling the electricity crackling in the darkness, the magnetic force between them drawing him even closer.

Zeke was beginning to feel a bit light-headed. Maybe it was the altitude. Maybe it was the intoxicating nature of summer nights. Or maybe it was just Olivia. Zeke knew for certain now: he was falling for her.

'I could finish those dishes?' he said, glancing over at the sink.

'You could. Or I could show you an even better view of Athens from the balcony,' she said, pausing for a moment. 'In my bedroom?'

40

Olivia

*Early hours of the morning,
day six of the 2024 Olympics*

When Olivia opened the big glass doors and stepped out into the summer night air, a silence fell between them. The view from her balcony was magical. The sky was a deep dark blue that perfectly contrasted with the warm yellow lights of the city. Olivia could see the tiny shapes of people walking down the main roads of Athens and crowds moving down the brightly lit streets of the city centre. She could hear the faint sounds of music leaking out of the late-night restaurants and see a group of performers dancing in the middle of a distant square. The jacaranda trees and bougainvillea bushes below them were decorated with warm twinkly lights. It felt like the whole city was celebrating.

She looked over at Zeke. He was gorgeous, the lights of the city reflecting on his skin, and he seemed completely content, more relaxed than she'd ever seen him inside the Village. And he was looking at her like they'd known each other for much longer than just a few days. She was a thousand miles away from London, but with Zeke, she felt right at home.

'This is my first time coming into the city at night, you know,' said Zeke.

Olivia fixed the sight of him in her mind, because she knew that her future self would want to come back to this moment over and over again.

'Really? Are athletes not allowed to leave the Village at night?' she asked.

'We are, it's just not really recommended until the Games have ended. You can't predict what a crowd is going to be like,' he said with a shrug, remembering what brought him up to the apartment in the first place.

'Or if paparazzi will follow you to a club,' she added.

'Or if a strange girl is going to lure you into her bedroom to "see the balcony",' he said.

She could feel them drifting closer towards each other.

'It's late,' she said.

'It is.'

'And I start at seven a.m. tomorrow.'

'You do.'

'And you have training in the morning.'

'Yeah,' he said, taking a step nearer.

'So why did you stay?' she asked softly but with a sliver of danger in her voice. It was less a question and more a challenge. 'You didn't follow me out on to the balcony because you wanted to see Athens, did you, Zeke?' The air felt even more charged.

'Olivia,' he said, his voice so deep and rough that it sent a hot, delicious thrill down her spine. She touched his shoulder and felt his muscles contract at her touch. The first few buttons of his shirt were undone and so her hand moved gently across his shoulder, grazed his neck and slowly began to make its way down the bare patch of skin on his chest. Before she could overthink it, she placed a finger on one of the buttons on his shirt and undid it. He looked down at her with an intense look of desire that almost stopped her in her tracks. But she knew what she wanted. She moved closer, until their lips were just about to touch. His hands slid a trail down her back and around her waist. He slowly guided her away from the balcony and back into the dim, warm light of her bedroom, the lights of the city getting further and further away.

'Is this okay?' he asked as he led her inside until they were standing next to her bed.

'Yes,' she said as he slowly wrapped his hands around her waist then laid hot, breathless kisses along the length of her arm, from her hand all the way up to her shoulders.

'Why didn't you go to the party?' she said. She didn't need the reassurance, but she wanted to hear him say it out loud. It came out as a whisper as his warm, rough hands gently traced the curves and bends of her body. It was slow, sweet torture, and she didn't want him to stop.

'Olivia,' he said. The sound of her name on his lips made her eyes flutter, and she wanted to hear it over and over and over again. 'You . . . know . . . why,' he continued, his breath uneven.

'I don't,' she said with fake innocence as he left another tantalizingly slow trail of kisses up her body and casually set her on fire with just the tips of his fingers. He stroked the side of her face and looked into her eyes with an equal mixture of desire and adoration that made her feel deliciously light-headed.

'Zeke. Don't show me . . . tell me,' she said, looking

directly into his eyes. She wasn't going to fill in the blanks for him this time.

'I want . . .' he said, his voice breathless as he swallowed, 'I want . . . you.' His eyes looked into hers with a burning intensity that melted away all her bravado.

'Oh,' Olivia said, feigning surprise as her lips gently curved up again. Then she looked back up into his eyes, 'Okay, now you can show me,' she whispered.

Their lips crashed into each other, and it felt like lighting a match. The sensation of his hands against her skin was intoxicating, she wanted more. She wrapped her legs around him, tugged his lip between her teeth and sighed as she felt the effect she was so clearly having on him. She grazed the skin of his bare arms with the tips of her nails and unbuttoned the rest of his shirt. Then he lay quick, hot, tormenting kisses down her shoulders and across her chest. His eyes were wide open, learning her, taking in every part. Then he turned her around and slowly, agonizingly, began to untie the delicate strings of her dress. Olivia let go of her need to control things and just let her skin, lips and hips do the talking as they succumbed to the pleasure coursing through their veins. Tracing lines of desire across the curves, contours and soft edges of their bodies, savouring each touch until they were completely, dreamily undone.

41
Zeke

Day six of the 2024 Olympics

'Coach, we're supposed to be celebrating – I came first!' said Zeke, wrapping a towel around his shoulders. Zeke could still see his glorious semi-final win playing back on the big screens and hear the sound of the crowd cheering. But as soon as he'd crossed the finish line, Coach Adam had told him to go straight back inside.

'Yes, Ezekiel, you came first, but that's not what the world is focused on, is it? Why? Because you decided to spend the night before your semi-final . . . partying,' said Coach Adam as they walked into the changing room.

'We were just celebrating Valentina's win,' said Zeke.

Coach Adam gave him a stern look. '*Valentina* can go out and celebrate. Why? Because *she* has her medal. *She* went out last night because *she* did not have a competition the next day. But you, Zeke, *you* did,' said his coach, shaking his head in annoyance.

'But I wasn't drinking or getting into trouble or anything,' Zeke said. It was a weak excuse.

'I don't know how many times I have to tell you all. Have fun and enjoy your life, but don't let it distract from the work!' Coach Adam let out an exasperated sigh. 'Yes, it's the race that matters, but do you know what also matters? Professionalism, the athlete code of conduct, *your* sponsorships and the whole team's reputation. The sprint is a solo event, but this is Team GB, not Team Zeke. When you do something irresponsible, it tarnishes the whole team's reputation.'

'But, Coach—'

'Don't *but Coach* me. Do you know who I got a call from at six a.m. this morning?'

Zeke had no idea.

'The *Greek City Times*, and then the *Sun*, and then TMZ, and then I was put in a conference call with the Team GB PR team,' said Coach Adam.

Zeke grimaced. That was never a good sign.

'But I kept all that away from you so you could focus on your race, and congratulations – you were great on the track. But look . . .' Coach reached for his desk and pulled out a stack of papers and his iPad.

He read the headline on the first newspaper cover: A GOLD-MEDAL-WINNING BAR CRAWL.

The photo on the front was a shot of him, Haruki and Valentina running down an alleyway to escape the paparazzi.

'*Zeke and Valentina's hot, wild night on the town*,' Coach Adam read aloud as he flipped to the next paper. '*A very Olympic run-in?*'

'We didn't run, just power-walked,' said Zeke, trying to diffuse the situation.

'I'm not having this any more, Zeke.'

'Sorry, Coach, I won't do that again,' said Zeke.

'You know I have to make an example of you, right?' he said.

Zeke just nodded and waited for the verdict.

'You're not allowed to leave the Village for the rest of the Games. And you've just earned yourself a curfew,' said Coach Adam. 'I want you back in GB House every single night at seven p.m. sharp and you're not allowed back out until six a.m. for your first training session.'

Zeke had known Coach Adam since he was fourteen years old. So, he knew him well enough to know that when he'd made his mind up about something, trying to convince him otherwise was futile.

'All right, Coach,' Zeke said, accepting his fate.

'Right, get some rest. Training starts tomorrow morning at six thirty,' Coach said as he got up. 'And, Zeke? I hope whatever made you stay out late last night was worth it,' he added before leaving the room.

Zeke sat down on the bench and drank another bottle of water. Last night was *definitely* worth it. He'd been texting Olivia ever since he'd kissed her goodbye at the gates of the Village that morning, and thinking about her every other moment in between. Waking up next to her left him feeling the kind of joy he'd only felt a few times in his life. He couldn't stop thinking about how much he liked her, how beautiful she was, how perfect last night had been. They'd kissed like each other's lips were their only lifeline, gripped on to each other's bodies as if the world was seconds away from ending, held each other through the night like there was nobody else in the world except for them. It was passionate, it was tender, it was hot, sweet, reckless pleasure.

But then, instead of falling asleep, they'd spent the whole night talking. Telling each other about their favourite memories and the moments that had shaped their lives. The longer he stayed there, the clearer it became that he was falling for her. He wanted to take her to all the places he loved, introduce her to his favourite people, and get to know every part of her mind, body and soul. He'd seen a flicker of for ever. Imagined what it would be like to dance with her in the kitchen and wake up to her on Sunday mornings.

But the fear always came back around again.

Whenever things were really good, his immediate reflex was to start listing every single thing that could go wrong. The euphoria and the anxiety were dancing hand in hand. But the memory of the way the moon lit up her eyes wouldn't let him go.

42

Olivia

Day six of the 2024 Olympics

'You're different today,' said Arlo, looking over at Olivia.

'What do you mean?' Olivia asked as she took a sip of her coffee. She and Zeke had left the house at the crack of dawn that morning so that Zeke could sneak back into GB House and Olivia could get to the Village for her seven a.m. start. She and Arlo were scheduled to help the volunteers at the registration desk hand out press passes to the photojournalists covering that day's competitions.

'I don't know, you seem more peaceful than usual,' Arlo said, looking at her. Arlo knew what she looked like after her busiest days on the walkie-talkies. So, there was no doubt this was probably the first time he'd ever seen her look relaxed.

'I'm like a sleeping newborn before eight a.m.,' she said truthfully. Olivia *was* at her most peaceful in the morning before the day clouded her clarity. But there was something else on her face and Arlo could see it.

'Did you really end up spending last night filling in job applications?' Arlo asked, raising an eyebrow.

'Well . . . I got distracted.'

'Distracted?' he asked curiously.

'Yeah, you know how it is,' she said, shrugging her shoulders.

'Olivia, you're doing a bad job of trying to sound casual,' Arlo said, scanning her face to try to figure her out, but she turned away so he wouldn't see the story in her eyes.

'Has it got anything to do with why you keep looking at your phone?' he asked.

'I'm not looking at my phone,' she said indignantly. But she was definitely looking at her phone. She and Zeke had been texting back and forth ever since they'd left each other. About last night, about his semi-final win, about when they would get to see each other again.

'Has it got anything to do with that tall, gorgeous hunk of an athlete who's clearly obsessed with you?' Arlo said, teasing her.

Olivia hadn't told him about the kiss in the lift, or all of the overwhelming thoughts and feelings that had been bubbling ever since. About how last night she'd felt like her body had been set alight. She was pretty sure the image of Zeke kissing her inner thigh would be seared into her memory for the rest of her life. And that when she'd woken up this morning in Zeke's arms, to the tender sensation of him gently running his fingers through her hair . . . she'd realized with complete, unflinching certainty that she was in way over her head. And that it was unlikely she'd be able to shake the feeling off.

But Arlo was good at reading people.

'Did you even go to sleep last night?' he asked, tilting his head to the side in amusement.

She opened and then shut her mouth.

'Olivia!' he shrieked, excitedly peppering her with questions as they began their shift.

It quickly became her busiest day yet. Her walkie-talkie went off non-stop. She spent the whole morning and afternoon on her feet going back and forth across the Village. She went to South Korea House to deliver a stack of VIP tickets for that afternoon's archery contest, then rushed off to the equestrian field to help a truck of delivery men figure out where to drop off thirty-eight boxes of hay. After hours of running around, she finally got the chance to sit down for a few moments and drink a glass of water but then her walkie-talkie buzzed again.

'On a scale of one to ten, how busy are you right now?' asked Arlo. 'Because there's another evening reception that forgot to . . .' She already knew how Arlo's sentence was going to end.

The Olympics was all about sports, but the sheer scale and scope of it meant that there were always at least a dozen different non-sporting events happening in the Village on any given day. Receptions for international diplomats, tours for kids from local schools and huge marquee events for big-money sponsors. Each event required catering, risk assessments and security checks. But everybody always forgot to order goodie bags until the very last minute. Which is when Arlo or Olivia stepped in.

The office at the back of the Hub was essentially a Santa's workshop-grade goodie-bag packing room. There were boxes and boxes of official Olympic merchandise: shirts, pens, notebooks, sweets, water bottles and basically anything you could print a logo on to. So, Olivia grabbed 150 paper bags and began to fill them up. And as she did, she thought about Zeke. If she was honest with herself, she hadn't once stopped thinking about him. While running errands, she'd replayed all of their conversations. Each time she saw a Team GB uniform, she hoped it was him. She even found herself smiling at lifts.

Olivia wasn't naive; she'd heard rumours about the love lives of Olympic athletes. How they treated the athletes' quarters of the Village like a dorm in one of those raunchy noughties' university movies. She knew that, despite what he'd told her last night, to Zeke this was probably just a summer fling. A casual situationship. She knew better than to fall for the blind hope of a sun-soaked romance. Even though she really wanted to. So, despite how tempting it was to imagine that things would last beyond their time in Athens, she brought herself back down to earth. August wouldn't last for ever and, when it ended, she'd hopefully be too busy with a new job in a new city to be heartbroken. She shook her head, packed the last of the goodie bags and drove to the fancy restaurant on the other side of the Village.

It was a lot more glamorous than she'd expected it to be. There were fresh flowers and flickering candles on every table. Hand-calligraphed name cards and relaxed jazz music playing as she walked in. It all looked so elegant and put together that Olivia instantly felt out of place with her bright blue-and-yellow uniform and multicoloured goodie bags. It was her last call-out of the day, though, so she was too tired to be self-conscious. When Arlo had called her about the event, he'd only told her where it was and how many bags to bring. So, it wasn't until she looked up at the screen that she realized what she'd just walked into. The screen read 2024 OLYMPICS DIPLOMATS DINNER. Olivia's heart sank.

She looked to the other side of the room where two men in suits were talking and, after a second glance, she recognized them as OOT officials. She read the name cards on the tables and saw they were for the national ambassadors she'd dreamed of working with.

Olivia could feel the dull ache of sadness starting to settle in. Imagining how things could have turned out was one thing, but there was something uniquely cruel about walking in on an alternative version of what her summer, and future, could have looked like. She should have been standing over there with the officials, wearing one of the many formal dresses she'd packed for occasions just like this. She would have arrived early and spent the whole night impressing them with how much she knew about international relations. She'd fantasized about excelling at the job and being offered her dream full-time job at the Olympics. Instead, she was standing at the door in her now-creased volunteer uniform looking like a delivery lady. She was ready to quickly drop off the bags, buggy back to the Hub and catch the next shuttle home. But then she heard a voice from behind her.

'Are those the goodie bags? Thank God, I was going to get into so much shit if I didn't get them.'

Olivia knew that voice. Her mood curdled.

It was Lars Fucking Lindberg.

And, all of a sudden, she was back at university again. Olivia hadn't had many interactions with Lars back then. He'd barely spent any time on campus that didn't revolve around partying or schmoozing with the visiting speakers that his parents always got him a meeting with. Their paths rarely crossed so she had no reason to think about the big name on campus whose wealthy, influential family's generous donations funded the library refurbishment. Except for that one night during her second year.

Olivia had been in fierce 'get a good summer internship' mode. She'd spent the start of the year going to open days, setting up coffee meetings and making sure that hers were the highest grades not just in her class, but in the whole faculty. On paper, she'd had everything going for her, so one of her favourite lecturers invited her to the fancy annual reception the university held for its most influential alumni. She'd run to the high street and used a chunk of her overdraft to buy an outfit to make her feel like she fitted in. And then she'd put her braids in a ponytail and headed to the reception. The room had been filled with CEOs, company founders, law firm partners, politicians and tech entrepreneurs. And, while Olivia was only twenty and still felt out of her depth whenever she was surrounded by such successful people, she'd given it her best shot. She'd walked around introducing herself to the kinds of people who could change the trajectory of her career. She'd done her very best to act like she belonged there. And then one of her lecturers had introduced her to Christian Millar, head of Millar and Partners, the top law firm in London.

Her lecturer sang her praises then left her to hold her own in a conversation with Christian about a big legal case in the city that she'd spent weeks reading about. But then Christian had looked past her. She was familiar with those moments – when the person she was speaking to absent-mindedly glanced away, looking for someone else that they'd rather talk to. She was used to it, especially at events like this. But rather than going to speak to another founder or businessperson or successful peer, Christian Millar had turned away from Olivia while she was in the middle of a sentence to speak to . . . Lars Lindberg. The son of one of his most important clients.

Olivia quickly became the invisible third wheel in a conversation above her tax bracket. She'd listened with her glass in her hand as they talked about skiing season and the Lindbergs' golf club. Then she'd watched in silence as they scheduled in a dinner at Lars's favourite restaurant in the city and the two of them walked away from her, too caught up in their conversation to say goodbye. Olivia's lecturer had cast her a sympathetic look from the other side of the room, but they both knew this was just the way it was. Boys like Lars, who'd grown up in rooms like this, were always going to have an easier time getting to where they wanted to go.

The logical part of Olivia knew that if she'd grown up with Lars's wealth, access and opportunities, she would have made the most of them too. And she knew that Lars probably had no recollection of that night or any knowledge of the fact that he always seemed to be the perfect fit for the places Olivia couldn't get a seat in. But seeing him here, in the Village, doing the internship she'd wanted, felt pretty brutal. So as soon as she saw him, she began to pick him apart.

She hated his expensive tailored suit. Hated the watch on his wrist, which definitely cost more than her parents' annual salary. But more than anything, she hated the way he spoke to her.

'Lifesaver, you really got me out of a sticky situation,' he said, before looking back down at his phone and beginning to walk away.

'You're welcome. I do need to take this trolley back with me, though,' she said.

'That's fine, you can take it away when you've placed all the goodie bags,' Lars said, still on his phone. Usually, when she arrived at events with last-minute goodie bags, the interns and assistants who'd ordered them quickly thanked her and hurried to collect the bags and place them on the tables, ready for their guests. But as she watched Lars scrolling through his phone, she realized that he expected her to pick up each of the 150 bags and go around the venue placing them on the guests' chairs for the event he was clearly supposed to be coordinating.

Usually, she would help the other interns and assistants. In her quest to be more like Arlo, she'd met a bunch of people her age working in the Village and enjoyed the walkie-talkie calls that let her hang out with someone new for more than fifteen minutes. But Lars was just standing there on his phone, waiting for her to unload the goodie bags.

'I only pack and deliver the bags,' she said curtly. He looked up at her. She refused to break eye contact. It was a stand-off, but it was completely one-sided. Lars wore a blank expression.

'It would be such a help if you could just put the bags on each seat with a name card – it shouldn't take too long,' he said with a nod before turning away again.

Then he turned back and said, as if it was an after-thought – as if it was a special kind gesture instead of just the bare minimum – 'Thank you,' with a wink and then walked away to talk to the other men in suits.

Olivia felt the quiet, searing rage begin slowly. It started in her fingers, travelled up her arms and then created tension in her shoulders and neck. She gritted her teeth and swallowed. She knew the voice he'd just used with her like a second language. Knew the contortions in the appearance of politeness, the facade of familiarity that coated the truth of professionalism. It was polished, and it was practised. She knew that he wasn't asking her, he was telling her. It was the voice that rich, well-raised people used when they were talking to the help. She could already imagine the way Lars's mother used it. She was probably an elegant woman in her late fifties whose hair was always freshly blow-dried and who wore Diane von Furstenberg wrap dresses like a uniform. Lars's mother probably thought that the people who cooked her food, mowed her lawn and cleaned her toilets considered her a friend. Olivia imagined that Lars's mother came from a long line of ladies who hired people like her to clean up the messes they made, but then felt good about themselves for giving them Boxing Day off. Because, of course, they needed all the help they could get on Christmas Day.

What Lars said wasn't that bad. But in his voice, Olivia heard all the blue hyperlinks to other wealthy heirs in his family's Wikipedia page. She'd imagined all the years he'd spent being pampered by the servants who'd waited on him in one of his family's eight (she'd checked) houses around the world. She knew that another person might just call her bitter. But that didn't do anything to stunt the growth of the resentment she felt towards Lars. So instead of picking the goodie bags up and placing them on the seats one by one like he'd asked – no, *told* her to – she picked them up in bunches, placed them on the ground and turned to leave. As she did so, she heard Lars call out to her.

'Hey, I thought you were going to help me—' he was saying but she cut him off. She looked back at him and smiled politely.

'I only pack and deliver the bags . . . but it shouldn't take too long,' she said, echoing his words with a shrug as she turned around and rolled her empty trolley out of the restaurant.

But like most things, that small act of defiance didn't feel the way she'd wanted it to feel. She thought that leaving the bags on the ground and echoing his words back to him would make her feel badass. But it didn't.

Yeah, Lars would have to lift a finger for once in his life. But he was still the guy in the expensive suit talking to other powerful men in suits at the fancy diplomatic dinner. He was already in a position that would fast-track him to wherever he wanted to go. He had a billion-dollar safety net and the kind of big-name family connections to raise him up before he could ever fall. Meanwhile, Olivia was just another anonymous face to people like him, working for free in her slightly-too-big, blue-and-yellow uniform. There was no victory in that.

43
Zeke

Day seven of the 2024 Olympics

Zeke had texted Haruki, but he wouldn't reply to any of his messages. He tried to phone him, but each time the phone rang out until the call was declined. Haruki didn't want to speak to Zeke, and Zeke couldn't blame him. Zeke was tortured by the memory of the blindsided look on Haruki's face. The look he'd ignored. Zeke didn't regret a single thing about his night with Olivia, but he felt a deep sense of regret about what he'd done to Haruki.

Zeke hadn't set out to betray him. Yes, Haruki had been telling him about the girl he liked all week, but he'd never mentioned her name, so there was no reason for Zeke to think it was Olivia. Maybe if he'd asked more questions and put the clues together, he might have realized that they'd been thinking about the same person all along. If that had been the case, Zeke could have stopped it before things went too far. But by the time they'd got to Aditi and Olivia's apartment, Zeke knew the truth. So, there was no excuse. He should have explained things to Haruki or gone home at the end of the night. But Zeke had stayed at Olivia's apartment. *What kind of person did that to his best friend?*

Zeke was about to skip dinner and head over to Japan House to convince Haruki's housemates to let him up the stairs to apologize in person, but then he heard a familiar voice and lost his train of thought.

'Mukoma Ezekiel, is that you?'

Zeke turned around. 'Simba? Why didn't you tell me you were here!' he said, genuinely surprised to see the man. Simba was the captain of the Zimbabwean field hockey team.

'We didn't know we were going to qualify, did we?' Simba said with a laugh. Zeke pulled him into a hug and went around shaking hands and catching up with the rest of the team. He was so glad to see them. While the athletes on Team GB were like family to him, there was something different about hanging out with the Team Zimbabwe athletes. It felt like spending time with his cousins, or his oldest friends. They shared the same language, upbringing and history. Every conversation with them felt effortless.

The Zimbabwean Olympic team wasn't very big. In fact, it was one of the smallest delegations of athletes of any country that year. But what they lacked in size and funding they made up for in energy. They grabbed food from the canteen and headed outside to eat dinner on one of the big garden tables near the lake. Zeke felt a wave of comfort. Eating with them as they all told jokes in Shona felt like a brief interlude at home. Simba got his speakers out and there was something about hearing old songs he'd grown up with, while eating Zimbabwean food and listening to them tell him exaggerated, full-gestured stories about how they'd only just about made it to the Games, that made him feel completely at ease.

You could find the feeling of home anywhere in the world. Zeke had learned that at his very first international competition, an athletics tournament in Toronto he'd travelled to with his dad when he was twelve years old. He'd been feeling homesick on his second night until his dad started blasting his favourite Zimbabwean songs in the hotel room. When he was in London, he found the songs grating. His mother would play them at the crack of dawn every weekend to not so subtly announce that it was a cleaning day and she was waiting for him and his brothers to come down and help her. Back in London, the sound of the marimbas, acoustic guitars and Shona lyrics symbolized waking up earlier than he wanted to and having his mum and dad quiz him about school while he did his chores. But when his dad played them in the hotel room on the other side of the world during his first big trip away, the songs wrapped him up in comfort.

But then the song coming out of Simba's speakers changed.

An electric guitar started playing, a piano came in and then the lyrics began. Zeke knew every single note and word but he hadn't been able to bring himself to listen to it in years. It was his dad's favourite song.

If the song had played on shuffle, Zeke would have immediately pressed skip. If it had come on at a family party, he would have gone to the bathroom. And when it started playing on Simba's phone speaker by the land-scaped lake, Zeke immediately got up to leave, trying to get as far away from the canteen and the music as he possibly could. Because Zeke knew that as soon as the chorus hit there would be no way to stop the effect the song was going to have on him. He was already getting flashbacks to the last morning he'd ever shared with his dad. To the joy on his father's face, and the way the sun came through the window. Zeke had spent the past ten years wishing he could step back into that moment and relive the memory one more time. But he couldn't and the grief was threatening to overwhelm him.

He ignored the confused and concerned looks on his friends' faces as he promised to come along to the next Team Zimbabwe meal. He ignored the sound of Simba calling out to ask him if everything was all right and walked away because, in that moment, Zeke's biggest concern was checking if everyone back home was okay.

He pulled out his phone and called his brothers, but neither of them picked up. Athens was two hours ahead of the UK so if it was five p.m. in Athens, it was only three p.m. back in London. Why weren't they picking up?

He called his mum, and she didn't pick up either. His mother usually spent the whole day sending Bible verses, old photos and chain-mail conspiracy theories to the family group chat. But she hadn't messaged once that day.

He called her again and again. Then he called his brothers again and again. He stood still in the middle of the path and texted them, the discomfort in his neck growing.

It spread into his arms and tightened his chest. He stretched and tried to shake it off, but it was getting worse. He counted to try to regulate his breathing, but it only made him feel like he couldn't get the air in fast enough.

His first panic attack wasn't the one he'd experienced the night after he won his first medal; that was just the first time he'd been conscious of the fact that he was having a panic attack. His first panic attack was when he was fourteen years old, after the call that turned his whole life upside down.

Zeke could feel the pangs and pains of what he'd been dreading ever since he was a child as he walked through the Village. The fear took hold of him and he couldn't disentangle himself from its ropes. It constricted his body and made it difficult for him to stay standing up. Each time he had another panic attack, he felt the exact same fear and clarity that he'd felt all those years ago. Like what happened to his dad was about to happen to him.

Zeke tried to remember all the techniques he'd learned over the years. But his mind went blank. He desperately tried to control his breathing, but he felt like he was struggling for his last gasps of air. Standing was becoming too much to bear, his legs weakened and his body descended to the ground. But before he could fall and hurt himself, he felt someone's hands against his back. Gently breaking his fall and helping him to sit down on the grass. She smelt like vanilla and spoke with soft words. Olivia.

'Hey, you're okay, you're okay,' she said gently as she helped him lower himself to the ground. Zeke tried to speak but it came out as a strangled mumble.

'I'm not going anywhere, you don't need to say anything,' she said as she rubbed his arm. 'You're okay. I'm here, okay?'

He mumbled something that sounded like an 'okay' and then he closed his eyes.

Zeke was at practice when his father had the heart attack that killed him. So, Zeke didn't know what it looked or felt like to have a heart attack. But whenever he experienced a panic attack, he felt like he was on the verge of the same thing that had taken his dad's life that afternoon ten years ago.

His panic attacks always started slowly. He would feel the familiar sense of anxiety that he could usually manage in his day-to-day life. But then it would go from an emotional sense of anxiety to a physical one. Slowly, uncomfortably seeping through his body. Usually, if he reassured himself quickly enough, he could manage it. But every once in a while, it escalated so quickly and deeply that even his best attempts couldn't stop the fear from taking over. And, boy, did it take over.

Zeke felt dizzy. He felt nauseous. He felt like his chest was clenching so tightly he couldn't breathe. He felt hot. He felt cold. He felt like his heart was beating so fast that it was only a matter of time before his body would no longer be able to keep up. He was shaking and his breathing was coming out in short, irregular, disjointed breaths. The only sensation he could hold on to was the touch of the cool hard ground he was sitting on and the warm, soft hand that was holding his.

Olivia was speaking, but Zeke couldn't really make out all her words. He didn't have the capacity to make them out. All he could do was try to keep on breathing. And so he did. In and out, in and out.

'I'm not going anywhere, okay? I'm right here,' Olivia said. Zeke breathed in and out, in and out. Then he opened his mouth. 'One hundred . . . ninety-nine . . . ninety-eight . . .' he said, taking deep strangled breaths as he tried to get the words out.

'You've got this,' she said after he struggled to catch his breath between seventy-seven and seventy-six.

'Seventy-six . . . seventy-five . . . seventy-four,' he said. Each word felt like a battle and each breath felt like a fight for survival. But, slowly, he counted down.

'Three . . . two . . . one,' he finished, his mouth trembling as the tears rolled down his face.

'You did it, you're doing so good,' she said reassuringly. 'Tell me five things you can see?'

Zeke took a deep breath and rolled his shoulders, trying to relieve the tension, then answered her as best he could. He knew where she was going with this: it was the 5-4-3-2-1 method that Fiona had told him to try.

'Four things you can feel?' she asked.

He tried to focus on all the sensations outside of his body rather than the sensations inside of his body. 'The fabric on my shirt . . . the soles under my feet.' He took a deep breath in and then a deep breath out. 'The ground under my left hand . . . your hand on my right hand.' Her hand was soft and warm, with a firm grip on his. He slowly uncurled himself from his slouching position and leaned against the wall she was sitting by.

'And what can you taste?' she asked.

'I'd say tears, but I like you too much to admit I cry. Even though that's exactly what I'm doing now, so . . . I can taste . . . saltwater,' Zeke said, making Olivia laugh. Her laugh sounded like honey. It was the lightest he'd felt all day, and he experienced a short, temporary sense of relief.

'You can just say tears, Zeke,' she said, looking over at him with a softness in her eyes.

They sat there for a little while longer, side by side, watching the evening go by. She was still holding his hand. He didn't need her to, but he didn't want her to let go yet.

Zeke was grateful. The scariest thing about panic attacks was that he always felt like he was about to die. No amount of rationalizing would shake the feeling until it passed. Having someone there with him as he went through it helped bring him back sooner, to see a glimpse of reality through them before he could find it for himself.

Still they sat there, just holding hands and staring out across the Village. Olivia made him feel safe. He didn't ever feel like he had to be anybody other than himself with her. He'd been his truest, most unfiltered self with her from the very first time they'd met. For some reason, there was no need to pretend with her. He didn't feel like he had to be charming or polished. Sitting next to Olivia, he could just be who he was.

44
Olivia

Day seven of the 2024 Olympics

Olivia felt the same way. So much that it scared her. Zeke was still holding on to her, so she gently lifted her arm and kissed the back of his hand. It was an act of tenderness unfamiliar to her, but it felt completely natural as the sun made its slow descent, leaving blurry pink and orange lines in the sky. Zeke wrapped his arm around Olivia's shoulder and she shuffled closer towards him until they were sitting side by side. He placed a soft kiss on her head and then slowly rested his head on hers. They sat there in comfortable silence for a while. Zeke's heartbeat slowed down and his breathing returned to normal.

The rest of the Village was still bustling with activity, but with all the other athletes out training or at competitions, the athletes' quarter was strangely peaceful, like the world was in slow motion.

'You know that feeling you get when you're a kid and your parents don't come home on time?' Zeke asked.

'When you start to think something bad has happened to them?'

'Yeah. Exactly that. When I was a kid, I used to think about what I would do if something bad ever did happen to my parents,' said Zeke, looking into the distance. 'I made a plan. My older brothers would move back home to look after me, we'd stay living in the house that we grew up in and then, when we got older, we'd all grow up and buy houses on the same street. I felt like if I imagined and prepared for the worst thing that could happen, the worst thing couldn't happen.' He spoke with a clarity about it that he'd never really experienced before. 'But it still happened.'

Olivia nodded and gently squeezed his hand. He squeezed back.

'I thought by now I wouldn't need a plan to get me through a missed call. That knowing I'd gone through loss and survived it meant that I'd be able to handle the fear of it happening again. But all it took was two missed calls to my brothers and my mum to reduce me to . . . this,' he said, waving his left hand.

His right hand was still holding hers. They sat in silence for another moment. Olivia didn't feel the need to fill it. Then Zeke's phone rang. He answered the video call and his phone screen lit up with the image of an older woman wearing a glamorous dress at what appeared to be a party.

'Ezekiel! I've already packed my bag to come and see you,' she said, grinning as she chatted away about how she and Zeke's brothers were planning to fly to Athens at the end of the week in time to watch his final. Zeke looked so relieved. It turned out that his mum was at her half-sister's cousin's niece-in-law's Zimbabwean traditional wedding that afternoon.

'Mum, I was just calling to see if you're okay,' Zeke said, putting on a cheerful voice.

'I'm brilliant, excellent, fantastic,' said his mother,

emphasizing each word by lifting her phone up and down. 'Wait, wait, you need to say hi to your Auntie Chipo,' she added, getting up.

'I don't have an aunt called Chipo,' Zeke said, looking over at Olivia, who laughed as she saw the perplexed look on his face.

'Chipo! Chipo! Ezekiel is on the phone, come quick,' the woman said, waving her phone in the air.

'Chipo! Chipo! Ah, here she is,' said Zeke's mother as another equally glamorous-looking older woman walked into the frame.

'Ezekiel! Is that you? Your mother said you'd grown up, but I didn't know you would be as handsome as your father,' said the other woman.

'Thank you, Auntie Chipo,' said Zeke, looking embarrassed as he noticed Olivia grinning at him.

'Wait, wait, is that a girl? Ezekiel?' said his mother, her eyes growing wider. 'Ezekiel, have you found a girlfriend? Oh, Jesus Lord, you have answered all of my prayers!' She put one arm in the air.

'Mum, stop it,' said Zeke, looking even more embarrassed.

'Chipo, imagine. I have a whole twenty-four-year-old son. An athlete, scholar and superstar, but he gets embarrassed when I say that he is a very eligible bachelor,' said Zeke's mother.

'Imagine,' said Auntie Chipo, shaking her head. Olivia smiled as she thought about what family dinners must be like in the Moyo household.

After passing the phone around to a dozen relatives and calling his aunties over to interrogate him about his love life, Zeke's mum was finally convinced to let him hang up. Then he and Olivia lay back on the grass, laughing as they talked about the summers they'd both spent with their grandparents back in Zimbabwe, and swapped the wildest stories from both of their family trees.

'What's your family like?' Zeke asked.

'Quiet? I don't have siblings, but I've known Aditi long and deep enough that she feels like my sister,' Olivia said, thinking about how lucky she'd been to find her.

'And your parents?'

'They love me a lot,' said Olivia, remembering all the texts they'd sent asking about her internship. *And* the calls she'd avoided and blamed on time zones. 'They're not stereotypically overbearing Zimbabwean parents, but sometimes I feel like they've put too much hope in me,' she said.

'How so?' he asked.

'They have the classic immigrant story, you know? Came with a dream, got disappointed, think their daughter is going to be the one that makes it. And I will,' she said.

'Of course,' Zeke nodded, looking at her with affection.

'But I don't know. Sometimes I wonder who I would have become if wanting to be their success story didn't matter so much to me.' She shrugged. 'I wonder if I would have put so much of who I am into becoming the person I'm trying to be if I didn't want to make them happy.'

'You know that they'll be proud whatever happens, but you still want to do right by them,' he said thoughtfully.

'Exactly. And I want to do right by all of the past versions of myself who wanted the things I'm getting closer to achieving,' she said.

'I have a younger cousin named Rumbi,' said Zeke. 'And

every couple of days she sends me a new article about something problematic one of my sponsors has done or some issue I'm supposed to be speaking out on.'

'How old is she?' asked Olivia.

'Seventeen,' said Zeke.

'Tough crowd,' said Olivia.

'It's that age when you finally have your adult values but haven't had the adult experiences to make you lose sight of them yet,' Zeke said, staring out into the distance.

Olivia nodded in agreement. 'When I was seventeen, I figured out this whole vision for my life. For who I wanted to become, what I wanted to do and what I believed in. And I've basically spent all the years since then trying to become that idealized version of myself.' She paused. 'But I've made all of these small compromises along the way to get there.'

Her mind flicked through all the times she'd averted her eyes – from the toxic environments to the whispers about bad people in high places. She'd accepted the uneasy gut feelings as an occupational hazard.

'But sometimes you've got to make compromises, right?' Zeke said softly.

'Yeah, but when does it stop, you know?' Olivia said, thinking of how much her personality had shifted since she'd left school. 'When I was Rumbi's age there were so many lines I thought I would never cross. But sometimes I can feel myself moving the net, getting more comfortable with small compromises if they get me to where I want to be.'

Ever since she'd seen Lars at the diplomats' dinner yesterday, she'd been thinking of ways she could manoeuvre the situation to get to where she wanted. She'd thought about marching straight to Noah's office and highlighting the conflict of interest that had clearly got Lars the job over her. She'd toyed with the idea of having an anonymous, on-the-record conversation with a journalist about how convenient it was that the son of a billionaire sponsor in the midst of serious legal proceedings magically got a job at an organization that so loudly and publicly praised themselves for bias-free hiring. But the fact that she could want something enough to happily burn someone in her way made her feel like she'd already strayed too far from who she'd once thought she was.

'When I was seventeen, I had this airtight, unshakeable sense of right and wrong and knew everything I didn't want to be. And now a part of me is like *Yeah, of course you did, because you'd never experienced anything that pushed against your belief system*. It's easy to be idealistic when you've never had to compromise. But then the other part of me is like *If you're willing to make all those compromises just to get where you want to be . . . did you ever actually value the things you thought you did?*' she said.

'Me too,' said Zeke. 'Sometimes I wonder if I would have mapped out the path I did if I'd known all the ways it would change me.'

Olivia felt the same way. She'd always believed that she could get to where she wanted and keep her hands clean. But maybe she'd have to get a little bit of dirt in her nails to get into the boys' club and climb to the top. The clarity of that thought – and the realization that she was more than willing to make those compromises – shook her up a bit.

'I'm terrified of gradually losing sight of who I once was, but being so far gone on my road of compromises that I don't even realize I've turned into the kind of person I didn't want to become,' she finished.

'Have you become someone you don't like?' There wasn't any judgement in Zeke's eyes, just a question.

She paused to think about it. 'No, not yet. But sometimes I can feel myself chipping away in small chunks, losing myself in real-time. Like, even here in the Village, there are things I could do to get ahead,' she said, thinking about all the ways she'd imagined getting back at Lars and Noah. 'And doing those things would get me where I want to be but . . .'

'But at what cost?' he said with a nod. And then he turned around with an uneasy expression.

'I hope Rumbi never changes, because me and you, Olivia . . .?' he said with a chuckle.

'We're way too far gone,' she said, grateful for a moment of lightness in the weight she'd been carrying all day. A part of her wanted to just stay there and sit next to him until the sun went down.

'What were you doing before you found me?' he asked.

'Walking to the shuttle stop,' she said, having long forgotten her 5.15 p.m. shuttle.

'I'd call you a taxi, but I think you'd give me a look and say—'

'I can order my own taxi?' she said with a smile. 'The shuttles run every fifteen minutes on competition nights, I'll be fine.'

They walked together to the bus stop.

'Olivia, let's go out. On a real date,' Zeke said suddenly. 'Just name the day. I want to know when I'm going to see you again.'

She wanted to make a joke and jump on the bus. Act like everything was just casual to protect herself from the threat of completely letting herself go. But August wouldn't last for ever. In just over a week, the Games would be over and everyone in the Village, including Zeke, would be gone. This summer was too short to stop herself from experiencing what it would be like to put all of her cards on the table.

'The day after tomorrow?' she said. He looked directly into her eyes and the intensity she'd grown used to craving was replaced with something softer, more tender. *Oh no*, she thought. She was too happy and too far gone to turn back.

45
Zeke

Day eight of the 2024 Olympics

Zeke spent the whole night thinking about Olivia. The dates he could take her on, the stories about her life that he wanted to know and the parts of himself he wanted to share with her. He'd liked her from the moment she'd convinced him to sing in the middle of that opening ceremony after-party. And his thoughts had been consumed by her since that night in the lift.

He hadn't felt this way in a long time. And he'd never felt this way so soon.

As he walked into his bathroom, he caught a glimpse of himself in the mirror. *Uh oh*, thought Zeke, as he saw the dazed look on his face and the smile he couldn't hold back. He was falling for Olivia, plain and simple. The free-fall felt like flying.

But then he remembered that Haruki had been screening his calls or texting to say he was in training ever since that night at Olivia's apartment. Zeke hadn't got the chance to explain himself or apologize. But he knew that they needed to talk about everything that had gone down the other night so he called him up again. This time Haruki did pick up the call, but said he was too busy to speak and promptly hung up. When the call ended, Zeke just stared down at his phone, feeling the guilt. He tapped Haruki's contact page and looked at the photo he'd saved to his profile. It was a photo of them laughing at the Tokyo Olympics. He couldn't remember the joke any more and the details of the day they'd taken it were fuzzy and distant now. But they looked happy, comfortable with each other, like family. He'd done his best to repress the guilt enough to continue things with Olivia, but he couldn't deny it any more. Zeke had seriously messed things up with his best friend. He had to make it right, and the only way to do that would be to find Haruki and have a conversation long and honest enough to apologize. But Haruki was about to go into a swimming session so he couldn't hunt him down until the evening. And Zeke was scheduled to be at the athletics track in ten minutes. He had to make things right with his best friend and do it as soon as he could, but that conversation would have to wait until after training.

In the days leading up to his race, Zeke's schedule got tighter and his routine got stricter. He knew he was supposed to channel his energy into increasing his speed, perfecting his stride and doing all he could to run better than ever before in the final. But he spent the whole of practice distracted, going back and forth between trying to come up with ideas for his date with Olivia and forming a game plan for apologizing to Haruki.

After training, he bumped into Valentina. She was on her way to get some gelato, so he decided to tag along.

'By the way, Olivia's flatmate gave me this the other night when I got cold,' Valentina said, giving him a blue cardigan.

'Why are you giving it to me?' asked Zeke. Valentina liked to fairy godmother her way into people's lives.

'To give you a reason to go and see Olivia again, duh,' she said, like it was the most obvious thing in the world. 'Because I know you'll wait six months to text her.'

'I asked her out yesterday,' he said.

'You did?' asked Valentina, sitting up in surprise. Zeke's friends always teased him about moving too slowly when it came to a crush.

'This is not the Zeke I know,' she said, sounding impressed. 'Usually you take two weeks to ask for her number, spend six months just being her friend and then ask her out after ten months once you're already in love.'

'I don't do that,' he protested.

'You either do that or meet a girl you only half like, hook up that night and never see her again,' she said, making a not-so-subtle reference to the brief romantic encounters he'd had in the last year that had been documented on gossip accounts and blind items.

'That's kind of a pattern, isn't it?' Zeke shrugged.

'So, if you're already texting her, making plans with her, and aren't tempted to run away . . . you must really like her,' Valentina said. It was a statement, not a question.

'I do . . . really like her and I've told her that,' he admitted.

Valentina squealed. 'Really? And what did she say?' she asked, loving every part of this conversation.

'That she liked herself too.'

'Oh, you've met your match,' Valentina said as they both laughed. She put her head between her hands to listen while he told her everything – well, almost everything. The first time they'd met, what he liked about Olivia and how he felt about her. Then he admitted that, as delicate and risky as it seemed, he wanted to give this – whatever it was – his all.

Zeke could still remember the day Valentina had broken up with him. He'd kind of seen it coming. Long distance was always hard, but in the months leading up to 'the talk', Valentina was unusually distant. Their FaceTime calls became fewer and further apart and he'd sensed an uncharacteristic heaviness and detachment. So, when she'd sent him a text saying 'this isn't working any more' and then arrived at his apartment with tears in her eyes, he'd just sat down and listened as she told him everything. About her first childhood crush, the girl she'd kissed at gymnastics camp when she was fourteen and all the worries that held her back from living the life she truly wanted. Staying friends had been a complete no-brainer. And as they sat outside on the grass now, Zeke realized that he was probably going to know Valentina for the rest of his life. And he was so grateful things had turned out the way they did. Friendships like this only came around once in a while. So he bought them another pot of gelato and they sat and talked some more. She told him about Leila, how they'd met and the day she'd introduced her to her family. He told her about Haruki and how guilty he was beginning to feel about the way things had gone down, and she gave him advice on how to approach the situation. Then Valentina's phone started ringing.

Zeke got his phone out and used the moment to research places he could take Olivia on a date without breaking his Village ban or his ridiculous seven p.m. curfew. But then Valentina got off her phone call and looked up at Zeke with a grimace.

'Umm, Zeke? How much do you like Olivia?' she asked.

The truth was, over the past couple of days Zeke had realized that he was starting to fall in love with her. Each time he was beside her, he felt safer than he ever had before. When she laughed, or met his words with some quick remark, he began to wonder what for ever would look like. But it was way too much and too soon to admit that, so instead he answered –

'I like her . . . a lot.'

'And how certain are you that Olivia likes you back?'

'I . . . think she does?' he said, ignoring the persistent, nagging doubt he seemed to feel about everything these days.

'Yeah, I think she does too. Which means that you have a problem. That was my publicist on the phone. She just told me that we've picked the worst possible place to get gelato.'

A couple of metres away from them was a group of teenagers in school uniform who were probably there for a tour of the Village. They were taking photos of Zeke and Valentina on their phones and not being covert about it at all. But there were hundreds of photos online that had been taken when Zeke wasn't looking. It made him uneasy, but it wasn't particularly out of the ordinary.

'Look,' said Valentina, sliding her phone across the table to show him the photos her publicist had called to talk about.

Zeke immediately saw the problem. In the photo, he and Valentina were sitting so close together it looked like they were about to kiss. In reality, they'd just moved over so they could hear each other above the music that was playing from the ice-cream truck's speakers, but Zeke automatically saw how it could be misperceived. Their faces, the gelato, the way the sunlight was trickling through the leaves. It looked romantic, like they were just as in love as the rumours said they were. Zeke glanced down at the cardigan in his hands and then over at Valentina.

Zeke had to explain it all before Olivia saw the photos.

46
Olivia

Day eight of the 2024 Olympics

As Olivia walked into the laundry room, she smiled at all of the random things she'd done since she'd arrived at the Games that she could now put on an alternate version of her CV. She'd become an expert in horse-hay delivery, stacked up hundreds of miles' worth of golf-buggy trips, learned how to get 200 journalists through the accreditation office in less than ten minutes and could pretty accurately guess what sport someone did just by glancing down at their shoes.

Since unfollowing Lars Lindberg, she'd stopped fixating on the summer she'd anticipated and allowed herself to focus on the summer she was actually having. And it had made all the difference. She'd spoken to Sierra Leonean sprinters about their favourite TV shows, helped Peruvian badminton players get new keys to their apartments and tried Indonesian food for the first time with a group of weightlifters who'd given her a spoonful of everything they'd cooked for their team meal. Her walkie-talkie calls allowed her to really explore the Village and she couldn't count how many interesting conversations and experiences came from just saying yes.

In a break between replenishing bath towels in the gym that the Serbian women's basketball team had just used, she picked up her phone to scroll for a few moments. And as she did, she saw a picture of someone she recognized. Zeke.

She clicked on the photo to be sure, and there he was. Sitting out in the sun, eating gelato. He looked so good. His face was lit up and he was leaning forward with that expression that she'd grown to hopefully anticipate whenever she walked past a guy his height and complexion in the Village. His smile felt like summer and the slight sparkle the sun was casting on his eyes made her even more excited for their date tomorrow. She was about to press the 'like' button when she realized that the photo was just one in a long series of photos of him. She scrolled through them and then she froze. She didn't want to believe what she was seeing, but she couldn't pull her eyes away.

The photos were grainy, but the facts were clear. Right next to Zeke – looking gorgeous in a green dress – was Valentina Ross-Rodriguez. They were sitting so close together that Olivia had no doubt that the photographer had captured a private moment. She looked down at the grass and saw that Valentina was holding Zeke's hand. She flipped through the photos and zoomed in to check that what she was seeing was really true. She knew that ice-cream truck, it was just a ten-minute walk away from where she was. At first, she tried to tell herself that they were old photos, taken right at the start of the Games. But there on the grass next to Zeke was something that Olivia immediately recognized: Aditi's favourite cardigan.

She'd given it to Valentina the other night so it was clear that the photos were taken in the last two days.

Despite herself, Olivia scrolled through the comments from self-proclaimed 'Zekentina' stans celebrating their favourite couple's reunion. Olivia tried to come up with an excuse for why Zeke would be sharing a pot of gelato with his ex-girlfriend and holding her hand . . . platonically. But there were limits to what she could convince herself of. It was Tiago all over again. Zeke had told her there was nothing going on between him and Valentina. But as Olivia zoomed in on the other photos and saw the way Valentina looked at him, it was clear that Zeke wasn't as honest as she'd hoped he was.

Her fears confirmed, she turned her internet off, put her phone on 'do not disturb' and pushed it down to the very bottom of her bag so it couldn't hurt her feelings any more. She lay down on one of the benches in the gym and stared up at the ceiling, pinned to the spot as she felt an overwhelming wave of sadness.

Of course he still liked Valentina. Who wouldn't still like Valentina? She was beautiful — so beautiful that if she hadn't become a gymnast first, she would have been snapped up by some modelling agency. She was success- ful — she'd literally won an Olympic gold medal three days ago. And the whole world was rooting for them to get back together. She'd seen the fancams and viral tweets. She didn't need to be a Zekentina stan to know that Zeke and Valentina just made sense. They were both athletes and famous and beautiful and charismatic. Valentina was ambi- tious but in an inspiring way, impressive but with humility, beautiful but oh so effortless.

Olivia stood up and began to push the cleaning cart out of the gym. She felt her eyes well up but immedi- ately blinked the tears away. She shook her head in embarrassment. Didn't she know better than to trust a boy in the summertime? How could she have let herself get carried away so quickly? Zeke had told her that he liked her. But that didn't mean anything. He was an athlete, and this was the Olympics. She was just another girl watching from the stands. How could she have been naive enough to think she was the only one?

She left the gym and walked back out into the Village, silently berating herself for losing sight of reality so quickly. Then she began to cry. Slow, quiet tears. She stopped rolling the cleaning cart and sat down on a bench outside the gym, looking out as the Village moved on without her. Olivia hated that she'd allowed herself to care so much. It was like Lisbon all over again.

She could still remember locking eyes with Tiago's girlfriend as she explained that Olivia had wasted her summer with a boy who did the same thing with different girls year after year. She'd spent the whole plane journey home crying. But they'd been tears of embarrassment more than anything else. She'd been angry at herself for getting so caught up in the romance of it all that she hadn't been able to spot the glaringly clear signs that Tiago wasn't the dream boy he'd made himself out to be.

But this time, with Zeke, was different. She wasn't embarrassed and she didn't regret a single moment. Because, despite her instincts to run, over the past couple of days she'd started to imagine what it would be like to be in love with him. It was too much and it was too soon, but she could already feel herself falling, which made the realization that she couldn't trust him hurt more than any other disappointment she'd ever experienced.

Olivia could feel the heartbreak setting in, making the world look different and shaking her sense of self. She knew from experience that there was no use in trying to out-swim the wave. She'd have to let it wash over her and distract herself enough that she didn't drown. So, she wiped away her tears and headed back over to the Hub, hoping that pouring herself into errands and walkie-talkie calls would take her mind off him for long enough to get her through the rest of the day.

But, when she got there, Zeke was standing right in front of the door.

47
Olivia

Day eight of the 2024 Olympics

Olivia immediately turned around. She wasn't ready for
him to see her red eyes.

'Wait! Olivia!' Zeke said, following her.

'I'm busy, Zeke,' Olivia said quietly as she gripped on to
her cleaning cart and tried to manoeuvre away from him.
She couldn't bear the thought of him lying to her face;
she'd already seen the pictures.

'But I need to talk to you,' he said.

'And I need to deliver two hundred towels to the west
gym,' she said, looking ahead because she knew that if she
looked at Zeke she'd find a way to change her own mind.

'You saw the photos? Just let me explain,' he said,
speed-walking after her.

'I don't need your explanation. It's fine. You don't owe
me anything and I don't owe you anything,' she said. She
didn't sound angry, she sounded defeated.

'Liv, it's not what it looks like,' he said.

'It's always what it looks like, Zeke. You don't need to
force it to protect my feelings. I can do that all by myself.'

'You've got to at least give me a chance,' said Zeke. Olivia
stopped and closed her eyes. He was right. She decided to

give him one chance to say whatever it was that he had to say.

But as she turned around to face him, she saw someone else she recognized. Olivia froze. Because right there, walking towards them, wearing a perfectly tailored suit and a staff lanyard . . . was Lars Lindberg.

'Zeke! How's it going? Congratulations on the big race,' said Lars, patting Zeke on the back like they were old friends. Olivia could feel herself deflating.

'Thanks, bud, I appreciate it. Looking sharp as always,' said Zeke. 'Don't say you've gone corporate on me?' Olivia looked at Zeke and she could see the version of himself he turned into when he had to play the role of Ezekiel Moyo. She didn't like it.

'It was either this or the old man was going to get me to take over the London office,' said Lars. Olivia bristled at his nonchalance.

'Let me introduce you,' said Zeke, but when he looked at Olivia she could see the worry in his eyes. Tell that he was desperate to get rid of Lars and finish the conversation they'd been about to have. But it was too late.

'Olivia, this is Lars, one of my old friends,' he said. 'And Lars, this is Olivia, who's going to be running this whole thing in a couple of years.'

She knew that Zeke thought he was doing her a favour by introducing her to one of the most powerful people (pending his father's death or retirement) in the sporting world. But the sight of Lars made her nauseous.

'Nice to meet you, Olivia, I'm Lars Lindberg,' Lars said, reaching his arm out to shake her hand.

'You know we've met before, right?' Olivia asked.

'We have?' said Lars.

'I gave you the goodie bags two days ago,' Olivia said. She hated that she immediately wondered if her tone was too harsh. She could feel herself slipping back into the version of herself she'd been during all those hours spent in offices and rooms that made her feel invisible.

'Sorry, I don't remember you. Are you sure we've met?' he asked.

'We were on the same course at university for *three years*,' she said, tracing his face for a hint of recognition. She couldn't see any. Lars didn't remember her and why would he? To a guy like him, she was just another faceless, nameless uniformed girl there to make his experience of the Village easier.

She knew the only reason he'd gone to shake her hand was because of Zeke. Zeke talking to her gave her value in Lars's eyes. She had to be somebody, or somebody adjacent, to know Ezekiel Moyo, right? As she looked at Lars, she could see him assessing her, trying to figure out if she was worth his time; whether she could help his climb. But then he glanced over at her cleaning cart and lost interest. She withdrew her hand and wiped the sweat from his palm on the back of her shirt.

'Thanks for everything you're doing for the Village. The Games wouldn't be the same without incredible volunteers like you,' said Lars dully, like it was a line he'd been trained to repeat.

His practised politeness left such a vile taste in her mouth that she put both of her hands on her cleaning cart and started to push it away. This was all too much to handle right now.

'Olivia, wait up!' said Zeke.

She shook her head and kept on walking. 'Zeke, I get it. This, us? It was a glitch, a mistake, I don't need your explanations,' she said, waving him off.

'A glitch? Olivia, come on, you know it was more than just a glitch.'

'A summer thing, then. Everyone's reckless in the summer,' she said, walking ahead without turning to face him.

'So, I was just a reckless decision?' said Zeke flatly. Olivia kept on walking, but she could hear the answer in her head. No, he wasn't a bad decision, he was one of the best decisions she'd made all year. But for the first time in a long time, she'd made a decision based on how she felt instead of what she knew. She couldn't believe she'd let herself be led by something as fickle as feelings.

'Zeke, I don't want to talk. Just leave me alone, please,' she said, walking faster, trying to hold back the sting she could feel in her eyes.

'If I was a mistake, I don't want to get in your way,' Zeke said, slowing down as he fell out of step with her.

'Fine,' she said, speeding ahead without looking back. He'd got so good at making her feel safe enough to let her guard down that he'd started to do it without even trying. But now he'd stopped walking after her. So, she powered on ahead. Pushing her cart as she bit her lip and refused to let herself turn around. She couldn't let him see her cry. She couldn't let him know how much she wished he'd carried on walking by her side.

48
Zeke

Day eight of the 2024 Olympics

Zeke wanted to run after Olivia. He'd gone to the Hub to explain everything, to tell her that the photos of him and Valentina weren't what they looked like.

But when she said it was 'just a summer thing', he'd frozen. Because he had allowed himself to believe that she felt what he'd felt too. The chemistry between them whenever they spoke, the tenderness that filled their quiet moments, the raw passion when they kissed. But as he watched her walk away, the hopeful lovestruck feeling he'd had all week curdled into anxiety. And, as he headed over to his afternoon training session, the worry that he might have got ahead of himself began to chip away at him.

'You need to get those legs higher, Zeke,' said Coach Adam. Zeke was jogging on the spot while trying to get his knees up as high as he could. But every leg lift took more effort than the last as he worried over Olivia's admission that everything between them was just a 'summer thing'.

There wasn't a specific set of rules for what a sun-fuelled situationship should be, but there were sure-fire rules of what it shouldn't be. They weren't supposed to talk about shared futures or old wounds. They weren't supposed to meet each other's friends and families. And they weren't supposed to allude to any sort of lifespan beyond August. But if all Olivia wanted from him was someone to play the other part in a summer fling, he'd already broken so many of the rules. Maybe too many.

'All right, rolling planks,' said Coach Adam.

Zeke got down and pulled himself into a plank position.

She'd jokingly called him a distraction the other day and he'd laughed, but he knew there was some truth to her words. He *was* pretty distracting. He was always battling with an intensely packed schedule, training sessions and public appearances. Maybe Olivia had realized that she didn't want the constant complications that came with his world. The scrutiny, the pressure and all the cancelled plans.

'Zeke?' said Coach Adam. 'Are you all right?'

'I'm good,' said Zeke. But he wasn't.

'It's taking you a lot longer to do things than it usually does. Are you tired?' Coach asked with concern. Coach Adam was usually a pretty easy-going guy, but he became very protective when it came to his athletes. They were like his kids.

'I'm fine,' said Zeke.

'You seem a little off. Are you still seeing Fiona?'

'Yes, Coach,' said Zeke with a hint of irritation. Asking for help was supposed to be a choice, not a mandatory element of his place in the team.

'I'm just looking out for you, kid,' said Coach Adam.

'You don't need to,' said Zeke. It came out a little more sharply than he'd intended it to. There was a pause.

'Do we have a problem here?' asked Coach Adam, firmly but not unkindly.

'No, Coach,' Zeke said. Coach Adam looked at him. Zeke tried his best to look normal, but Coach Adam had known him long enough to tell he was going through it.

'Go for lunch,' said Coach Adam.

'I've already eaten lunch.'

'Okay then, take a walk.'

'We've *just* started training,' said Zeke. His voice was thick with annoyance.

'We have, but your head is clearly not in it, Moyo. You make mistakes when your head's not in it.'

Zeke stood up. 'I only have five more days before the competition.' Heartbreak began to mingle with the anxiety he'd been feeling on and off all week.

'Clear your head, Ezekiel. Take. A. Walk,' said Coach Adam with measured, no-nonsense finality. It wasn't up for discussion.

Zeke let out a frustrated breath. He was about to reply with a quick remark, saying that it was *his* training session and that *he* would stop when *he* was finished. That Coach Adam had no right to tell him what to do, that he wasn't his dad, or his uncle, and that Zeke could and would do whatever he wanted. But as he felt the words bubbling up, he realized he might say something he didn't mean. Which probably meant that he really did need to clear his head. So, he picked up his bag and left the gym without saying another word. Then he did what he always did when he was feeling emotions he didn't know how to handle. He went on a run.

He began at GB House and then turned left. He pressed

play on a news podcast, but the sound of political chaos and natural disasters wasn't enough to distract him from the thought of Olivia.

Zeke had gone years without really talking to anybody about his dad or all the complications that came with grief because he'd been worried about what would happen if he opened himself up too much. He didn't want people to look at him differently, to go from seeing him as Zeke Moyo the star athlete to Little Z, the fourteen-year-old boy who'd just lost his favourite person and had no idea how to handle it. It had been over ten years now and he still wasn't sure he knew how to handle it.

He ran past the athletes' apartments, over the bridge and into a park filled with trees. He'd found a way to cope with his grief, to distract himself with running and competitions and the relentless drive to constantly outdo himself. But the truth was that talking to Olivia about it had lifted a bigger weight off his shoulders than anything else. Maybe that was the problem. That sitting on the ground with her while he gave her a glimpse into his insecurities had changed things for her. Maybe she *had* liked him, but the panic attack and talking too much about his feelings spooked her. Had it been too much emotion, too much fragility? Girls said they liked a guy who could talk about their feelings but maybe only when they did it in a contained enough way to still seem manly.

The photos with Valentina didn't help but perhaps they'd just given her an easy out to end things. It was a lot simpler to finish something because you suspected some-one was untrustworthy than because the guy you thought you'd liked had come on too strong with his emotions and complications. Zeke ran faster, annoyed with himself for revealing too much about the inside of his head.

As he circled back to the athletes' apartment to end his run, he saw a guy wearing a white-and-red tracksuit walking towards Japan House. Zeke was already feeling pretty low, but as he realized it was Haruki, he felt himself deflate even more.

Zeke had been raised on loyalty. He treated his closest friends like siblings. If he'd been friends with somebody or they'd been there for him when he needed them the most, Zeke took them in like family. So, as he walked over to Haruki, he felt the sharp pain of knowing he'd let down someone he loved. Haruki normally had a smile on his face, but as he turned, all Zeke could see was disappointment.

'Hey, I tried to call you,' said Zeke, knowing that he could have done a lot more than that.

'I was busy,' said Haruki with an unfamiliar coldness.

Zeke knew he'd made a mistake, but it wasn't until he saw Haruki's face that he realized just how bad things were. He had to apologize.

'About Olivia. I'm sorry. I didn't know that you were talking about—' started Zeke, but Haruki cut him off.

'No, *we* weren't talking. Because we don't talk.'

'We do talk.'

'*I* talk to *you* all the time – I tell you about work and who I'm seeing, my family and what scares me. But you never tell me *anything*. Not really,' said Haruki, his voice a mixture of sadness and anger.

'I call you all the time,' said Zeke defensively.

'No, I call you. Do you know, your brothers and your mum call me more than you do?'

'My mum calls you?' Zeke was surprised.

'Yes, your whole family does. Whenever you're sad and distant and refuse to tell them about anything beyond how your last race went, they call me to figure out if you're okay because you don't talk to them either,' he said.

'That's not true.'

'Yes, it is. You never tell us how you're feeling. Sometimes I see you and know you're going through it, but you just force yourself to handle all the bad things alone. And so you don't let people into the good things either,' Haruki said.

Zeke was speechless.

'And if we hadn't bumped into Olivia that night in the city, would you have even told me about her?' asked Haruki.

Zeke was silent.

'No, you wouldn't have,' said Haruki, with a disappointment that made Zeke wonder how long his best friend had been feeling this way about him. How long all of the people around him had been feeling that way.

'I'm sorry,' said Zeke, because it was the only thing he was sure of. Then he said, 'You really liked her, didn't you?'

'Kinda,' said Haruki with a shrug, but his expression was so dejected that Zeke knew Haruki was holding back. They stood in silence for a moment.

'Haruki, you're my best friend. And I like Olivia, a lot. But I'd never let a girl get in the way of our friendship. If that's going to make this weird between us, I won't—'

'Zeke, come on.' This time Haruki didn't sound sad, he sounded annoyed. Really annoyed. 'I didn't even know her second name until the other night. Is that why you think I'm mad?' he said, shaking his head like Zeke was completely missing the point.

'I thought—'

'Zeke, I kind of liked Olivia, but that's not the real issue here.' He looked Zeke in the eye. 'You're my friend, my best friend. But you don't tell me *anything*. You don't talk to me about your anxiety even though I know you feel it all the time. You don't talk to me about your feelings. I'm pretty sure you would have dated Olivia for six months before even dropping a hint that you were seeing someone. Bro, you're a great friend to me, one of the best people I know, but you don't let me be a good friend to you.'

Haruki was right. Everyone had been so worried about Zeke when his dad died that they'd started treating him with kid gloves. And Zeke resented it. He loved being the centre of attention when it came to races and competitions. But he'd hated the well-intentioned but suffocating attention he'd received the moment his identity became that of a boy who'd lost his dad too young. So, Zeke did his very best to act like none of it affected him. But somewhere along the line, that desire for people not to worry about him had shifted into not letting people in. And in doing so, he'd shut his best friend out.

'I'm . . .' Zeke thought about it. 'I'm sorry. I didn't even realize,' he said honestly. Thinking of all the things he hadn't told Haruki.

'It's all right, I get it. The insides of our heads are complicated. Just let me in sometimes, okay?' said Haruki, patting his shoulder.

'I'll try,' said Zeke, nodding. He knew it would take him a while to readjust, but the weight that lifted from his shoulders each time he talked to Olivia was enough for him to understand that he'd feel better if he didn't force himself to carry it all alone.

'We're good, Zeke,' Haruki said. Then, with a look of pure annoyance, added, 'But you do know that I'm *never* going to forgive you for leaving me to sneak off to the kitchen to make out with a girl you knew I liked.'

Zeke's eyes widened. He couldn't even defend himself.

'While I was playing Uno. You're a bit of an asshole, you know that?'

'I am, aren't I?' said Zeke.

Haruki laughed at the guilty, embarrassed look on Zeke's face. 'You really do like her, don't you?' he said after studying him for a moment.

'I . . . I do,' Zeke admitted.

'She likes you too. I could tell as soon as I saw you together. So . . . you have my blessing, I guess,' said Haruki with an exaggerated sigh.

Zeke felt a wave of relief; he was so glad to have his best friend back.

But, he still had to fix things with Olivia. And before he could fix things with her, he would have to face himself.

49
Olivia

Day eight of the 2024 Olympics

When Olivia called Aditi with tears in her voice, Aditi immediately caught a taxi, picked her up and dragged her out of the Village. Olivia protested, but her best friend insisted that spending the rest of her lunchbreak drinking an iced pistachio latte far away from the Village was exactly what she needed to process it all. And she was right. Olivia hadn't stopped talking since they'd driven out of the gates past the Olympic rings. But she didn't want to talk about Zeke. It was too complicated, and it hurt too much. So, instead, she focused her energy on the much simpler act of trash-talking Lars.

'Imagine what my summer would have been like if he hadn't just called his daddy for a favour,' Olivia said, shaking her head.

'I hate him as much as you do,' Aditi said as they found a table in I Cafe.

'I see Lars Lindbergs everywhere,' Olivia said. 'These silver-spoon-fed boys who just glide through life and collect shiny friends to make themselves look good.'

'And by "shiny friends" do you mean Zeke?' asked Aditi, who'd been listening patiently as Olivia talked about everything except for the person she was really thinking about.

'Yeah, because the fact that he's pally with Lars Lindberg makes me question what kind of person he is. Like, who willingly hangs out with *that* spoilt nepo baby? Lars doesn't even have a real personality. What does that say about Zeke? *Probably* that I had him all wrong from the start,' said Olivia, taking a furious sip of her iced latte.

'Liv,' said Aditi in a gentle voice, 'do you think that maybe you're focusing on how much you hate Lars to distract yourself from the fact that Zeke hurt your feelings?'

'No,' Olivia said unconvincingly. She twirled her straw and stared at her glass, hoping she'd find answers in the pistachio-flavoured froth. But none appeared.

Aditi was right. Olivia had spent the past ten minutes picking Lars apart because it was easier than facing what was actually upsetting her. At least she knew how to deal with *that* part of her life. She'd just work harder and keep doing everything she needed to do to get a seat at the table. Her future would be filled with rooms of people who made her feel invisible and dream jobs that left her disillusioned. That she could handle, but the way she felt about Zeke was a lot more complicated.

'The photos aren't even the worst thing,' she said – even though the photos felt like a rough punch to the gut. 'It's the fact that he didn't run after me.' Now that she'd stopped channelling her emotions into being annoyed at Lars, she could no longer avoid how hurt she was.

'Liv,' said Aditi, handing her a tissue. Olivia hadn't even noticed that she was crying.

'Part of me is devastated because I still really like him,'

Olivia said, the present tense not lost on her. 'But this other twisted part of me is almost relieved because the photos gave me a quick, easy out before I fell in way over my head.'

'Was it starting to feel a bit too—' started Aditi.

'Real? Yeah.'

Ever since she'd met him, Olivia had felt her guard coming down around Zeke . . . And it scared her. She didn't want to get sidetracked and didn't particularly fancy getting her heart broken at the end of August, again. But what really scared her was letting someone in enough for them to see every part of her. It wasn't like that summer with Tiago when she'd felt like another person for a few weeks. No, it was quite the opposite. Whenever she spent time with Zeke, she felt herself opening up beyond the point that she'd allowed herself to be comfortable with. She felt herself becoming lighter, freer and more herself.

Falling in love was fun, until it wasn't. Even with Tiago, a part of her had been relieved she could blame the end on him. A sharp, quick ending was always better than a summer spent watching affection slowly start to fade away. So, whenever she felt someone's interest begin to wane, she was the one to cut things off. She wouldn't let her heart be so easily broken.

'With Zeke, I don't know, it was different. And maybe I ran away from it. But if he'd wanted me enough, he would have run after *me*,' she said, unable to hold the tears back as Aditi came over to her side of the table to hug her.

Olivia's lunch break was only an hour, so, despite Aditi's attempts at persuasion, she had to go back to the Village. Once there, she distracted herself by attacking the huge pile of goodie bags waiting to be filled. She'd only planned on working on the goodie bags for as long as it took to get ahead of tomorrow's events. But without meaning to, she spent hours in the packing room. By the time she looked up at the clock on the wall, it was already 6.41 p.m. Her shift should have ended an hour earlier. But she wasn't ready to go home and face her feelings yet. So, she increased the volume on her headphones and picked up her phone.

The phone was where her problems had started in the first place, but she couldn't help but absent-mindedly reach out for it. She was scrolling while trying not to think about Zeke when her finger landed on an image that sent a bolt of adrenaline through her body. Olivia clicked on it and froze. Because she was looking at a post that Valentina had just sent out to the world. It was a four-photo carousel with the caption 'People I love'.

The first slide was a black-and-white photo of her with her gymnastics teammates holding their medals up and throwing their winners' wreaths into the air. The second was a photo of her, Zeke and Haruki dancing at a bar the night she'd won her gold medal. And then Olivia saw the third picture. It was a photo of Valentina dancing hand in hand with a girl who was looking straight into her eyes. She wore the gaze of someone in love. The final photo was a picture of Valentina with that same girl, kissing as they stood in colourful outfits right next to a parade.

Olivia stared at the photo, her thoughts racing. Zeke had asked her to just give him a chance, to believe in him rather than jumping to the worst-case scenario. But she had jumped to the least-trusting conclusion. However, as she looked down at the photos she felt a small flicker of hope. It wasn't too late to fix things.

She glanced around the goodie bag room and then back down at her phone. It was 6.48 p.m. She had to find Zeke, and she had to find him fast.

50

Zeke

Day eight of the 2024 Olympics

'Zeke?' she said, looking up from her desk in surprise.

'Is it okay that I came here?' he asked as he walked in, much more nervous now than he had been when he'd decided to walk to the other side of the Village to see her.

'Of course, I'm glad to see you,' said Fiona, the Team GB therapist, as she left her desk and made her way over to her usual seat.

'I can make an appointment,' he said.

His plan had been to search the whole Village until he found Olivia. To apologize for not running after her, to explain the photos and tell her how he really felt about her. But as another wave of anxiety washed over him, he'd decided to do what he'd been putting off for years – actually have a conversation with his therapist. Now, before he could change his mind, he opened his mouth and started to talk.

He recounted the moment the ambulance had driven his father away. Told her that he'd received his offer to run for Team GB less than a month after. Talked about how he'd numbed himself to negative emotions so he could live alongside the grief. She listened as he explained the ways he'd fallen short of being the man he thought his father wanted him to become. How his dad always dreamed of him competing for Team Zimbabwe, but he'd never had the guts to leave the security of what he knew. Zeke explained that sometimes he got a tightening in his chest when he thought about his competitions and that while he wanted to win his final, the thought of how it would change his life kept him up at night. He'd seen the way Haruki and Valentina's lives had changed after winning their gold medals. The brand deals and the late-night talk-show appearances, but also the intense online scrutiny and pressure not to just represent their country, but to be the kind of public figure on to whom people pinned their hopes and hatred.

And then he told her about Olivia.

The tightness in his chest began to ease. Things were a mess, but he couldn't help but smile as he talked about her. Shared the story of how they'd met, confessed the feelings he had for her and explained how they'd left things.

'Why didn't you follow her?' Fiona said, not a hint of judgement in her voice. Zeke had been thinking about that all day. He paused for a moment, and then he found his words.

'I think that . . . it was almost easier to let her walk away now than to fall in love with her and watch her change her mind,' Zeke said. 'Because people change their minds. And the thought of that is so hard to take that I'd almost rather not let myself go all in.'

He knew that it probably had to do with losing his dad so suddenly. He'd realized at a young age that grief was an inevitable part of love.

Fiona looked at him for a moment, holding space for what he'd just revealed.

'Sometimes we act against our better interests so we can control the situation,' she said. Zeke tilted his head as he listened. 'Not chasing the things we want allows us to know the outcome.'

He'd read about athletes who let themselves lose races they could have won easily. He understood the feeling. Sometimes it was easier to hold himself back and lose than give something his all and risk losing. It wasn't right, but there was something comforting about being able to blame a loss on himself instead of becoming a victim of fate.

'Throwing the game,' he said with a nod.

'Exactly,' said Fiona. But before they could finish their conversation, there was a knock on the door; it was time for Fiona's next appointment. So, Zeke said goodbye, booked another time to see her and then stepped back out into the Village.

Zeke had been running for as long as he could remember. His mother always told their friends that he'd learned to run before he could walk and, when he saw home videos from his childhood, he could see what she meant. Since childhood, he'd been moving his feet faster than his body could handle. His toddler-self had always been running across the house, around the garden and after his older brothers. Falling over his tiny baby shoes in glee. At primary school, he'd discovered his competitive streak and just how much he loved the overwhelming joy of winning a race. Back then he'd always been running towards something: to his family, to his friends, to the finish line.

But when his dad died, something shifted. Running

stopped being a thing he did because he loved it and started to become the thing that kept him afloat. The steady sound of his feet pounding against a running track had felt like a heartbeat; a constant amidst a time of such internally turbulent uncertainty. Whenever he was feeling anxious, he went for a run. Whenever he felt the grief creeping up, he went for a run.

As he walked through the Village that day, he realized that he'd spent the first fourteen years of his life running towards what he loved and then the last ten years running away from all of his fears. The realization came with such clarity that he stopped in his tracks.

What was he waiting for? He needed to go and find Olivia. She hadn't picked up any of his calls so either her phone was off or she'd blocked his number. If she was still in the Village, his best chance at finding her was to go to the Hub. But as he launched into a sprint, he came face to face with . . . Coach Adam, who was leaving the canteen after dinner.

'Twelve minutes before curfew,' said Coach Adam in a sing-song voice as he walked past. It was already 6.48 p.m.

Zeke looked down at his own watch then around at the Village. It would take him at least eight minutes to walk to the Hub and another twelve minutes to walk back to GB House. If he broke curfew, he'd never hear the end of Coach Adam's lectures about *thinking he was above the rules*. Once you got a bad reputation amongst the Team GB coaches it was almost impossible to shake it off and he knew that the ramifications would follow him for the rest of his career. Zeke already had two strikes. He was walking on thin ice.

But Olivia was worth it, way more than worth it. And Zeke was quite literally one of the fastest men in the world. So, he ran.

He had spent the last ten years running away from his fears, his anxiety and the persistent feeling that he was doing it all wrong. But now he had something to run towards. Someone to run towards. There were no guarantees in life. No sign that Olivia would hear him out or that the sparks he'd felt would be reciprocated past the heady haze of the summer. But this thing they had, this electric, romantic, overwhelmingly tender thing that kept drawing them together, was more than enough for him to temporarily stop running away from everything that scared him and run towards the hope of all that he and Olivia could become.

51

Zeke

Day eight of the 2024 Olympics

Zeke put one foot in front of the other, and ran faster than ever before, reaching the Hub in record time. He put his hand out to grab the door handle but, before he could make contact, the door opened. And there she was.

'Zeke,' she said, looking up at him in surprise as they stood in the doorway. The warm early evening light was pouring in through a window behind her, framing her silhouette with gold.

'Olivia,' he said, feeling his heart swell. He was *so* happy to see her.

'Did you run here?' she asked, looking at the sweat on his arms. It was scorching in Athens, but running in the heat was worth it for her.

'I needed to tell you . . .' he said, catching his breath. Her eyes were slightly red. He couldn't bear to see her sad, especially knowing he was the reason. 'The photos aren't what they look like . . . I can explain—' he began.

'I know. I saw Valentina's post. I'm . . . sorry I jumped to conclusions,' said Olivia.

'I'm sorry I just stood there,' he said. A silence fell between them for a moment. He watched as she nervously tugged at one of her braids. He could see the sadness on her face. 'I should have run after you,' he admitted. 'But — did you really mean what you said back there? That it was just . . . a summer thing? Because if you did, that's fine, I understand. But for me, it was always more than that.'

She looked slightly panicked. Zeke felt a bolt of fear, but then she began to speak.

'Zeke, I never meant that you were *just* a summer thing. I mean that I feel the most myself in the summer . . .' she said, looking up at him. 'And, lately, I've started to imagine what it would be like to feel this way all the time. To be with you all the time. I like you, Zeke Moyo. So much that it kind of terrifies me.'

He could feel his heart beating faster.

'I'm not always my summer self, Zeke. And as much as I like you, I'm not going to change myself to be some perfectly warm, sunshine dream girl. Because I like who I am,' she said, hesitating for a moment.

'I like who you are too, I like you a lot,' said Zeke. 'And I know it's summer, and everyone's always trying to be easy, carefree and nonchalant when the sun comes out—'

'I'm none of those things, by the way,' Olivia said with a solemn shake of her head. 'I'm not easy or nonchalant or carefree. I care a lot. I am very chalant.'

'I would *never* call you carefree or nonchalant. And I don't want carefree or nonchalant.' Zeke looked into her eyes. Standing under her gaze felt like stepping outside and feeling the sun on his arms on the first day of spring. Like waking up to a bright-blue sky in the depths of a long winter. He already knew that it was too late to stop the fall.

'Olivia, I'm terrified of messing this up,' he admitted,

looking at her. 'I know I seem confident and sure of myself . . .'

'Handsome, charming *and humble*,' Olivia said, unable to hold herself back.

'I'm the full package deal, baby,' he said with a smile. But then it faded, and Olivia gave his hand a small squeeze as he started to speak again.

'But I spend every night terrified I'm going to do the wrong thing . . . in every part of my life. That I'm going to disappoint someone, waste my potential, make the wrong decision, go down the lesser path or let people down. I don't want to mess things up, and it's easier to not get things wrong by not giving anything a real try,' he said, allowing himself to be honest in a way he never had.

He gently pulled her closer to him; she raised her hand to slowly stroke the side of his face. He brushed a loose braid away from her cheek and tucked it behind her ear so nothing could obstruct his view of her.

'I really like you, and I'm going to give this my all. Because I think we could really have something . . . be something.'

As she heard his words, she leaned forward and closed the distance, their lips finding a soft, safe, tender place to land. The sun began its slow descent, coating every surface it touched in a warm, bright, golden light. But they were so focused on each other that everything else was reduced to a blur in their periphery. Summer wouldn't last for ever, but when it ended – no matter how it ended – at least they would know they'd given it their best shot. In that moment, it was enough just to live for the hope of it all.

52

Olivia

Day thirteen of the 2024 Olympics

When Olivia was eight years old, she'd run a tactical campaign to become class president. With the strategy of someone way beyond her years, she'd written out a list of the most influential people in each friendship group, starting with the girl who ran the lunchtime book club and the goalie of the KS2 football club. She'd subtly befriended them all over the course of the two months before the vote, told them about all the things she wanted to change at their school, alluding to campaign promises with the strategy of a seasoned politician. It would be a piece of cake to get the librarian to order some 13+ novels for the book club girls. And, of course, the football boys should be allowed to play whatever they wanted during PE. She'd whispered and promised, charmed and calculated her way to the ballot paper, and won the presidential election by a landslide. Olivia could take any situation and make it work in her favour. She knew exactly how to get what she wanted.

So, when she walked into the Village that morning, she did so with clear-eyed focus. She had a goal, and nothing was going to get in her way. First she had to find Noah – the weaselly head of HR – and, as she told Arlo, 'Make him bend to my will.' Because, you see, Olivia was *that* girl. She'd just temporarily lost sight of it.

She and Arlo walked past Olympic prison and Olivia made what she hoped was intimidating eye contact with the security guards who had detained her on that first day. But they didn't seem to notice. Then they walked into the offices, using the security clearance that Arlo had somehow acquired by being friends with virtually everybody in the Village.

'I don't know if I can do this,' Olivia said as she walked up the stairs, her nerves threatening to get the better of her.

'Olivia, I've seen you coordinate an eight-hundred-goodie-bag-drop operation and single-handedly convince a team of burly, kind of intimidating but also really hot Australian rugby players to take their post-match celebration back into their apartment. I've seen you persuade the canteen chefs to bake a birthday cake for the Holland House receptionist and I've witnessed you find a way to transport eighteen bales of hay across the Village by yourself. Olivia, you can do *anything*.'

'You're right, I can,' she said, summoning up every possible drop of confidence in her body. She went up to Noah's office and knocked on the door.

'Come in,' said Noah.

Olivia slowly turned the handle and walked in. Noah was on his laptop, typing with a pen in his mouth. As he looked up, she could feel his instant recognition.

'Olivia, it's nice to see you again,' he said, looking panicked. She hadn't forgotten her Olympic prison detainment and, from the expression on his face, he hadn't either.

'Hello, Noah, may I take a seat?' she asked calmly.

He looked alarmed but put his hand out to say yes. 'How have you been getting on? I wanted to apologize again for the—' he began, the guilt pouring out of him, but Olivia didn't have time to console him.

'I've moved on from my unnecessary detainment,' she said plainly, and then, more pointedly, 'I've also moved on from the fact that my internship was *quite clearly* given to someone whose family has strong affiliations with the organization.' Noah squirmed. She sat back in her chair and took up more space as she realized that, for maybe the first time in her life, she was the one with leverage. She liked it.

'I know that the OOT have made a pledge towards diversity, inclusion and representation in and out of the stadiums. And I know how much the Olympic Organizing Commission stands against corruption.' She paused to let the words sink in, looking directly at Noah. He flinched, calculating the scandal Olivia could cause if she started speaking to the press.

'And I know how much you care about the future of the Games and the next generation of Games Makers,' she said with a small smile. 'Right?'

'Right,' Noah said, too smart to say anything that she could later use against him.

'Which is why I wanted to ask if you could help me with something.'

When she left the office and closed the door, Arlo was outside waiting to hear what had happened. She shook her head and they headed down the corridor. They walked down the stairs and then out of the office building. Down the path past Olympic prison, until they were far enough into a neutral area of the Village that Olivia could grin at Arlo and tell him what had gone down.

'You are looking at a girl who just landed a job at the United Nations,' she said.

'No way!' said Arlo in disbelief.

'Yep. I was only planning on asking him for tips on how to apply for the autumn internship. But then he looked *so* terrified that I had to see how far I could take it,' she said, before explaining it all.

A deep stalking session with Aditi the night before had revealed that Noah was only working at the Olympic Organizing Commission on a temporary attachment for the year. His main job was overseeing graduate jobs at the United Nations. So, Olivia pulled her CV out of her bag, slid it over to Noah and told him all the reasons she was qualified – if not overqualified – for a job listing that she'd seen go up on their website a few days before. It was a graduate position in the UN office on Sport for Development and Peace that consisted of working with sports organizations around the world to make recreational and professional sports more accessible to children from different backgrounds. She immediately knew that it was the job for her.

So, she'd spent a day running around the Village trying to convince every senior volunteer and department manager she'd helped since she'd arrived in Athens to write her a glowing recommendation. The head of transportation for the Village gave her a rave review, listing all the compliments he'd heard from athletes she'd buggied around the Village. The head of facilities sent her a two-page-long reference detailing all the crises she'd helped them avert. And the equestrian stable master wrote a letter praising how she was 'always willing to get stuck in, even if that meant scooping up horse poo'. Noah had read every reference she'd handed over to him and then left the room to make a call.

When he returned, he'd told her that he'd made the call because he genuinely believed she was perfect for the role. And then he'd told her, in no uncertain terms, that if she ever tried to blackmail him again, he would find a way to put a permanent Olympics life ban on her.

She'd smiled and said that if she ever suspected he was trying to blackball her, she'd find a way to slowly but effectively leak every salacious piece of OOT gossip she'd heard to the press.

Noah had laughed, shaken her hand and said she would make a great politician one day. Olivia said she'd see him when she got to the top. Then she left the room, triumphant that she'd got the job, uneasy about all the compromises she could already see in her future, but at peace in the knowledge that at least now she was brave enough to negotiate for what she wanted *and* deserved.

At some point, she'd taught herself to stop actively wanting things. To work hard but never want it *too* much. Girls weren't supposed to want power too much; Black girls weren't supposed to actively, shamelessly fight for it. But Olivia wanted it, and so she'd finally allowed herself to reach out and get it. She knew that guys like Lars had no qualms about making calls and asking for favours, so why should she? Of course, at some point, someone would use it against her; call her power hungry or 'difficult'. But smoothening down her edges only made her feel like she was losing herself. Olivia *was* hungry and wanted it all. It was who she was and there was no need to deny herself any more. There were already enough glass ceilings – she wasn't going to allow her own thoughts to be another.

'Olivia, I always knew you had a Machiavellian streak,' Arlo grinned.

'I've just been waiting for the right opportunity to use it,' she shrugged with a wicked smile.

'I'm ninety per cent sure this is going to become your villain origin story . . . but I'm so here for it,' he laughed. 'So, when do you start? Where do you start?'

'October in Geneva,' said Olivia excitedly, realizing that for the first time in her life she had a whole month of unplanned time. Usually not knowing what she was doing the next day filled her with dread. But as she thought about all the activities she and Aditi could tick off their check-list, all the places Arlo had recommended and all the adventures she'd begun to dream up with Zeke, she felt a wave of joy. She could make the summer stretch out all the way into the autumn.

'And how are you going to celebrate?' Arlo asked, excited for her.

'Well, nothing can top the volunteers' bar opening cere-mony watch party,' she began, recalling the day she'd first met Arlo. 'But do you want to go to the *second-best* watch party in town?' she asked as she took two VIP tickets out of her pocket.

An hour later they were outside the gates to the stadium. At long last it was the day of Zeke's 100-metre final.

53
Zeke

Day thirteen of the 2024 Olympics

Most athletes had good-luck charms. Things they carried into the changing room before every competition that made them feel at ease when the whistle blew. For Haruki, that was an old hoodie he'd worn the day he won his first gold medal. And a lot of athletes were superstitious about the things they would and wouldn't say in the lead-up to a competition. Valentina never said the words 'win' or 'medal' the day before a competition and always recited the serenity prayer before she walked out into the arena. In fact, almost all of the athletes in the Village had tried-and-tested game-day routines that started as soon as they woke up on the morning of a big event.

Zeke had spent years perfecting his. He woke early in the morning and started his day with a jog around the perimeter of the Village. Then he took a long shower and grabbed his notebook to write down everything he was worried about to avoid carrying it out into the day. Then he would make time for his family.

The Moyos had landed in Athens the night before and that morning they descended on GB House.

'Little Z, you've got this,' said his oldest brother,

Takunda, as the three of them walked into Zeke's room.

'Just put your whole heart into it, leave it all on the track,' said Masimba as he pulled him into a fierce bear hug. 'Dad would be so proud of you.'

Zeke nodded and hoped it was true.

'All right, we have only a few minutes before that Coach Adam of yours starts trying to tell me how much time I can spend with my own son,' said Mai Moyo, who treated the coach like he was one of her troublesome nephews, despite being only ten years older than him. 'My son, you make me proud every day. Kick those small boys to the ground and bring home gold, in Jesus's name,' she said, pulling him into a tight hug before insisting that they spend the last few minutes singing one of her old favourite hymns. Then she began to pray.

'Almighty King and Saviour!' she said, ready to begin the non-negotiable ten-minute-long prayer that marked the official start of each competition. Once his mum was done, Zeke said goodbye to his family, ran downstairs to meet his teammates and then headed over to the other side of the Village to go to the next part of his race-day ritual.

Every single year Coach Adam hosted an annual team breakfast. Usually, it ended up being on a random Saturday in the off-season when none of the team was competing, but in Olympic years, he always scheduled it to happen on the morning of the athletics finals. It seemed counter-intuitive, and Zeke's friends who competed for other countries always raised an eyebrow when he told them that their head coach got them all together for a celebration on the morning of the most important competition of their lives. But the reasoning was pretty clear. By the end of the day, all of them would have competed in their final competition of the Games. For some of them that meant the day would end in a victory, a medal ceremony and a new personal or world record. But for others, the day would end with them finishing in last place, getting injured or making a small mistake that had the potential to derail their entire career. They all knew how high the stakes were, so Coach Adam threw the team breakfasts to remind them to celebrate just how far they'd come.

Coach Adam reserved a private section in the athletes' canteen, decorated it with Union Jack flags and covered the walls with printouts of all the pictures he'd taken of them since they'd arrived in Athens. Funk and soul blasted from the speaker. Tables were covered with healthy, colourful breakfast platters, fruit bowls and jugs of fresh juice.

When Zeke got there, he was instantly engulfed by the excited energy in the room. The whole athletics team was there, walking around and catching up with people they hadn't seen since the airport. Village days felt like lifetimes and they'd all been so busy with training and competitions that breakfast was a reunion. They talked about how much of Athens they'd seen since arriving, made plans for everything they wanted to do before the closing ceremony and spent the morning taking photos, telling stories and eating breakfast. And they did it all without talking about their competitions. It was Coach Adam's only rule: no field talk at the team breakfast. They were all hyper-aware of what lay ahead of them, all the things they'd been working for, and all the hopes they were running towards. But for that hour, at least, it was just about being together on one of their last days of the Games.

'Okay, I know what happens in the Village stays in the Village,' said Coach Adam to a collective groan. 'I know you've all been so focused on your competitions that you haven't even thought about parties.' He looked over at Camille as he said this, who had thrown a hall party at the start of the week. 'That you've all put so much of your attention into training that you haven't had time to befriend a sheik *and* a crown princess.' Anwar laughed and pretended to zip his lips. 'And that you've all been so disciplined with your routines that none of you were grounded and given a seven p.m. curfew.' Zeke looked sheepish.

'All right, team. Give it your all, be braver than you've ever been and know that you've already achieved everything you needed to by getting here. Whatever happens in that stadium is just the icing on top. You are some of the most hard-working, determined, excellent athletes I've ever had the privilege to work with.'

'Oh, Coach,' said Camille with a hand on her heart.

'And the most annoying, arrogant, infuriating bunch of people I've ever had the displeasure to meet,' he said, making them laugh. 'But I'm *so* proud of you. Of what you've achieved, what you've sacrificed and, most importantly, the incredible people you've all become. So, drink enough water, make sure to stretch and don't get into too much trouble at the after-party I'm going to *pretend* I didn't just hear you planning.'

Everyone clapped and cheered before they all headed out to one of the most important competitions of their lives.

54

Olivia

Day thirteen of the 2024 Olympics

When she got to the stadium, Olivia became Arlo and Aditi's designated photographer. The two of them had clicked immediately and so Olivia spent the whole afternoon laughing. They bought overpriced shirts and merch, which Olivia justified by reminding herself she would have a full-time job by October. Arlo sourced a bunch of whistles and foam fingers from one of the audience management volunteers, so they were fully embracing the spirit of the Games. And then an usher guided them up the stairs, out into the stadium and over to the VIP section to sit next to all of the Team GB family, friends and officials there to support the athletics team.

Olivia was looking around in awe, taking photos of the stadium from every angle and promising herself she'd paint a few of them into postcards. But then she saw an incoming call. *Oh no*, she thought as she saw the caller ID. It was her mum. Olivia had been blaming her lack of video calls on time zones and how busy she was. But the truth was, besides a few reassuring texts and photos, she hadn't spoken to her parents on the phone since her first day in the Village. She hadn't wanted to tell them about her internship falling through. That she'd only worn the suit they'd bought her once. Or that the self-belief they'd done their best to instil in her had taken so many hits in the past two weeks that she'd started to question every aspect of who she was. But she knew it wasn't fair to hide from them just because she felt like she'd fallen short of her own goals. So, this time, she picked up.

'Olivia!' her mum shouted, her face breaking out into a joyful grin as she popped up on the screen. Olivia felt a sharp sense of relief as she heard the warm lilt of her mother's voice and saw the cosy, familiar background of the house she'd grown up in.

'My superstar!' said her dad, bringing his face into the frame. Well, half of his face. He wasn't wearing his glasses, so he was holding the phone up so close that she could only really see his grey, but surprisingly full, head of hair. Olivia hadn't even realized how much she'd missed them.

'Look! I'm in the stadium,' Olivia said, feeling her child-like excitement rise up the way it always did when she was with the people who'd known her for her whole life.

'I'm so proud of you, baby,' her mum said.

Olivia needed to tell her the truth. About the internship, about Lars and Noah. To ask her to stop telling their family and friends that she'd made it big, because she hadn't – at least, not yet. Olivia didn't want them to get their hopes up. She didn't know if she could fulfil the dreams *they* hadn't been able to. And she was no longer sure that she wanted to let her life be guided by the pressure to do so. But before she could explain and manage their expectations, her mum put her hand up.

'We're always so proud of you,' she said. 'Especially

when you're happy,' she added with a warm smile. 'Of course, you're ambitious and brilliant, you're my daughter, after all' – Olivia's dad chuckled beside her – 'but sometimes I think, wow, Olivia is doing all these great things, but is she happy? Is she enjoying it? Is she truly living for herself? But now I can see that you really are.'

'That's all a parent could want,' her dad said, nodding along.

Olivia could feel herself softening. She blinked back the happy tears in her eyes and beamed back at them. She wasn't entirely there, but she was well on her way. She knew there was a part of her that was always going to work to make them proud – she wanted to give them something to tell their students and colleagues about. To make them believe all the obstacles they'd endured had been worth it. Even though she knew she didn't need to, she still wanted to be her mum and dad's success story. But as she showed them the rest of the stadium and told them about everything she'd got up to since she'd arrived in Athens, she realized there was so much more to her, and the future she was stepping into, than the goals she'd set all those years ago.

Nothing about this summer had gone the way Olivia had expected it to. She hadn't done the internship she'd come here for or visited a single landmark in Athens. But things had turned out so much better than she ever could have planned. And while it was too early to claim a complete transformation, she could feel herself coming home to herself. Returning to the unashamed excitement and ambition that had propelled her through her girlhood. She didn't want to forge a path in silence or to spend her energy trying to make all the things she'd spent years planning seem effortless. Nothing about her or her life was effortless. And finally allowing herself to admit that gave her more freedom than she'd ever felt before.

She looked around the stadium and took in just how many people were in the audience. It made her feel like just another dot in the ocean. She felt unbelievably at peace.

'Olivia?' came a voice she recognized.

'Haruki!' she said, excited to see him again. She congratulated him on the medal he'd won the night before and then watched in amusement as Arlo and Aditi swept him away to pepper him with questions about his race. Then Valentina came running down the steps.

'I am so glad Zeke finally got it together enough to just tell you he liked you,' she said with a big grin. 'He'll hate me for telling you this,' she went on, 'but it usually takes him at least six months to get out of his head enough to even admit that he likes someone to *himself*.' She laughed as she pulled Olivia into a hug.

Then Olivia saw three other people she recognized coming towards them. Two tall men wearing Team GB shirts with Zimbabwean flags painted on their cheeks and a majestic-looking older woman. She was descending the stairs in a bright multicoloured dress and a shirt with Zeke's face on it. The woman looked over at Olivia and her whole face lit up.

Olivia knew those eyes, she knew that smile. She'd spent the last week seeing them on the boy who had occupied every inch of her mind. Zeke's mother came over and pulled Olivia into a warm embrace, as if they'd known each other for years.

'My son has told me so much about you,' the woman said, nodding her head in delight. 'Well, no, he hasn't. He and his brothers don't tell me anything because they think I interfere too much and scare girls away. *But* my son's face has been telling me everything I need to know.' She laughed and Olivia grinned.

'Mama, don't embarrass him,' said one of Zeke's brothers in amusement.

'No, we should,' said Zeke's other brother. 'Do you want to see photos of Zeke when he was a baby? He was not a cute baby, trust me,' he said, laughing, as the whole Moyo family came down the stairs. But before Olivia could get a glimpse of those photos, the stadium filled up with music and light.

'Ladies and gentlemen, distinguished guests, Olympians of the world, welcome to the 2024 Olympic Games Men's One Hundred Metres Sprint Final!'

55
Zeke

Day thirteen of the 2024 Olympics

Walking out of the changing room, through the tunnel and into the stadium never got old. As Zeke stepped out, the crowd roared. Zeke waved and the crowd got even louder. He turned around and, without even realizing that's where they would be, he spotted his mother, brothers, Haruki, Valentina, Aditi and Arlo waving at him from the supporter stands. Then he made eye contact with Olivia.

Zeke lifted his arm, put his hand up to his face and blew her a kiss. Her face lit up as she blew one back. Zeke's body relaxed as he realized that, no matter what happened that day, everyone he loved would be right there in the audience ready to embrace him when it was over. Well, almost everyone.

He put his headphones back on and turned up the noise-cancellation switch until all he could hear was the sound of his own breathing. He did his stretches, reassessed the track, nodded at his competitors and smiled at the field volunteers, whose eyes widened in excitement.

Zeke's pre-run rituals meant everything to him. He wasn't usually superstitious, but he knew that the steps he took the morning of each run were what helped him to completely focus on the task that lay before him. Which was why what he did next made so little sense to him. In fact, if he'd been thinking, he would have concluded that it was the worst possible thing he could do on the day of a competition. Never mind just four minutes before he was scheduled to compete in the 100-metre final of the Olympics. But it wasn't an active choice, it was an impulse he couldn't fight.

He picked up his phone, readjusted his headphones and pressed play on the song he'd been avoiding for the past ten years. And as soon as the opening guitar strings began, he was taken right back to that morning ten years ago. The very last time he'd seen his dad.

It was an ordinary Saturday in the summertime. Zeke was fourteen and he was getting ready for a regional athletics race. He hadn't known it then, but it would be the very last competition his dad would ever take him to.

Zeke had woken up late, again. And he'd run down the stairs ready to receive a lecture on the importance of always being on time. But, instead, he'd found his dad listening to the mixtape of old Zimbabwean music that formed the soundtrack to his entire summer. The one he'd been playing that morning was an Oliver Mtukudzi song that sounded like sunshine. It was lined with the gentle sound of a mbira, the upbeat strum of an acoustic guitar and warm, soulful percussion. Instead of a lecture, Zeke was greeted by the sight of his dad dancing around the kitchen. Sunlight poured through the windows and on to his father, bathing him in a golden light that made him look years younger than he was. The joy on his face was so palpable that Zeke started dancing too.

Zeke was well accustomed to grief. To the knowledge that he could never get the person he loved the most back. He worried that recalling those perfect, sunlit memories would plunge him into a sadness so deep that he wouldn't be able to claw himself out of it. And so, he had done his very best not to remember, until this moment. Now, Zeke sat on the ground of the Olympic running track and smiled. As the final guitar strings of his dad's favourite song played through his headphones, he let himself sit in that one perfect memory. Then he whispered the advice that he'd carried like a guiding light: 'Just put one foot in front of the other, but faster than you ever have before.'

Zeke knew what he had to do.

He and his competition lined up across the track. Everyone around the world tuned in to watch the most anticipated race of the year. The stadium held its breath.

It was midnight in Hong Kong. A group of university students were crowded around the TV in their apartment. Eager to watch the competition they'd been waiting for ever since the opening ceremony.

It was one p.m. in Buenos Aires and a group of eighty-something-year-old men who'd known each other since they were kids were watching it outside on their neighbour's porch. Talking about how it was only a matter of time before one of their grandsons qualified to compete for their national team.

It was six p.m. in Harare and the whole extended Moyo family were congregated in their grandmother's house to watch their grandson, nephew and cousin run his race. The house was filled with food, joy and British and Zimbabwean flags. They'd been pre-celebrating for hours. But as soon as the camera panned to Zeke, the room became completely silent, pride pinning their eyes to the screen as they waited for the announcer to call out *his* name.

'Ladies and gentlemen, prepare to be seated for our final competition of the day, the Men's One Hundred Metres Sprint Final!' said the announcer and the whole stadium roared.

This was it, thought Zeke as he took off his headphones, letting the noise of the crowd rush in. Some athletes felt a surge of adrenaline when they got on to the track. Some started to shake with nerves. And others were calm and focused under the lights. But Zeke became quiet, completely quiet. His thoughts cleared, his muscles relaxed and he felt completely weightless.

The moment unfolded in slow motion. The words of the announcers started to sound fuzzy and far away. Zeke became more aware of his breathing and took each step forward with quiet but determined intention. Everything except the track faded out.

'On your marks!' said the announcer. And everything came back to Zeke in sharp focus.

'Set!' He lifted his body, heard the audience quieten in anticipation and held his breath. He could hear the memory of his father saying, *Just put one foot in front of the other, but faster than you ever have before.*

Zeke nodded, heard the shot and *ran*.

Running was the closest thing to flying. STEP STEP. Dancing felt like flying too. His mother started every Sunday morning by cleaning the house and dancing. STEP STEP. The sky was the same shade of blue as the first beach he remembered going to when he was six years old.

The joy of each step felt like all the nights he'd spent out in cities around the world with Haruki and Valentina. STEP STEP. Joy was the colour green. Green like the juice he'd spilt on Olivia. STEP STEP. There had been a hailstorm the day he'd got the call to say he'd been invited for Team GB try-outs. His brothers had thrown him in the air, and he'd landed on the sofa with a beaming smile. He'd cried as soon as he'd gone upstairs to his bedroom. STEP STEP. His dad had died before he'd ever got to see how far putting one foot in front of the other, faster than he'd ever done before, would take him. STEP STEP. The wind on his face felt like the breeze that blew his shirt back when he rode a bike through Richmond Park in May. STEP STEP. The first time he'd seen Olivia, she'd looked at him with the sun silhouetting her head like a halo. STEP STEP. His feet pounded against the track like they had on stadium fields every summer before this one. It was pure, peaceful bliss. It was chaotic, overwhelming euphoria. It was like his whole body lit up and propelled him forward. STEP STEP. It was over before he'd even really realized it had begun.

'In first place is . . . Ezekiel "Zeke" Moyo!' shouted the announcer as the whole crowd roared. 'He is the winner of the hundred-metre final. Zeke Moyo is the fastest man on the planet! Breaking his personal record *and* the world record! Finishing at an extraordinary nine point two nine seconds!' The whole stadium cheered his name.

Zeke couldn't take it all in. It was so quick. Before he knew it, he was surrounded by photographers. Fuelled by pure adrenaline, he ran another lap with a Union Jack wrapped around his shoulders.

The whole stadium was going wild. Coach Adam and his

teammates threw him up in the air. Then his family, who'd somehow managed to defy security and make their way down on to the stadium grounds, ran to hug him.

But before he could find Olivia in the stands, he was ferried off to a press conference where he was immediately greeted by camera flashes, microphones and shouted questions. After all the usual post-victory questions, a reporter asked him if he planned on coming back to the next Olympics to defend his new record. Zeke paused for a moment, looked directly into the camera and said:

'I'm so incredibly grateful to have won this medal. I'm so grateful to my phenomenal coach, my best friends and teammates at Team GB and to all the people who have supported me so fiercely. It's been the greatest honour of my life to run for my country . . . but I won't be running for Team GB at the next Olympics.'

The whole room erupted into shouted questions and camera flashes as people speculated about an unreported injury.

'I'm twenty-four, I'm definitely not retiring yet,' Zeke said, quelling the murmurs around the room. 'But for the past few years – the last decade in fact – I've been running from something. A dream me and my dad had before he passed away. It felt so important to me that it was easier to run away from it than face the reality of doing it without him. But someone really important to me reminded me that while we're all scared of things not working out, the only way to find out is to try. To put your heart on the line.

'So instead of running away from what I care about so deeply that it scares me, I'm going to run towards it and take the next few years to live out a dream I've always wanted to fulfil.' He took a pause as the whole room leaned forward. He gave himself one last chance to change his mind, but as he searched for reasons, he realized that he was completely at peace with his choice, there was no fear telling him to turn back.

'At the end of this year, I will be joining Coach Chikepe and his incredible team of athletes as I compete for Team Zimbabwe. The country my parents were born in and that I've dreamed of competing for ever since I walked on to my very first running track.'

Each row of journalists was taking photos and shouting out questions, but Zeke didn't need to explain himself. So, he didn't. Instead, he looked over at Coach Chikepe, who was sitting in the front row. They had so much to achieve together. Then he locked eyes with Coach Adam, who was standing at the side of the room beaming at him. Zeke smiled back as he remembered the advice Coach Adam had given him when he'd gone to his office that morning to tell him about the decision he was about to make. Coach Adam had given Zeke his full support and encouragement. Telling him just how proud he knew that Zeke's father would have been to see him come this far.

'We'll talk about all of that in the new year, but right now, I just want to go out and celebrate,' Zeke said as he stood up and left the press conference to the cheers of his friends and family who were waiting in the wings. But there was only one person he wanted to see at that moment. As he spotted Olivia in the crowd, the sight of her smile was more glorious than any gold-medal-winning victory.

Olivia

Day fourteen of the 2024 Olympics

Olivia was sitting on her bedroom balcony with her paint pots on a table and her iridescent notebook in her lap. Every time she sat on the balcony, she was struck by just how beautiful Athens was. The bright-pink bougainvillea bushes growing around each building, the sounds of people filling up the streets below her and the warm sun on her bare arms.

As the sun rose higher, she realized with complete clarity that this summer hadn't put even the smallest of dents into her ambition. While the past couple of weeks hadn't gone quite the way she'd expected, the vision she'd stuck up on the wall five years ago had served her well. It led her to the Village. And to Zeke.

She still wanted it all, the influence and the power. But she didn't want it just to prove she could or because she still believed that anything other than perfection meant failure. Now she wanted it so she could enjoy it all.

For the past five years, the plan had been a checklist. A clear road map to some future perfect version of herself. But as she opened her notebook, she decided that the next plan would be an adventure. A list of all the fun she could have, the memories she could make and the ways she could become the woman she'd always dreamed of growing up to be.

She made a list of goals, and then she made a list of all the things she'd once loved but let go of. Her younger self had decided that she needed to be excellent at something to justify spending her time doing it. But that summer changed her mind. So, she wrote 'Do things you love badly!' and then underlined it three times. She let everything she wanted spill out on to the page. The plan became a manifesto on how to live a full life, not just a successful one.

'Five-year plan?' asked Zeke, opening the door and coming over to join her on the balcony. She looked up and saw the brightest smile she'd ever known. A face so handsome, so deep with warmth, that she could have sat there looking into his eyes for hours.

'I figured I owed you at least one of these,' he said, reaching into the paper bag he was holding and pulling out two tall plastic cups of green juice. Olivia couldn't help but laugh.

'I'll need at least twenty to make up for how much it cost me to dry-clean that suit.' But she smiled as she drew him close to press a soft, sweet, gentle kiss on his lips. He put an arm around her shoulder, and she moved closer until she was cosily snuggled into the gap between his shoulder and chest.

'So, this new five-year plan,' began Zeke, looking at her open notebook. 'Is there any space for you to finally let me take you out on that date? Any gaps between now and your path to world domination?'

Olivia tilted her head from side to side, pretending to think it through.

'Well, I do have a lot of plans for the rest of the summer,' she said.

'Oh, I can see that,' Zeke said, planting a kiss on her right cheek.

'And I'm very busy with walkie-talkie calls.'

'Mmm-hmm.' Zeke softly kissed her left cheek.

'Lots of plans to make, very important meetings to go to,' she said unconvincingly.

'Very important.' He kissed her neck.

Her eyes closed involuntarily. 'But I think I could pencil you into my diary,' she said, biting her lip as he carried on kissing her neck. The sensation was electrifying.

He drew her closer to him and kissed her with a sweetness that felt like stepping outside to the first warm air and blue sky of spring. She kissed him back, marvelling at the soft tenderness of his lips. They sat like that for hours, telling each other their favourite stories in the warm, golden daylight. Until the sky melded into pinks and purples, eventually deepening into that magical, familiar shade of blue. Bright enough to still see each other, but dark enough for the yellow street lights to turn on and line the roads with a warm glow. The air ripened with possibility. Another sunset settled over the Athens skyline and, as the rest of the city began to dim, Olivia and Zeke realized that they'd happily spend every night for the rest of the summer just like this, watching the day fade into the night by each other's side. In a couple of days, the 2024 Olympics would come to an end, but Olivia and Zeke's story had just begun. And what they had was definitely more than just a summer fling.

Olivia knew that one day she would love him. Love the

way he smiled in excitement before every run, how he reverted to his teenage self around his brothers and how, one day in the future, he'd sweep her off on spontaneous adventures that would make their hearts fill with wonder.

Zeke knew that one day he would love her too. Love the way she made every idea that came to her at two a.m. into a seven-page spreadsheet, how she laughed until she cried at old sports movies she'd watched a dozen times and how, one day in the future, she'd turn their kitchen into a dance floor, twirling to the sounds of old love songs as they danced together every night.

They didn't know who they would be by the time the summer came to an end. There were still so many sunsets to watch from the roof, golden hours to spend walking through cobbled streets and long deep-blue nights to get swept into. They didn't need certainty. It was enough to know that they found home whenever they sat beside each other. It was enough to know that they were falling in love.

Olivia let her head fall against Zeke's shoulder. He smiled and laid his head against hers. The blue sky turned to black and, as the city fell asleep, Zeke and Olivia held each other and closed their eyes. Finally, it was safe to just be who they were.

Acknowledgements

It took A VILLAGE to write this book. A vast community of people who came in and out of my life at the right moments and changed it for the better. Many of the people who've had the biggest impact on me are people I don't know very well; people who I met in passing, glimpsed from afar or only briefly bumped into, whose words marked an inflection point in my life. But there are a few people, *my* village, who shaped me and this story in ways I can't even begin to explain. So, if this was the end of the closing ceremony, and the credits were beginning to roll over the final fireworks above the stadium of my time writing this book, these would be the names on the screen.

Mom, thank you for taking me to the library every other week, letting me get lost in the shelves and giving me cutouts of the children's stories in your magazines. Dad, thank you for bringing home copies of *Reader's Digest* and *Pride and Prejudice*, and giving me the unshakeable (to a fault) belief that I can basically achieve anything. Thank you for the prayers, lectures and love. I wouldn't have written this book if I hadn't lived with you for three summers longer than I'd planned to. Having you as my parents is the greatest privilege of my life.

Ruvimbo, thank you for hyping me up, making me laugh and for all the hours you've spent listening to me talk through every single thought process I've had since 2020 on that little white stool. Takomborerwa, thank you for always understanding the vision and pushing me towards my potential. The two of you are the most supportive people in my life. You bring out the best in me. You're true blue.

Lydia and Kukuwa, thank you for being the best editors and readers I could have ever asked for! There are not enough exclamation marks to express how grateful I am for your insightful notes, thoughtful edits and the in-doc comment reactions that made me smile during all of my two a.m. edit sessions. Thank you for helping me make this the best version of the story it could be and making this such a fun process, truly a dream team.

Jemima, I can still remember where I was (the third floor of Sports Direct on Birmingham New Street) when I got your Sunday afternoon email reacting to the end of this story and offering to become my agent. Thank you for being so enthusiastic from those first emails until now and championing the book through the most exciting year of my life.

A huge thank you to Allison Hunter, Natalie Edwards and everyone at Trellis for guiding me across the pond and making my dream of walking into a Barnes & Noble and looking for my book come true. And a really big thank you to Giulia Bernabe, Sophia Hadjipateras, Georgie Smith, Emmanuel Omodeind, Sanskriti Nair, Kim Meridja, Sam Norman and everyone at David Higham who made this a reality.

Sam Chivers and Sandra Chiu designed the breathtakingly gorgeous UK and US covers for this book. Thank you for portraying Olivia, Zeke and the Village more perfectly than I could have ever imagined.

And the biggest, most heartfelt thank you to every member of my own personal Team GB (Viking) and Team USA (Flatiron Books) for everything you've done to bring this book together in less than a year! It's been the race of a lifetime and I'm so grateful to have had you cheering me on and championing this book the whole way. Like with every team, there are way more people than I can name or even know, but a special thank you to Ellie Hudson, Juliet Dudley, Brónagh Grace, Lucy Chaudhuri, Karen Whitlock, Maris Tasaka, Bria Strothers, Emily Dyer and Isabella Narvaez.

Thank you to the librarian at JHNCC for always sending me out of the school library with three more books than I planned to borrow, Ms Moran for being my first favourite English teacher and Ms Crehan for being my last favourite English teacher. Thank you to the librarians at Kents Moat Library and Yardley Wood Library for creating spaces filled with magic and wonder. Thank you to Rachel at the University of Surrey for teaching me the story structure I've used for everything I've written since February 2017 and Amy, Paul, Liz, Claudia and Angela for leaving comments on my assignments that I saved and read whenever I needed a little reminder that I've written a few good sentences.

Thank you to Izzy, Liljana and Yoanna for being the first to read this book. Juweyriya, Brandon and Sophie, for always reminding me of what I'm capable of. Mia, for reading all my creative writing assignments. Arr for being endlessly supportive of everything creative I've ever done. The girls on Goldsmith Avenue for convincing me to run for five weeks. And thank you to Nyasha, Rhyanna, Charlie,

Natasha, Lucie, Hollie, Chiedza, Nicollah, Nancie, Demi, Megan and Erin for swapping books with me when we were little girls.

A ridiculous thank you to the assorted people and groups who have dealt with the Olivzekiel-like tendencies that have made me the person I am today. Including, but not limited to, my year three tutor group who elected me as school councillor 'by a landslide'. My year six lunch-time book club. The friends who weren't annoyed when I told them I had a book deal before I mentioned that I'd actually written a book. The social media team at Birmingham 2022 for giving me the closest thing to an Olympic summer. The TEDxSurreyUniversity team who accepted and encouraged my occasional intensity. The kind, smart and thoughtful writer friends who I've spent many a caffeine-fuelled afternoon writing with. And the volunteers at FoodCycle, Raindance, GRACE, TEDx, churches and schools for reminding me that volunteering is the most rewarding thing in the world.

All of the greatest opportunities in my life came from people who didn't know me that well but extended kindness to me when I needed it the most – who threw the ladder down, gave me a seat at the table, sent an email or lent me a book. I'm eternally grateful and will spend the rest of my life trying to do the same.

He just wanted a decent book to read ...

Not too much to ask, is it? It was in 1935 when Allen Lane, Managing Director of Bodley Head Publishers, stood on a platform at Exeter railway station looking for something good to read on his journey back to London. His choice was limited to popular magazines and poor-quality paperbacks – the same choice faced every day by the vast majority of readers, few of whom could afford hardbacks. Lane's disappointment and subsequent anger at the range of books generally available led him to found a company – and change the world.

'We believed in the existence in this country of a vast reading public for intelligent books at a low price, and staked everything on it'
Sir Allen Lane, 1902–1970, founder of Penguin Books

The quality paperback had arrived – and not just in bookshops. Lane was adamant that his Penguins should appear in chain stores and tobacconists, and should cost no more than a packet of cigarettes.

Reading habits (and cigarette prices) have changed since 1935, but Penguin still believes in publishing the best books for everybody to enjoy. We still believe that good design costs no more than bad design, and we still believe that quality books published passionately and responsibly make the world a better place.

So wherever you see the little bird – whether it's on a piece of prize-winning literary fiction or a celebrity autobiography, political tour de force or historical masterpiece, a serial-killer thriller, reference book, world classic or a piece of pure escapism – you can bet that it represents the very best that the genre has to offer.

Whatever you like to read – trust Penguin.